A Tale of The Feyra
Tale 2

Dee Of The Fontala

George R. Mead

E-Cat Worlds Press

Dee Of The Fontala

LCCN 2011927485

Mead, George R.
Dee Of The Fontala/
George R. Mead.
p. cm. – (A Tale Of The Feyra; Tale 2)
ISBN-13 978-0-9817446-5-0
1. Fantasy. I. Title. II. Series.

E-Cat Worlds established its publishing program as a reaction to the large commercial publishing houses currently dominating the book industry and the smaller intellectual clones. It is interested in publishing works of fiction and non-fiction that are often deemed insufficiently profitable or commercial or that are not necessarily reflective of literary trends and fads.

E-Cat Worlds, 57744 Foothill Road, La Grande OR 97850
www.ecatworldspress.com
SAN 255-6383

In the middle of nowhere - Creativity.

First Edition:
Printed in the United States of America

From Grandeville.

Portal
Lair
Search
Not Again
And Again.
Magiwitch
Rebirth
Offspring
Holiday
Treasure

A Tale of The Feyra

Jonathon and Dee
Dee Of The Fontala

Nonfiction

A History of Union County
The Ethnobotany of the California Indians

You must take us as you find us, as the saying is.

Charles Rushton – 1937

Book Tour and Adventure

Just Another Small Town.

She and her companion had been wandering the United States for a number of months, popping into a number of the larger urban areas, visiting the bookstores. It was a book tour that had been arranged by her publisher. The pair of them, the author and her assistant and tour organizer, were beginning to get just some small amount of tired from answering the same old questions, asked over and over and over again. It was interesting in a strange sort of a way. But tiring, very tiring.

She had suggested to her companion that maybe they could just create a handout with those same questions and the usual answers printed on it. That way, she hoped, someone would ask something new. Her companion had argued that it wasn't a good idea and she had agreed.

Finally, the author had suggested, quite forcefully, that she was going to visit some small towns and their bookstores, often the only bookstore, and give the stores and whoever might be there more of an unprepared show and tell than the usual thing that they did. It would be fun to be spontaneous and relaxed rather than programmed.

Her traveling companion had fussed, frowned, grumbled, and in desperation phoned the publisher's main office for guidance and help. But, as per usual, there was little guidance provided and no help at all. She was told to just keep the author happy.

So, there they were, two females, author and helper slash companion, in a small town in one of the western states, well off the main road, having a meal in the only restaurant.

"Much better than the usual hotel restaurant stuff." She licked the frosting off her lips and smiled at her traveling companion. "Much better."

Her traveling companion nodded. "I agree. But why are we doing this? Way out here in the middle of nowhere?"

"There is more variety out here, in the middle of nowhere. Or haven't you noticed? All those big urban book stores look alike. Out here I can see open spaces, talk with a few people at a time, listen to the quiet, and begin to think, ummm ah, about a new novel." She laughed. "So when you call home again, you can tell them that. It will make them happy."

She waved at the only waitress, who strolled over, and looked down at her. "Somethin?"

"Yes. I would like another piece of that pie. And more coffee, please." She looked across the table.

"Just coffee, please."

The waitress shuffled over to the pie case, a circular pie container with a number of shelves inside a clear plastic shell, cut a chunk from the appropriate pie, slid it onto a plate, and returned, and set it on the table.

"Here ya go, Dearie. Coffee is just finishing. I'll bring you some more." She winked. "I do enjoy seeing someone who enjoys what we fix." She refilled coffee cups and wandered into the back to speak with the cook.

The author smiled and cut a big chunk off the slice of pie with her fork. And finished her coffee. "Nice country. Lots of open space and mountains. So, Janice, how much more of this are we going to do?"

"Two more big places, and whatever else you want to do. "I am tired of sitting. Let's just stroll around for awhile. We can cruise the main drag, such as it is. Stretch our legs."

"Sure."

As soon as they were finished, they paid the bill, left a generous tip, and walked outside.

Janice pointed. "That way. I think that I can pretty much see the edge of town from here."

They strolled that way in the gathering dusk. And as they wandered down the sidewalk the sky darkened and the few street lights came on. They heard no traffic or any other sounds. It was a very quiet town.

"Small place," observed Dee. They had hit the edge of town. And looked out at the open fields. So they turned and wandered back toward the other edge of town.

"Certainly is," agreed Janice. "With one not too bad motel, one pretty good restaurant, and it appears one bar of a rather unkempt exterior."

As they approached the rather unkempt exterior, noticing the very clean and only window, a very large window, the door banged open and two big men straggled out, stopped, and stared at them. One mouth dropped open. Both men were wearing heavy, badly worn work boots, dirty denim jeans and denim jackets over faded shirts of some barely visible pattern. Both stomachs were threatening of overflow wide leather belts.

"Oh, my," said one, snapping his mouth closed.

"Very nice, Rance," said the other.

"Come into our parlor," said Rance, waving one very thick arm. "Have a beer." He smiled. "I am not a spider, and that is certainly not my parlor, and you two don't look like flies. But come in anyway." He smiled down at them.

She swung her arm and pushed Janice back. "Nope. But thanks for the invite. We are just taking a little stroll." She looked up and smiled back. "Perhaps some other time, Rance." She winked at him. "I don't think that you look like a spider either."

"NOW!" demanded Rance, reaching for her arm. Both jumped back out of reach.

"Bad idea, Rance!" She glared up at him.

Janice backed further down the sidewalk.

Rance grinned widely. "This one has spirit, Little Fred." He stepped toward her.

"DON'T HURT HIM, DEE!"

The two men spun and stared.

The man who had shouted had just stepped from the alley that ran past that side of the bar. He was neither fat nor thin, neither short nor tall. Just a rather ordinary looking fellow.

The two large men turned back toward the two young women, ignoring him.

"Who's Dee?" grumbled Rance.

She stepped off the curb into the street, turned, and faced him. "I am."

Rance grinned at her. She was a full head and a half shorter and weighed, maybe, he guessed somewhere around a hundred pounds or so, tops.

"Think that she will hurt me, Little?"

"Might hit you up alongside the head with a beer mug."

"Well then, I'll just have to carry her inside and see." He stepped off the curb.

Dee slammed the flat of her hand on his chest. It was a

house skill that she had been taught.

Rance stumbled backward and somehow up and into the large, newly cleaned and only window, and into the bar. The window blew into the interior and from the window frame just before he hit it.

Little gasped, stared at her, and hurried inside. A number of very angry and loud conversations had started up.

Dee spun. "Jonathon?"

He walked up to her. "Let's go elsewhere, Princess."

Dee pointed. "Motel's back that way. Shall we run?" And hurtled down the street.

Inside the bar, amidst some raucous merriment at Rance's unorthodox entrance into the place, Little ordered a round of refreshments for the few regulars that were still in the place, and handed Rance a large mug. "Guess that she didn't hurt you, huh?"

Rance emptied the mug in one long swallow, and grumbled loudly, "Not another word, Little, not one."

"Sure, Rance, sure." He set more money on top of the growing pile to pay for the replacement window.

"She?" The bar maid smiled at him.

"Pour, Paula," snapped Rance, sliding his empty her way.

Dee started the small coffee pot and then sat at the table with the others. "It will be ready in a moment." She looked at him. "This Janice. She helps me when we are on tour."

He looked at Janice and nodded.

Dee fetched the small coffee pot and poured three small cups full, emptying the pot. "Ummmmm?"

He sipped. "Family problem, ah ummm, Dee."

She stared at him. "What? Who?"

He sighed, a soft sigh, and pulled a folded newspaper from somewhere and pushed it across the table to her, and tapped an article. "Read."

She picked it up and did, then frowned. Handing it back, she turned slightly. "Change of plans, Jan. You will have to reschedule the last two stops. It is a family matter that must be seen to." She leaned forward and told her what to do when she returned to the main office, then hurried across the room and rapidly packed what little required packing. She always traveled light.

Straightening up, she spun around. "Well, that does for that. I will go with Jonathon. Don't hurry back. No rush. Just take it easy." She smiled at Janice and nodded at Jonathon. "Let's go."

Five days later, Janice sat in the main office and listened to her boss rant and rave. When he finally wound down, he glared at her, leaning his forearms on the desk top. "Why didn't you stop her from running off like that?"

"She said that this was a family matter that she had to take care of."

"What kind of family matter?"

Janice shrugged. "Dee never talks about her family."

"You should have stopped her!"

Janice laughed.

"You're fired!"

She leaned forward and looked him in the eyes. "Dee said to tell you that if you did that, that she would change agencies." She smiled at him. "She also said that she had some ideas for a new book."

He grumbled. And waved her from his office, and

mumbled to himself, "Damn authors are always a pain in the butt."

A Family Problem

House Darthar Na.

They sat in one of the smaller but comfortable rooms with a large outside window and sipped coffee.

She glared at him and tapped a finger on the newspaper lying open on the table. "How could something like this happen?" she grumbled.

He shrugged. "Sub-house Milaton is very isolated in a very empty spot deep in the Himalayas. Some group of people studying snow leopards had pushed into there and caught a Hamel, a young one. And were very much surprised by what they caught."

"And now it is on display in a zoo?"

"Just so. But not yet on display."

"And you want to steal it!"

"Not yet on display. They are studying it, some."

"And how will that change anything? They must have records and photographs or video or any number of other things."

"Ummmm."

"Steal everything?" Her glare darkened. "In the middle of one of their large cities you want to steal everything?"

He nodded. And took a sip. "There is no longer a trace of Sub-House Milaton. They removed it and found an even more hidden spot. Home, family, beasts."

She filled her cup. "But those people will still know."

"Ummmmm."

"What?"

"Other members of the people profession have already written disagreement about the reported find and some have suggested that this is a hoax to solicit great amounts of money."

She nodded. "Just you and me?"

"Hofga. He looks like the people as well. Ummm ah, that place is close to a fault line. He can make them think that it did it."

She laughed. "So all we have to do is steal the young Ice Cat, all their records, and destroy their building." She sipped from her cup.

He nodded. "We won't hurt the people investigators. Ummmmmm."

"What? Else?"

He sipped. "The Furleen."

She leaned back in her chair and stared at him. "You want my House Beast, you want Purr Cat, to come along, with us?"

"Someone has to tell that young Ice Cat how to behave. It is very young and probably very upset at being in captivity."

She sipped. "One small problem."

"Ummmmm."

"I can't walk down the street with an Ice Cat on a leash. How do we get it home?"

"You and Hofga can walk down the street without anyone paying attention to you."

"Uh huh?"

"Soon there will be a no moon night."

"Uh huh?"

"I will take it. It weighs less than you do."

She nodded. "O.K. When?"

"Six people days."

"Ummmmmm." She leaned forward. And began to tell him how she thought that they should proceed.

The Main Office.

Janice was called into see the Head Man and told to fly to the West Coast and meet up with Dee. He shoved a plane ticket, money, credit cards, at her and told her to go. And grumbled at her to do try to keep their author happy, please, on this book tour.

A Large West Coast City.

"Surprise," said Dee as she greeted Janice outside the security area of the airport. "After you gather up your things we can go rent a car." She thumped the stocky man standing next to her on the shoulder. "This is Hofga. He will be with us for the next week." She laughed happily. "Hope you like the zoo, Janice. We are going to spend a few days there. Luggage is this way." She started them in the correct direction.

The next day the trio wandered through the zoo.

Dee bought a map and a guide book. They had a snack here and there and lunch. They were some of the last folk to leave at closing time.

Dee nudged Janice as they headed down the street to where they parked the car. "You can rest tomorrow. I already set up an author thing with one of the bookstores. One afternoon reading and one evening reading. They were quite surprised, but very happy. Should make the home office happy as well."

Then they enjoyed a very good meal in a very good restaurant. "Just phone in, in the morning, and take all the credit." She poured more coffee for herself and Hofga as Janice sipped.

"Oh," she said to Janice. "And the day after, why don't you just relax, go shopping, and play tourist. Hofga and I are going to spend the day at the zoo. You would probably be bored at doing that again."

They all slept in and finally went to the bookstore after a leisurely lunch.

Janice talked with the owners. Dee entertained the audience. Hofga prowled the store looking for books about the zoo.

And so the day passed.

Dee was munching on a bag of popcorn while Hofga sipped from a large coffee, a tall insulated cup with the zoo logo on it.

She pointed at a spot on the map she had spread on the table where they sat. "This building. Let's go look and wander around over there. You can tell me what you think."

Hofga nodded and said very softly, "Certainly a lot of them."

"Who?"

"The people. It has been some long time ago since I was in one of these places." He nodded. "Tend to forget, living the way we do."

"You could live in a town. Some do."

"No. I like quiet and just a few to be around." He tilted his coffee container up.

"Well, big guy, you are always welcome to come and visit House Darthar Na." She stood, crumpled up her popcorn bag and tossed it into a trash container. "Shall we check out that building?"

"Ummmm hum. Let's check it out just before closing time as well. See if anyone stays to work at night."

Dee nodded.

And off they went, just two among the very, very many visitors at the zoo. One large visitor and one not so large visitor.

The pair stood in the gathering dusk and watched the lights go out in their target building.

Dee nodded.

The Furleen sat next to her, a lion-sized cougar looking thing with dark bronze fur and white tiger stripes on her neck and shoulders.

Dee indicated the building with her chin. "Can you slip in there, stay hidden, and tell that young Ice Cat we are going to get it out of there and that it had better behave while we are doing that?"

One large green eye winked. Purr Cat faded into the outside wall building pattern, it was a chameleon-like skill of her species, and then flowed around and though the open door just as a man stepped out, closed, and locked it, then hurried away toward the zoo parking lot.

Dee tugged Hofga away and in the direction of the entry gate. "So far, so good. Purr Cat will talk with the Hamel, the Ice Cat, and in two nights we can snatch it, take anything in there that looks like records, and then you can trash the place. No one will ever see her in there."

They strolled down the sidewalk and to their rental car. "We will just have to relax until then."

The sky was as dark as the sky ever gets in a large urban

setting with all the normal light pollution from street lights and all the other usual light emitting devices of a big city.

But, here, inside the zoo, it was a bit darker surrounded as they were by dark animal houses and unlit walks. It was also a bit more quiet here than outside on the street. Street sounds were somewhat muted in the zoo.

The three of them stood in dark shadow not far from the locked door to the building that housed the captive Ice Cat, and hopefully all the records and recording that the investigators had made.

"Can you open that door without a lot of noise?"

Jonathon nodded at her. "Both stay here until I am inside."

He slipped up to the door, listened intently, and twisted the door handle off, reached through the small hole and pried the metal outward, slowly, carefully, making a soft ripping sound.

Then he thrust one arm though the hole, turned the latch, and pulled the door open, and stepped inside.

Dee looked at Hofga. He nodded. They waited.

Jonathon slipped outside, something white held in both arms, and thrust it to Dee. "Here. Hold him. Back in a small moment."

She cradled the young Hamel in her arms. "Not too heavy, maybe fifty or sixty pounds."

Purr Cat oozed from dark shadow and sat by Dee's side and bumped the Ice Cat with her head. He rumbled soft at her.

Jonathon hurried back outside, a large box in his arms. "All we need." He set it by her feet. "I'll take the Hamel and leave."

Dee set him in his arms.

Jonathon was gone.

"Dee," whispered Hofga, "take that box, make your way out to the street. When you are on the street, touch me with soft call, and I'll start. We will meet at that rental thing, ah, car. Be ready to leave in a hurry. The people will get very, very excited."

Dee gently shut the trunk, heard it click, and touched Hofga with a very light call, got into the driver's seat, and started the engine.

The car rocked, just a little, as the shock wave passed by.

Watching the rear view mirror she could see lights popping on in the apartment house that lined this street. Then the bulky form of Hofga chugging down the middle of the street.

He yanked open the door and lurched into the passenger seat, slamming the door. "Hurry, hurry, hurry. Something in that building started a fire."

She headed down the street and turned at the first corner off the main thoroughfare and parked, switched off the car lights.

Two minutes later two police cars and three fire engines raced past.

She drove, here and there, and eventually arrived at their hotel and into the underground garage and parked

As they piled out, Jonathon stepped from dark shadows and waited for them to open the truck.

"I'll take that box and meet you in a couple of people days. Hofga and the Furleen will come with me. Careful cautious, Dee, careful cautious."

Slamming the trunk shut, she started for the elevator.

Janice was watching the local news on the room's television and looked over as Dee stepped in.

"Big excitement at the zoo," said Janice.

"Oh?" Dee started the coffee maker.

"Come look. It was a local earthquake that apparently started a fire."

"Really?" Dee pulled over a chair and leaned forward to watch.

"Started about thirty minutes ago, according to the announcer. Zoo officials are saying various things depending upon who is being interviewed, mostly the standard comments signifying nothing. A bunch of researchers are very unhappy about the fire and the zoo officials. It was their building that collapsed and burned. They are blaming the zoo people for shoddy construction."

"Anyone hurt?"

"No. Just that building."

Dee fetched a cup of coffee for each of them. "Oh well. They probably have insurance for that. What else is there on the news?"

"Not much." Janice clicked off the set.

Dee sipped. "Think that this will effect tomorrow's book event?"

"Shouldn't. Probably be back page news by then. No one gets every excited if a building falls over and burns."

"Good." Dee put her cup in the small kitchen. "Time to go to bed. See you in the morning."

"Nite."

Way Out West.

The very mountains moved. Violently.

It was that kind of place. It was where the earth was not quiet. One piece went up, one piece went down.

This sort thing is what had built these mountains. Sometimes these mountains gained many feet in elevation, all at once. Sometimes pieces of the landscape dropped, suddenly.

In a narrow crack of a valley slicing deep into the mountains flank, deep into the mountain range, a valley that indicated where the often agitated fault line ran, a great piece of the real estate sank, taking all the accumulated rubble above with it.

When the dust settled there was a new configuration to the landscape within that narrow crack of a valley. And not too far above the new debris there was a dark opening in the valley wall, a dark space leading into a cavern that had not seen the light of day for thousands of years.

Cool air flowed out and puddled on the floor of the valley and seeped past the boulder clogged rubble heap

Far out on the open plain people stood and stared at the not too distant mountain and pointed fingers at the dust cloud slowly drifting from the mouth of that very narrow, dark canyon.

A number of structures in the area had been damaged by those earth tremors and a small bridge had fallen into the dry gully, dry for this time of year, that it had crossed.

But soon the novelty of looking at the dust cloud wore off and people began to help people repair damages, telling one another that eventually the County would come out and fix the bridge. In the mean time Freddie was using his dozer to cut a notch in either wall of the arroyo so folk could drive down, across, and up the other side. This route would work quite well at least until Spring when the snow melt would turn the dry water course into a raging danger to man or beast.

But no one got too excited. Spring was a long way off.

But some people did get excited.
A little.
A few weeks later.

Randle lost three of his cattle. He knew that it was three because he had found enough remains to identify three animals.

Damn rustlers, he told one and all, jabbing an angry finger toward the west and the closest town.

Damn wolves said others. Mountain lions said still others. Damn rustlers, Randle insisted.

His place sprawled on the slope on either side of Trickle Canyon, so named for the slight amount of water that ran out and onto his property. He knew what cattle taken by wolves or mountain lions looked like. It happened every now and then.

But people did get excited.
A little more.
Another few weeks later.

Rest and Relaxation?

House Darthar Na

Dee sat in one of the small rooms on a large couch. A daughter sat on either side of her. The pair were taking turns telling her about this lesson or that lesson.

Dee nodded at the appropriate places and sipped coffee from her cup. She was still amazed, and was still getting use to the idea, that she was one of the Feyra, The Hidden Folk, a sub-species of humanity that had branched away from the main branch, Homo sapiens sapiens, millions of years ago. After all, her parents had raised her as if she was one of the people when her parents were hiding out among them.

They, we, she corrected herself, had extremely long lives, another fact that she was still getting used to, that and a number of skills that were unique to her house and that she had trained in. One of those House skills had thrown Rance through the window into that bar. Their longevity accounted for the Feyra having offspring very widely spaced in time as well as the small number of Feyra extent in the world.

Ar, her Advisor, Counselor, Teacher, walked in, a strange looking fellow with a light blue tinge to his skin, who apparently been in this house, or family, forever, the terms house and family were synonymous, and said, "Jonathon knocks at the door."

Dee set her cup down and hurried to the outside door not too far down the hall from the room where she had been sitting. Non-members of the house were not able to enter without being invited in.

She threw the door open. "Jonathon! Do come in." It was the normal and formal way of asking one to enter.

He nodded. And did. In one hand he held a tightly rolled newspaper. They walked down the hall to a different room for a private conversation.

She poured two cups full and handed him one, being the good hostess that she was. It was a very proper thing to do for the Feyra. As well as waiting until all had taken a sip or two.

He sat, sipped, and said, "The people newspaper speaks about the loss at the zoo and the rancorous debate as to whether the animal was actually real or some sort of a hoax. It is a big argument, apparently."

"And?" She refilled his cup. Also a customary good hostess thing to do.

"Ummmmm. Their notebooks indicated a very great caution as to how they ought to proceed and how they ought to study their specimen. It seems that they thought to publish about where and how it was found first and to allow the animal to acclimate to its new surroundings before they tried to actually handle it. Apparently one of the their group was mangled pretty badly during the capture, which surprised them all due to the small size of the beast."

He sipped and looked at her. "I left it in your House Beast quarters. I think that the Furleen adopted it."

"So there is no indication that what happened was anything other than a natural event?"

He nodded. "I didn't plan a fire. But it helped. There were

no remains, no records, just lots of ash and collapsed building parts that do not burn."

He sighed, a soft gentle sigh. "I have asked all the sub-house heads and your cousin-house heads to gather here. We need to discuss a more careful and more cautious life style. The people having that Ice Cat could have been a great disruption for us."

"Why?" She sipped and watched his face.

"I think that they would have eventually realized that it was a new breed, a new domesticated breed, rather than some undiscovered wild animal. That would have started a great hunt to find who was responsible for that."

"Ah." She nodded.

He stood and peered out the large window. "I am going to ask all to search their records for any other occurrence, and any other accidental touch between us and them in the past. We have to find out if anyone could possibly detect a pattern which might lead them to suspect that we exist. We need to know whether some extremely clever researcher might be able to do that."

He spun around. "I am also going to ask every House Head that I know to do the same thing."

She stood and walked close to him. "What if I had Janice do a search of that sort as part of the background for something that I am thinking of writing? She is very good at doing research."

"Ah ummmm. If you think that it would help."

"I will need your help."

"Ummmm."

"I can't move from place to place. It is one of your House skills, not mine. Tomorrow morning, their time, I need to get to my office. I'll have to stay for a few days."

"Ah ummmmm." He spun and looked out the window at the sky. "After last meal." And was gone.

Well, thought Dee, it should be nice to have a few relaxing days in the big city.

The Big City. The Main Office.

After two days of busy work, Dee sat at the small table, all shiny chrome and Formica top, and looked out the room's window at the city sprawling in all directions and sipped her coffee. She had been discussing exactly the type of search she wanted Janice to do. After some discussion, in the Main Office convincing the boss, so to speak, of the necessity of Janice doing that, the pair had returned to Dee's office to finish planning the research project.

So now, Dee sat, sipped coffee, and listened to her friend and organizer make phone calls and do computer searches, more or less at the same time.

And while Dee was musing about things she suddenly realized that she probably had, maybe, three or four years left before she no longer could maintain the association to her friend, the publishing company, and her career as an author. It had been a good long time and lots of fun since she had first been published. But now it had dawned on her that she would have to stop soon.

It was a problem of being one of the Feyra, their extreme longevity. Janice would finally notice Dee's apparent agelessness and start asking who or what was responsible for her unchanging appearance.

She sighed, stood, and fetched them both more coffee. Staring out the window she wondered how her parents had thought that they could hide her among the people and keep their unaging daughter away from questioning eyes. Of course she had aged until she had reached her adult size. So growing up was normal, in a manner of speaking, but now, here she was, the equivalent of Methuselah, the long-lived character from the people's mythology.

Her parents had fled out into the world of the people away from something inside the Feyra world of loosely organized Houses. The thing that they had feared had eventually killed them and had come close to doing the same thing to her. But Jonathon had been there, helping her, teaching her, sharing with her all that she really was.

And now, staring out the window at all that sprawling mass of the people it had finally dawned on her, what it really meant to be one of The Hidden Folk, The Feyra, the stuff of mythology and superstition.

"Dee, what's wrong?" Janice was standing by her side. Dee hadn't noticed her do that, she was so deep inside her new understanding of herself.

"Huh?" She jerked around, and then realized that tears had been running down her cheeks.

Janice grabbed a box of tissues from the desk and shoved it at her. "Here! What is wrong? You suddenly looked so sad, so terribly, terribly sad."

Dee shook her head. "It is impossible to explain, really is." She hugged her startled associate. Then she stepped back, wiped her eyes, and wobbled a rather weak smile into place. "Finding anything?"

"Sure. From a rather elderly gentleman who seems to have specialized in dealing documents, mostly very old documents, on what he calls the true fairy world. He has a large private library of his own and cabinets of clippings dealing with things like that. We can visit him at his home tomorrow afternoon."

The Wild Garden.

After a very leisurely breakfast, Dee and Janice had piled into a rental car and zipped out into and through the traffic. Well, given the state of normal traffic here, they didn't exactly zip, more like plod. But, eventually, they were free of all that congestion and alone on a rather narrow road traveling through a mostly rolling open countryside dotted here and there with rather large houses set well back from the lane.

Janice was driving and following the directions that she had been given so they wouldn't get lost and would eventually arrive at their destination.

She turned their car into a driveway and stopped in front of a large and heavy ornate gate set into the very high walls. She got out, pushed a button, spoke softly into a small grill, and climbed back in.

"Well," she said, "here we are."

Dee looked up. "Interesting name."

The gate slowly opened and they drove under the arch with the name, in ornate script, telling one and all who would look up that the name of the place was *The Wild Garden*.

Janice laughed and headed the car up the long drive, around the long curve, and parked near the house looming over everything on top of the low hill.

"Ummmmm," said Dee.

They climbed out and walked up the steps to the large double door, dark wood totally decorated by intricate carving.

Janice knocked.

The door, one half, slowly swung in on silent hinges. "Yes?"

Janice smiled. "I talked to you? On the phone? I am Janice, this is Dee Grant. We came to talk to you about your knowledge of certain happenings."

He nodded and stepped back. "Do come in."

Dee stared at him as she followed Janice inside.

"This way." The not very elderly looking gentleman led them down the hall, past several wide staircases, and finally into a large library, all the walls lined with bookcases.

Waving one hand at a table set with three chairs, he sat and poured three cups of coffee from an over-sized carafe. He sipped and waited while they did. Then he nodded.

"Most welcome to my house, D. Grant."

"Thank you."

He smiled at her. "I knew your parents. The daughter reflects the mother."

She stared at him. "You knew my parents?"

"Yes."

She set down her cup. "Who are you? Exactly?"

"I am Helsing." He smiled. "A small joke."

He refilled their cups, then stood and bowed to her. "Most welcome to the Head of House Darthar Na."

Dee leaped to her feet, her eyes jumping from him to Janice.

"Ummmmm," he said. "Janice is my Third Daughter. You are in House Hinterane."

Dee stared from one to the other and nodded. The four Inferno Hounds and the Furleen appeared. "Watch them both," she ordered.

Purr Cat sat by her side and stared wide green eyes at

Janice. The great hounds settled around the room and stood ready, red-brown coats now beginning to glow with soft red internal fire.

"No harm, no harm," gasped Helsing, dropping into his chair.

Dee sat. "Explain. Please."

Helsing nodded and began.

Long before Dee's parents had fled out into the people and hid themselves and their daughter among the people, erasing all her Feyra memories and replacing them with people knowledge, trying desperately to protect her from the Dark Group, Helsing had placed his house on this very spot. He had wrapped grey shadow over it. No other house among the Feyra had this house skill or even knew of its existence. Grey shadow kept any of the Feyra from seeing it unless the caster wished them to.

In this manner, House Hinterane had removed itself from all that turmoil, that which occurred many long ago, and that which occurred not so long ago.

He refilled cups, took a sip, and continued.

Because he had known her parents from many a long ago time, and had known what they had done to their only daughter, Helsing had watched her life among the people very closely.

He had seen to it that his Third Daughter would be in a position to protect D. Grant, the author, if it was ever required. Fortunately, it had never come to that as Dee had come into contact with Jonathon and from that point on she was very well protected.

So, Helsing had watched and wondered. Word had come of Jonathon's worry and then, much to Helsing's surprise, the search that Dee had instigated in and on the libraries of the people.

He leaned back in his chair and nodded at Dee. "Now you know. Almost everything." He sipped. "It would be seen as a great favor to this house if you never told any, including Jonathon, about our grey shadow skills. It has kept us well guarded for ever so many long."

Dee nodded and smiled at Janice. "Your secret is safe. I was beginning to feel very sad at losing your friendship. My career as author and as D. Grant the author must soon end and I thought that I could not keep as a friend one of the people."

She looked at Helsing. "Now explain. Why am I here?"

"Ah ummmm, yes, that."

"Yes, that!"

He sipped. "Your true name is Daliera Fontala, called Daleira of the Fontala by many. Your parents told me your true name. As you know, we rarely ever use a person's true name. It is a long and honored custom." He sighed heavily. "We were very close, your parents and I. Those responsible for their deaths had a great price to pay. Word says that you delivered that." He nodded and smiled at her. "The house heard much of those events and that you have two daughters as well."

She nodded. And took a sip.

He stood. "I have a book, given to me by your parents to keep safe hidden. It is your's. Only you can read it. Or those who have been touched. Your parents saw to that before they fled out into the people." He stopped by one of the shelves, pulled out a purple bound volume, turned and slid it across the table to her.

Dee looked at it. It had a plain purple cover of some sort of soft material. She gasped. A title, a light green title, suddenly was there among all that purple background.

"The Fontalan?" she said.

"Good!" said Helsing. "Your parents told me the name but it was merely a blank book to my eyes. Inside that volume, I suspect, is your true heritage." He leaned back, took a sip. "Now I have fulfilled a promise given ever so long ago."

He laughed. "Oh, do tell Jonathon that I doubt that there is anything among all the stuff the people have in their many library collections that should direct their attention to us. Anything they ever glimpsed in the ever so long ago went into their mythology and was blended badly into folk superstitions. That creature that those people investigators caught will soon become known as another Piltdown Hoax, a hoax of that sort in most minds."

Dee touched the purple book. "What do I do with this?"

"I have no idea. It is for Head of House Darthar Na only to understand. But I would suggest, if I may do so, that a mother with two daughters has an obligation to see that they also are touched, or given the touch, or whatever you ought to do. My obligation was merely to see that the book came into your hands. And now it has."

Helsing straightened up and looked into Dee's eyes. "Do not blame my Third Daughter. She merely did what a father demanded of her."

Dee nodded and smiled at Janice. "A friend is a friend." The Hounds and the Furleen disappeared.

Helsing nodded. "One did hear of the House Beasts of House Darthar Na. It almost felt like some of the people's mythology."

Janice stood. "We have to get back to work." She bowed deeply to her father.

He stood. "Yes." And bowed to Dee. "Do visit again. You now know where we are."

She stood and returned his bow. "I will."

The Big City. The Main Office.

Dee watched Janice as she filled their cups.

"Sorry, Dee," she said. "I couldn't tell you."

Dee nodded.

"When your people house was blown up, we thought that we had failed, that you had died." Janice sat across the table from Dee. "Then, in some little time, word came of you and Jonathon moving about and all that came from that. We then felt that D. Grant the author was over and done with." She laughed. "But you came back with a new book and a well thought out explanation for you still being alive."

Dee sipped. "One more book, maybe two, and then D. Grant the author will retire. Good thing that I have been so camera shy with no portraits on book jackets. It would have been hard to explain."

"Yes. It is always a problem for the Feyra if they move among the people. So, what now?"

"I think that we, you and I, shall take a working vacation in my oh so very secluded cabin that no one knows the location of, to work on my next book. We won't tell them that it is maybe the last one." She nodded.

Janice smiled. "Sounds good to me."

Jonathon walked into the room.

"You remember Janice."

He nodded. "Yes."

Dee grinned at him. "This is Janice. Of House Hinterane."

He stared at both of them.

Janice stood and bowed deeply to him. "Now we are well met, Lord."

He dropped into a chair and grabbed the cup Dee shoved over to him and took a sip. "Surprise," she said. "I'll tell you all about it. At home. Take us, both, there. Please?"

He nodded, stood, stepped into an open space, waited until they stood close, and threw his arms around them.

House Darthar Na.

Dee ran up the outside stairs and pushed open the great door, and spun around. "Do come in, Jonathon and Janice."

As they walked down the main hallway, Janice said, "One heard of House Darthar Na but no word told of how it truly was." The hall glowed soft yellow in reflected sunlight from the golden oak paneling of the walls.

Two daughters and two Ice Cats hurtled down the hall toward them.

Dee was hugged from both sides by the daughters. The Ice Cats just sat and watched carefully.

"Tiela First Daughter and Winala Second Daughter," said Dee indicating each in turn. "Janice of House Hinterane, a friend."

Ar, Dee's Official Advisor and Counselor, and Teacher, joined them.

"Everyone studying hard?" she asked him.

Tiela frowned. Winala smiled. Ar nodded.

"Ar?" Dee held out the purple volume.

"Oh my!" gasped Ar.

"What?"

"When your parents fled out into the people world, taking them with you, that book disappeared." He turned so he could look into her face. "Can you read it?"

"Yep."

"Ummmmmm."

"Yes, Ar, I can." She laughed. "Well, at least the title on the cover. I haven't opened it yet."

He nodded. "You can read it then." He sighed loudly. "A great treasure, that book and what it can tell you. There are things in there that can only be shared by the one that can read it."

Dee yawned widely. "Not today. Today is nothing but R'n'R. I will start tomorrow."

Ar frowned at her. Once again some of what she said he didn't understand. It was the language choices, the ones that came from her being raised as if she was one of them.

"Rest and relaxation, Ar. It has been a few tiring days out there. We, Janice and I, need bedrooms with an adjoining comfortable room in between and connecting."

Ar bowed. "Follow me, please."

He led them up one of the staircases to the appropriate floor and down the hall to their rooms.

Dee sat in one of the small rooms off the main hall in a comfortable chair, coffee pot on a nearby table, and sipped.

It was after breakfast and she had started to read the purple covered book.

By the end of the introductory chapter she was beginning to grumble to herself. It seemed that this thing which could only be read by her was essentially some sort of treasure map. She had found a small slip of paper that had been tucked between the Introduction and the First Chapter, labeled *The First Key*. It was a note written by her mother. Apparently her parents had intended to get the first key but had to flee out into the people world before they could. The Dark Group that was forming was threatening everything that they held dear.

Dee thumbed through the volume. All the other pages were blank. The first paragraph of Chapter One had stated that each key would unlock the next instruction.

So, she thought, one has to fetch each key in the proper order and there didn't seem to be any indication as to how many of these so-called keys there were.

Setting down her cup, she left the room and headed for the library hoping that there was a really good atlas among all those books.

Janice stepped from a door just ahead, saw her, and smiled. "Morning. How goes the reading?"

"I've read all that I can. The rest is just blank pages."

"Oh. That doesn't sound good."

Dee explained what she had read and what they had to look for. "Want to go on a scavenger hunt?"

"Sure. Will it be safe?"

Dee shrugged. "No idea." She grinned. "I could ask Jonathon and Hofga to come with us." She pointed. "I need to see if the library has a good atlas so we can figure out where the first key is, where the first stop is."

They pawed through the atlas they found in the library.

"Here!" Janice pointed. "That volcano right on the border, more or less, between Chili and Argentina. It seems to be twenty thousand feet tall." A very high mountain had been a marker of some sort in a certain region as mentioned in the very obscure text. Somewhere around it was where they needed to go.

"Well," grumbled Dee, "that key had better be at a lower elevation. There is no way we can wander around on top of that."

"Ummmmm," agreed Janice. "So what are we looking for, on the ground?"

"Fairly cryptic. Three lines pointing at the eye that cannot see. The mountain is supposed to being indicating where there is something like that."

"Huh?"

"What it said."

Janice scanned the maps again, looking for the correct spot. "OOOOOP! Over here!" She laughed. "Might have known. It is right near this town in Peru. Nazca! Well, this will certainly be interesting. There are lines all over the place." She stood. "We need better information. We have to go to a certain library and look at lots of accurate maps and photographs."

Dee filled her cup. "Sit. I will call Jonathon. He can take us all there." She took a sip.

The Big City.

They sat at a large table in that certain library and poured over page after page of photographs and drawings of the multitude of designs left on the ground not far from the town of Nazca. There were straight lines running in every direction.

Janice explained that all these things, the Nazca lines, are really a series of lines, miles of them, geometric shapes, and large animal figures, some of which are as large as a people football field. They are all in and on the desert floor near the dry southern coast of Peru. There are parallel lines, spirals, triangles, trapezoids, birds, and other animals. Various of the people investigators had suggested all manner of reasons for their construction, everything from space aliens to maps of subterranean water sources. All of this is in what they call The

Red Plain which is around fifteen miles wide by thirty-seven miles long.

This area is a desert of dark red stone with a lighter colored subsoil. The designs seem to have been created from around 200 B.C. to 600 A.D. as the people measure time.

"What about this guy?" Janice tapped a finger on a photo of a figure etched into the side of a hill. "It has been labeled *The Spaceman.*" She pointed. "This is about the only one with eyes." The figure had a round head with two circles for eyes.

"This guy is around two hundred feet tall and is the only one that lies on a slope of this isolated mini-mountain. There do appear to be several lines pointing, in a manner of looking at it, at his mouth, with these round circle eyes just above."

"I don't see any lines," said Dee.

"Could just go and take a look." Janice looked at Jonathon. "What do you think?"

"We will have to be careful. From all these flyers it seems to be a very popular place to visit. Lots of the people there, locals and tourists of all kinds."

Dee nodded. "Ask Hofga to come."

He nodded.

Hofga stepped from a dark corner of the room. "What?"

"Taking a trip," said Dee.

"There is a coffee place just around the corner from here." Janice stood. "Let's stop there first."

So they did. Stop there, drank coffee, and ate a pastry or two.

"Nice place." Dee licked her fingers clean and finished the job with paper napkins.

"Umm humm," mumbled Janice, still chewing.

Hofga looked at Jonathon.

"Janice," said Jonathon, "of House Hinterane."

Hofga stared at her and took a big swallow from his coffee container.

"Surprise!" Janice grinned at him.

"Hao doata!" Hofga looked at Dee.

"Me too," she said. And laughed at his expression.

Janice walked over to a computer terminal, typed a bit, and returned. "Not too hot there. Cloudy with a temperature in the mid-fifties."

Dee looked at Jonathon. "Let's go."

He nodded. "Outside, behind the library. Lots of trees."

They hurried after him and soon stood inside the soft shadow of the grove of trees.

Nazca.

"WOW! That is some carving." Dee laughed.

Janice stared up the steep slope at the large figure carved into it, and at the large round eyes it had. "So how do we get up to one of those eyes to take a look?"

Dee looked at Jonathon.

"We are alone," he said. "For now. But one of those brochures said that they have airplane tours here." He frowned at Dee. "So if you hear motors of any kind, land!"

Dee nodded and launched herself upward, great white feather covered wings beating. And in a few wing beats she coasted ever so slowly down and across the great carved face, staring at the two circles that indicated eyes. Then she landed with a soft thump, grabbed a handhold, and pushed at a slight depression.

And fell inside.

Calling the others, she stared at the small chamber she

stood in. The place had a soft blue glow that seemed to emanate from the walls.

The rest appeared and stared. The opening grated shut.

Hofga stepped into dark shadow. "Here! A passageway."

They hurried over and stared at the opening. It was more or less seven feet high by three feet wide, all rough surface, apparently hacked from the surrounding rock by hand tools.

"I will go first," stated Jonathon. "Slowly."

Dee followed him, then Janice trailed by Hofga.

Within a few feet it was dark, pitch black. Dee shuffled her feet, seeking anything in the way to trip over.

"It bends to the right," whispered Jonathon.

Trailing her fingers lightly on the right hand wall Dee felt the sudden change in direction.

They turned and walked downward at a very steep angle.

"Turn left," hissed Jonathon. "There is a faint light ahead."

"Stop!" he whispered. "Stand and listen."

They stood. And listened.

All Dee could see past Jonathon was a faint glow ahead. She couldn't hear anything.

"Slowly," he ordered. "Slowly." Jonathon edged forward, one careful step after one careful step until they could see a room of some size coming into view.

"Wait here!" He slipped inside and to one side.

From what little Dee could see the room appeared to be empty.

They waited.

And after some time when all were beginning to wonder, Jonathon waggled one arm in the opening, beckoning them to come ahead.

They walked in.

"Prata!" snapped Hofga.

"Dee," said Jonathon, also banging into something he could not see, "step to the middle of the room and invite us in. Please?"

She stepped into the room and out to the middle of the room and turned. Everyone else was one step into the room, waiting.

"Do come in," she said. "Jonathon, Hofga, Janice." Then she slowly looked at the room.

It was a circular room, a large circular room with a low doomed ceiling. The light, soft faintly yellow diffused glow, seemed to radiate down from the high doom.

She frowned at Jonathon. "I don't see anything in here."

"Ummmm." He was carefully walking around the room, trailing his fingers on the walls, eyes searching for anything that might help them. "Ummm."

"What?"

"Have you looked in your book? Yet?"

"No."

"Please."

Dee shrugged off her small back pack and opened it, sliding out the purple clad volume. She sat on the floor, crossed her legs, set the book on her lap, and opened it.

"Oh." She looked up. "The next chapter is there now."

"Guess this room is the key," said Janice.

Dee shoved the book back into her pack and stood. "How come no one has ever found that button and come in here before?"

"Feels to me," said Jonathon, "that only the one who has been touched can see things like that and make them operate."

Dee walked over to Jonathon. "Let's go home, rest, eat, and see what this next chapter is all about."

House Darthar Na.

After a casual breakfast with her daughters, Dee found a small room with a large outside window and a comfortable chair.

Nestled in the overstuffed delight, coffee cup in hand, she opened *The Fontalan* and began to read the now visible chapter.

In the dawn of our existence it came upon us to know who we were. This was a new thing. The Others would not become as we for many a long change in the world.

For many a long change in the world around us, The Others struggled and form altered and spread ever widely. We, the first to know who we were, broke apart and spread ever widely.

Great were our numbers. Greater was the carnage as cluster tore cluster. A small number faded into the darkness of night.

Small then were our numbers. To know who we were changed. The First House shaped itself and so said, this was the way for existence.

The way for existence was true and houses formed for many a long change in the world around us. Smaller numbers remained as clusters. The Others struggled and form altered and spread ever wider and it came to them to know who they were.

The First House, Darthar, The Bringer of Order, said to the ones who first knew who they were, we are The Feyra, The Hidden Ones. And for many a long change in the world around us it became the way for existence.

Some of The Feyra watched The Others and so said House to House, they, The Others, struggle and build and this is the way for existence.

Darthar, The Bringer of Order, for many a long time watched The Feyra do as The Others did, and said to all, this cannot be.

Darthar altered and struggled and changed and so said, now is become Darthar Na, The Protector of The Innocent.

The first Fontala armed with house skills strode from Darthar Na, terrible and swift. Houses who followed the way of The Other became no more.

Great was the carnage. Greater was the beginning of the gentle existence of The Hidden Ones.

For many a long change in the world around them, The Hidden Ones, did see nothing of The Fontala, and did forget the true meaning.

To read these pages is to know who we are.

To read these pages is to know of The Fontala.

To read these pages is to know.

To read these pages is to follow the path.

To read these pages is to be.

Fontala.

Well, she thought, taking a sip, well, well, well, the things one learns about themself, in a manner of speaking. That narrative certainly explained some of the things that Jonathon had told her shortly after they had met.

She took another sip and stared out the window, book lying open in her lap. These pages are strangely written. Perhaps it is an older, more archaic form of expression for The Feyra.

Setting her cup on the handy table, she turned the page. The next page was blank. With one exception. Right in the middle of the page was the exception, done in brilliant colors of ink.

It was a very stylized image of an antique rose. At least, she supposed that is what it was. The drawing was complete with leaves and thorns surrounding the central design. The image appeared as if it had texture, as if it had been embossed onto the page.

She stroked it with a gentle fingertip.

"OUCH!"

Jerking her finger back she stared at the drop of blood forming on her finger. Something had stabbed her. How could a drawing of a rose, leaves, and thorns do something like that?

The drop released and hit the page, making a splat shape of deep red.

"Oh crap!"

The page absorbed the blood splotch.

She tried it again, squeezing her finger. Another drop hit the page. It disappeared.

"Well," she mumbled, "isn't that interesting." And stared.

A line of script began to appear. A line of blood red

script.

A voice spoke to her. It read the line of script to her.

"Deep, deep, deep," it chanted. "The House is deep, deep, deep."

The lines faded away.

Dee sighed, and thought that whoever was responsible for this book was a ding-dong who was enamored of puzzles. The author could have just written straight forward instructions instead of all this indirect blather.

Snapping the book shut, she dropped it on the table and grumbled out the door and up to The Training Hall and stomped inside.

"Ar," she called to the small figure talking with one of her daughters.

He finished and hurried over. "Princess?" And frowned at her expression. "Oh my."

"Does the house have a basement, a space underneath itself of some sort?"

He nodded. "There is. No one has gone down there in many a long time since some long time ago."

"Is it safe? Down there?"

"Ah ummmm, I do believe that it would be, ummm ah, for you."

She nodded. "Let's go take a look."

"Now?"

"Yep." She smiled. Purr Cat appeared and sat by her side.

"This way." Ar headed out, along the hall, and opened a door. The stairs beyond headed down.

So did they.

Down.

And around.

Down.
    And around.

Down.
    And around.

And on and on and on and on and on . . .

Then they stopped. At the bottom, Dee hoped. At a door. At a large door that was the same color as the covering on her book, deep purple.

Dee swung the latch and pushed. The door swung in on silent hinges. "Interesting." She stepped through.

The room was large with recessed lamps all around flooding the space with a soft golden glow. A thick column of stone, waist high, protruded up from the exact center of the floor.

Dee walked over to it and stared. The same rose design as the one in the book covered the top of the stone cylinder. Purr Cat sat and watched her.

"Well, well, well." With a very cautious fingertip she ever so gently touched it. The design was soft, rose pedal soft. She could smell it, the sweet odor of roses.

Silently the shaft began to sink until its top was flush with the floor. Somewhere, something made a loud click, a section of a wall swung open. Inside that space lights popped on, one by one by one by one, into the distance as the hall was illuminated.

"Interesting," she mumbled. "Also."

She walked to the entrance and turned to Ar. "Did you

know about this?"

"No, Princess. Only that there was a beneath." He pointed at the cylinder top. "It opened for you. You, Daliera Fontala. It appears that this is your heritage also."

She started down the hall. "Strange, strange, strange, strange," she mumbled. The Furleen walked by her side.

Finally, around the far corner, they stopped and stared. The floor sloped downward in a great curve. They started down.

The curve tightened.

And tightened.

And tightened.

"It's a spiral."

"Just so, Princess."

At the bottom they stopped. At the door. At the purple door. With a rose decorating the central panel.

"Ummm," she said, reaching out and gently touching the design. And pushed the door open.

She stepped inside, stopped, and slowly turned around, staring at them. Racks and racks and racks of long cylindrical staffs glowing with a soft purple light.

Another rack appeared to be entirely shelves with piles of neatly folded garments. She pulled one free and shook it open. It was a short jacket covered with glistening purple metallic scales. She held it against herself, nodded, and slipped it on.

She laughed. "Perfect fit." And stared at Ar who was staring at her with his mouth open. "What?"

He dropped to his knees. "Princess."

"What? And get up. Please?"

He did.

"Now what?" She ran her hand over the material of the

jacket. "It is really comfortable." A patch of material flashed red and became a rose on her left sleeve, just above her wrist. "Huh?"

Ar gasped.

"What? Now what is it? Again? Tell me, Ar. Please?"

"Oh dear, oh my, oh dear me oh my. Not since ever so many long ago." He bowed, very deeply, he bowed to her. "Daliera Princess, you wear the jacket. Only The Word could do that, only The Word would be allowed to cause that. You are become that one, The Word of the Fontala."

She stared at him, frowning. "What word?"

He straightened up and looked into her eyes. "Only one of the Fontala may wear the Shield of Color. Only one of the Fontala may carry the Flame Blade. The first among the Fontala is The Word, umm ah, the Head, the one who directs that great force."

"Me?" She laughed. She barely knew what it meant to be one of the Feyra much less anything else. After all, most of her previous life so far had been as an author and as one of the people.

He nodded. "You wear the jacket with the rose on the sleeve." He pointed at the racks of long purple staffs. "Touch one of those."

She worked over and did. "O.K." Then she lifted one free and held it. "Not very heavy."

"What do you feel?"

"Not much. Ummmm, it is kinna warm. That's all."

Ar walked over to a bare patch of the rock wall and tapped it with a finger. "Princess, come over here and gently hit this spot." He hastily stepped back and away as she approached.

"Hit? Gently?"

"Yes. Very gently."

"O.K." Dee very gently tapped the wall with the tip of the Flame Blade and thought that it was a strange name for a staff. And carved a great chunk from the wall. The piece thumped to the floor as she jumped back.

"WOW!"

Ar nodded. "Indeed, Princess, indeed."

She bent over and poked at the piece with her fingertip, and straightened up. "It felt like, oh ah, soft, ah, like soft butter. But it is rock."

"Be very careful, Princess."

"Let's go upstairs, Ar. I need to sit and think about all this."

He stepped close. "Kiss the rose on your sleeve, Princess."

Carefully she lifted her left arm and did.

"Ho boy!"

They stood in the warm glow of the main hallway near the outside door.

She walked down the hall into one of the small rooms accompanied by Purr Cat, set the blade, her long staff, in a corner, and poured a cup of coffee, dropped into a comfortable chair, and stared out the window, sipped, and thought.

She was in the middle of her second cup when the door opened and they walked in, Tiela and Armilin, and stepped around to stand in front of her.

Tiela filled two cups, handed one to Armilin, and walked around to sit in a chair next to Dee. "What is that staff in the corner, Mother?"

Armilin gasped loudly, stopped, and stared at what Dee

was wearing. She crashed to her knees, just managing to not splash her coffee on everything.

"What?" asked Dee and Tiela.

"Only in whispered legend," sighed Armilin. She bowed her head. "My arms are your's!"

"Huh?" Dee stared at her. "What?"

Armilin look up at her. "The Fontala are once again come from the dark fog of the ever so long ago."

Tiela stared from her martial arts teacher to her mother. "What?"

"DOWN HERE STUDENT!"

Tiela jerked and joined Armilin.

"Stop that!" snapped Dee. "Just sit and have some coffee."

The pair hastily did.

"Mother?"

"Princess?"

"Let me tell you two about a book."

And then she did, very carefully, very slowly, she told her audience of all that had happened since she had been handed the purple book.

She leaned back, and sighed. "Now you two know all that I know."

"Ummmmm." Tiela nodded. "May I see this book, Mother?"

Dee pointed at the tome sitting on the small table set against the wall under the large window.

Tiela stood, walked over, and picked it up, and looked at it. "The Fontalan?"

"Well." Dee crooked a finger at her.

Tiela walked over.

"Wait." Dee called.

Winala walked into the room. "Mother?"

"Take a look at the book that Tiela holds."

Tiela handed her sister the book.

Winala took it, looked at the cover, and then her mother. "The Fontalan? What is it, this book?"

"Turn to the last page you can read, then show Tiela, but do not say anything." Dee was watching them very carefully.

Winala opened the book and slowly began to turn pages. She nodded and handed the volume to her sister, who looked and nodded.

"What did you read?"

Tiela cleared her throat. "Keep open gates."

"Gates open to pathways," finished Winala.

"Both of you read that?"

Two daughters nodded.

"Show me."

Tiela handed the book to Dee. She looked at the page and then turned it. "Guess we aren't done yet." Both of them had read the last entry visible on the page facing the rose design.

Handing the book to Armilin, she stood, walked over and grabbed her purple staff, and headed from the door. "Armilin, come with me. Daughters, go talk with Ar." Purr Cat went with Dee and Armilin.

Way Out West.

Jeff Jeffers lost some of his sheep. He only found a few remains, so he was unsure exactly how many he had lost.

Damn rustlers, he told one and all, jabbing an angry finger toward the west and the closest town.

Damn wolves said some. Mountain lions said others.

So he and his neighbor, Randle Edwards, a long time friend and neighbor, good friends even though they disagreed, frequently, on what was the "right kind" of livestock to raise, both phoned the state game busybodies and demanded that they send someone out to investigate, "to do something."

Two days later, a pickup truck arrived. It was the investigator sent "to do something." He inspected the sites of both events and spent two days walking all around the sites studying the ground.

Not wolves, he told the two ranchers. Not cougars, he stated. Lots of foot prints though, all made by boots of some sort or another. Then he climbed into his pickup and drove back to town.

So, Jeff and Randle both tossed some money into the pot and hired Sneaky Pete Dupar. He came by his nickname honestly, a strange term to use in conjunction with Pete, as everyone knew that Pete poached everything, domestic and foreign. But no one had ever been able to prove that, hence the nickname of Sneaky. His other skill was his accuracy with a hunting rifle.

Pete agreed to do the job, prowl around at night, something that he was very good at doing, and shoot anyone he saw that would be trying take one of Randle's cattle or one of Jeff's sheep. All the ranch hands on both spreads were told what was going on so they would stay inside at night for a few days. That way no one would accidently get themselves shot.

So people settled down.
Quite a bit.
For a few days at least.

Everyone heard the shot.

Everyone waited for morning to find out who had been shot, who the culprit was. Not who is it, but who was it? Sneaky Pete was known as being very deadly with that rifle of his.

He met with Jeff and Randle. And neither really believed what he told them. So they went to look and saw the footprints, footprints running toward the canyon.

Pete insisted that he hadn't missed. So Jeff and Randle paid him for one more week hoping for better results.

But people got excited.

Some. And wondered. And talked.

For a week longer.

Jeff and Randle made more phone calls.

And they arrived. Two men in a truck. State Police.

They all, all four of them, drove out to where Pete's rusty pickup sat.

The State Police carefully inspected everything and then they shrugged. Pete was gone all right, but everything else was still there. The truck, sleeping gear in the bed of the truck, Pete's rifle still leaning against the rear bumper. And no sign of anything else. Other than lots of footprints, some of them coming from, some of them going to, that canyon.

So the State Police drove back to town. And shortly returned with a van full of additional members who searched everywhere. For four days.

Then they packed up and went back to town having found neither Pete nor anything else.

Jeff and Randle started two-man patrols, heavily armed two-man patrols. And they didn't really care whether the State

Police liked it or not. As far as Jeff and Randle were concerned, somebody needed to be shot, a number of times.

People calmed down.
>Quite a bit. And talked about how strange things were getting.
For a few days.

Four very excited ranch hands told Jeff and Randle that they saw the poacher. And emptied four rifles and two handguns at it. It was at night, it was dark and all that, but all four agreed. Something was skimming along about six feet above the ground when they opened fire. They heard it thump to the ground and run away.

All four agreed that is exactly what happened whether Jeff or Randle wanted to believe them or not. And not only that, they were not going out there anymore at night.

As far as they were concerned, anyone, or anything, that could skim along above the ground the way whatever it was that they saw, could get shot full of holes, and then run away, was not something that they wanted to ever meet up with again. Especially at night.

People were upset.
>Lots of upset. And told far-fetched stories to each other.
For days.

Onward. Ever Onward.

House Darthar Na.

They stood in the hallway on the ground floor, the very empty hallway, the almost very empty hallway, and watched Tiela and Winala head up the staircase toward the third floor and The Training Hall.

"Stand very close," Dee said to Armilin, and waited until she did. Then she raised her left arm and kissed the rose design on her cuff.

Dee laughed. "Wondered if it would do that."

Armilin stared at her. Then she stared at the room they stood in, its contents, as she slowly turned around.

She stopped and nodded at Dee. "Our House, House Induna, has passed on to all of us the tale, the story. The telling of the story is a long some time ago tradition." She shook her head. "But all merely thought that it was just a story and a tradition of no known reason. Just a thing to hear at the proper moment."

Dee pointed at one of the shelves. "See if one of those will fit you."

Armilin nodded and stepped over to the shelf and started to pull her glittering chainmail shirt off.

"No! Ummm ah, leave it on. Please?"

Armilin tugged everything back into order, took a garment from one of the shelves, and shook it open. She looked at Dee.

Dee nodded.

Armilin carefully shoved one arm in a sleeve, hesitated, then yanked the jacket into place.

The short jacket glistened purple metallic scales making her silver chainmail appear even more brighter than it was.

"Well, so far so good." Dee pointed. "See if you can pick up one of those purple staffs."

Armilin walked over and did. "It is warm to the touch."

"They are called Flame Blades." She pointed at a depression in the store wall. "Just above that spot I want you to hit the wall with as soft a touch as you can."

Armilin nodded, walked over, and very cautiously did. And leaped back. "Ahpat!" A large chunk of the wall fell and tumbled to their feet. On her left shoulder the jacket flared, a red rose appeared.

"That's interesting." Dee walked over to inspect the rose on Armilin's jacket as Armilin twisted her head and shoulder so she could see.

Armilin's mouth was moving but nothing came out. Finally she gasped and cleared her throat.

"What?" asked Dee. "What is it? Are you sick?"

Armilin shook her head. "Our house, my house, can never repay such an honor."

"Ahhhh, you had better tell me. I think that you know a whole lot more of what ever is going on than I do." Dee waved her hand at the room and its contents.

Armilin nodded. "As The Word says, so will the deed be done."

"Huh?"

"I am House Induna, Armilin, Anointed One, now

wearing the title, The One of The All, one step below The Word of The Fontala, The Protectors of The Innocent."

Dee stared at her. "That is what the rose situated there means?"

"As legend so said, so it came to be."

Dee laughed, raised her left arm, and kissed the rose.

She stepped into the small room, poured two cups full of coffee, and handed one to Armilin, and sat. She sent Purr Cat back to the house beast quarters.

"I don't think that we should wear these duds or carry these staffs, ummmm, blades, until we really know what we are doing. Do you?"

Armilin shrugged off her jacket, hung it on one end of her staff, and leaned the staff in a corner. "Just so. The Fontala are called into sight only as great events come to be."

Dee stood and did the same thing with her jacket. "Perhaps you should return to your home and talk with them. We need to figure out what to do next. And I still have keys to find."

Armilin took her staff and jacket and carefully folded the garment into a small bundle. Her Flame Blade flared purple light and became what appeared to be a simple grey wood staff.

Dee followed her example. "Now that is truly interesting."

Armilin fastened the small bundle to the back of her belt, tightened her belt buckle, and grabbed her staff. "In some small time I will return." She strode from the room.

Dee walked down the hallway, up the stairs to her bedroom, and put her jacket and staff in a closet. Then she wandered downstairs to see if that book had anything else to read in it. As she walked along the lower hallway, she shook her head and thought that her life had certainly managed to get even stranger than it already was. Very strange, very quickly.

She stopped for a snack and found her daughters doing the same thing, Ice Cats in attendance and looking hopeful at the food.

"Daughters."

"Mother," they said in unison.

"Lessons going all right?"

Winala smiled broadly.

Tiela frowned. "Armilin went home in a rush."

Dee nodded. "She had some urgent family business to attend to. She will return when that is, ummm ah, taken care of." She looked from face to face. "Ummmmm."

Both looked at her and her expression, and squirmed, carefully controlled squirming. "Tiela, I have a very serious question that requires some thought and an honest answer from you."

Tiela nodded, a very careful nod. She couldn't think of anything she had done that required an honest answer presented in that tone of voice. She began to worry.

"First daughter," asked Dee, "do you really want to be the next Head of House Darthar Na?"

Winala's mouth fell open.

Tiela looked stricken and slumped in her chair.

"Well," insisted Dee.

Tiela finally managed to sit straighter, looked deep into her mother's eyes, and said, all soft voice, "No, I do not." And waited for the explosion. The First Daughter was expected to take on that role.

Dee nodded and smiled at her. "Then Winala is from this

moment in time and forever, The Anointed One, the Future Head of House Darthar Na."

Tiela nodded, and said, "Good! She will be ever so much more well trained in that than I would ever be, or would want to be."

"Winala?" asked Dee.

"I . . . me?" She gulped.

Dee nodded, very slowly she nodded.

Winala shoved her chair back and stood. Then she bowed to her sister and even deeper to her mother, and straightened up. "I accept." And dropped heavily into her chair.

Tiela leaped to her feet, stepped behind her sister, and wrapped her in her arms. "You will be ever so much better a House Head." And whispered soft as soft in a handy ear. "I really dreaded the whole idea of becoming House Head but was afraid to say anything."

Dee watched them and nodded.

Karanly and Jonathon walked into the room.

"Ummmmm," said Jonathon.

Karanly smiled at everyone and wondered about the strange expression on the daughter's face.

Dee explained.

When she finished, Ar walked into the room carrying a large tray of bowls, spoons, and a large tub of vanilla ice cream.

Karanly, smiling very broadly, and Jonathon, stood and bowed deeply to Winala.

Then they all enjoyed the ice cream and had coffee to go with it.

After two daughters went off with Ar for more lessons, Dee cleared her throat, eyes shifting from Karanly to Jonathon.

"Ummmmm."

"Umm." Jonathon watched Dee's face carefully.

"What is it?" asked Karanly.

Dee stood. "Wait here. Be right back." She hurried out the door.

Karanly looked across the table. "Brother?"

He shrugged. "The houses are quiet." And waggled one hand loosely. "As they ever are."

They sipped and waited. But not for long.

Dee walked in and stopped, leaned her staff against a wall, holding a small bundle in one hand. She looked from face to face.

"O.K. No excitement! All right?" She waited until they both nodded agreement. "Watch!" She shook out her bundle and slipped on the jacket.

The staff flared and became soft glistening purple where before it had been grey wood.

"OH!" gasped Karanly.

"Come with me, please." Dee grabbed the staff and stepped into the hall. As soon as they joined her, she lifted her left arm and kissed the rose design on the cuff.

"Where are we?" Karanly slowly turned as she inspected the room where they now stood.

Jonathon waited, calm as calm ever was.

"I suppose," said Dee, "you could call it the armory. Of The Fontala, The Protectors of The Innocent."

Jonathon bowed to her, straightened up, and smiled. "Ummm ah, the name, your name, was more than a name, it seems."

Dee pointed at the very center of the room and the rose

there and explained all that had happened.

"Armilin went home to talk with her mother and siblings." Dee waved a hand at the room and its contents. "Somehow all this has to do with finding the next key. Which the book suggests opens some sort of a gate that will then lead to a pathway of some sort." She laughed. "All vague as all get out!"

Karanly wondered what she was talking about this time. Her usage of various people ways of speaking at times didn't make much sense.

All carefully studied the walls of the room, seeking some clue as to where a gate might be.

"Nothing," grumbled Dee, becoming more and more convinced that the authors of that purple book had very twisted minds, to put it mildly. She walked over and stared down at the rose design carved in the middle of the circle on the floor.

"Oh well." She bent and poked it with a very careful fingertip.

Sighing soft sigh the stone cylinder began to rise from the floor. It stopped, the top waist high on Dee. Somewhere something clicked loudly.

"Over here!" Karanly waved at them. "There is a corridor over here. Now."

Dee and Jonathon hurried over and peered past her as light began to flow in soft waves from the entrance along the stone walls and around the not too far distant corner.

"Humpf!" grumbled Dee. "Here we go again." She stepped in and began to walk slowly toward the corner. She stopped and carefully peered around. "Just more corridor."

As they hurried toward the far corner, Dee looked at Jonathon. "Did you know all this was below House Darthar

Na?"

"No. I do not think any did. The Fontala are known by some as being only a legend. But none ever said that it was more than a very long ago time myth. The same sort of myths that the people have. Similar to their King Arthur stories."

"That book stated that the split in the house into Darthar and Darthar Na had to do with the creation of The Fontala."

"Ummmmm."

"It said," she continued, "that House Darthar was also called The Bringer of Order."

"Ahhhhh ummmm," he said. "One family, two functions. One for order, one for protection." He stopped walking and leaned back against the wall.

"What?" Dee stopped and hurried back to him.

"We, you and I, all here must be very careful with this knowledge. All this happened ever so long ago when we, The Feyra, were finally realizing what we were and learning how to survive in the midst of the ever expanding hordes of people."

He gestured at the staff she held. "That will unsettle some of us, The Hidden Ones. But I believe that it would really frighten any of the people who saw it. Do you know what it does?"

"Not really." She frowned at something. "That purple book doesn't really explain much of anything. The authors seemed to have been more interested in being vague and mysterious than in being informative. But I do know that it chops through stone as if the stone is soft butter."

Jonathon pulled his left hand into his sleeve so that the end of the sleeve hung loose. "Touch my sleeve with it, please."

Karanly danced backward and away.

"Please?" He watched the staff.

Ever so carefully Dee extended the staff and gently poked one end at the loose sleeve. The material wobbled, undamaged.

"Ummmmmm," said Jonathon.

"Strange," stated Dee.

Karanly stepped further away.

"One more, ummm ah, test," said Jonathon, thrusting his left hand back out of the sleeve, making a tight fist, with the small finger extended. "Touch the tip, just the tip of that finger, please?"

"Jonathon?" Dee stared at him.

"Brother!" gasped Karanly.

"Please? Ever so gently."

Dee held the staff just below the tip and slowly raised the weapon and gently, ever so gently, touched the tip of his finger with it.

He winced.

She jerked the staff away.

"Nothing," he said, carefully examining his finger tip.

"Maybe," suggested Karanly, "it doesn't work in here."

"Oh," said Dee. She reset her hand and swung the staff, ever so gently. And carved a chunk from the wall and danced back as the piece thunked heavily to the floor at her feet. "Nope. Works just fine."

"Ummmmm," said Jonathon.

And down the hall they went. And around the corner. To stare at the door.

"Oh, well." Dee shoved the door open and stepped through. "Now what?"

The ceiling in here was high over head. The wall in front of them was tall, maybe ten feet tall, with a clear space above it, well below the arched ceiling. The hall, if that is what it was, went to the left and to the right.

She went right. And then around the next corner. And then the next corner. Both were left turns. They stopped and looked at another intersection.

Dee pointed. "This is some sort of a maze. Wait here."

Her great white feather covered wings, long wings tips, appeared and up she went. Standing on top of the wall she looked around and called back down to them, "It certainly is a maze all right. A very big one. Come on up here."

Grey wings, bat shaped, popped open. Karanly and Jonathon floated up to stand next to her.

Dee pointed at the ceiling. "Let's get as high as we can. That way we can see where the path in the maze leads. We can just shortcut the whole thing."

The trio lifted up and slowly circled over the maze just below the ceiling. Karanly traced their path before the others had finished. "There!" She pointed.

They slowly drifted downward, landed on the wall and looked down.

"Another door," grumbled Dee, lightly landing in front of it, great wings disappearing as the others thumped down beside her. Once all were ready she slowly opened the door, peered at what she could see, and walked through.

It was another round room. A stone cylinder thrust up from the center of the floor. The top was waist high on Dee. All there was in this room was . . . nothing.

"Boy," growled Dee, "would I really like to have a conversation with the guys responsible for this!" She stomped over to the cylinder and looked at the top. "Another rose!" She gently, ever so carefully, with a fingertip, touched it.

The cylinder settled flush to the floor with a soft sigh. The rose glowed red. The room darkened.

To one side the wall dropped into the floor exposing a long rack of large, rectangular boxes.

The light returned to pleasant, soft pleasant.

Dee walked over and peered inside one of the boxes, and gasped. "Dead bodies. Someone has stored lots of dead bodies down here."

Karanly and Jonathon stepped to her sides and looked at the body.

He lay on his back, hands clasped over the mid-section, one hand curled over the long staff that ran from his feet up to his chin.

"Fontala warriors," stated Jonathon.

They walked along and looked at them, male and female warriors, all laid out in the same fashion, all wearing purple jackets, all holding one of the Flame Blade staffs.

Dee looked at Jonathon. "What do you do to preserve bodies this well."

"We do not!"

"Huh?"

"We do not do something like this." He turned toward his sister. She was bent over one of the female bodies, face almost touching face.

Karanly jerked upright and stepped back. "They are not dead!"

"WHAT!" Dee reached out and touched a face. It was warm, soft. She leaped back. "Whoa!"

Walls around the room dropped into the floor. The room was encircled with rack after rack of the large, rectangular boxes.

"What is this?" Dee stared around the room and then at

Jonathon and Karanly. One hand waved violently at the racks of bodies in repose.

Jonathon slowly shook his head. "I have never heard of any house having a house skill that was capable of something like this."

Karanly nodded. "Never."

Someone sighed. It was a very long, drawn out, slow sigh.

They spun in that direction and stared.

An arm had flopped over the edge of one of the rectangular boxes. Someone slowly sat up, shoving the long staff to the side. Then the head turned and stared at them, eyes squinting in the soft light. The person looked at Dee and then at her left sleeve.

"A little assistance would be nice." They ran over and helped him crawl out and then stand on wobbly legs, leaning back against the rack holding so many of the rectangular boxes.

He looked at Dee. "I am Andalur, Andalur of House Argonar." He bowed his head.

They introduced themselves to her.

Andalur smiled at Dee. "I am The First Hand." He waggled his hand at the room. "The First Hand of The First Stand." His eyes watched Dee's eyes. "Daliera Word, shall I waken them?"

Dee jerked. "Ummmm, no!" She took a step back. "We need to talk. First!" She looked around the room with no apparent door in any wall. "Do you know the way out?"

Andalur nodded and touched the rose on his left breast pocket.

They stood in the main hall upstairs.

Dee gestured and led them to a room, poured and

handed each a brimming cup of coffee. And dropped into a chair.

Andalur sipped, after watching the others do so. "Interesting liquid, this." He sat after the others had done so.

"OH, my," sighed Dee.

"Daliera Word?" Andalur stared from face to face. "For why do all stare so?"

Dee leaned forward. "Andalur, when did your, ah ummmm, Stand, ummm ah, go to sleep? In there?"

"In there?" Andalur frowned. "That is the place of The First Stand! Only!" He took another sip from his cup. "This is quite good. Does it have a name?"

"When?" asked Dee, softly, gently. "It is called coffee."

"Ahhhh," replied Andalur. "It was after The Great Straightening and after The Stands took down The Dark Nine Cluster, buried their dead, and retired to their places."

Dee set her cup down, stood, and said, "Wait here. I'll be back in a moment."

Andalur sprang to his feet and bowed his head. "Of course! As the Word says."

Dee beckoned Jonathon from the room and out into the hall. "Come on, come on." She hurried down the hall and up the stairs and finally down a hall and into her bedroom.

Snatching the book from a shelf, she dropped into a chair and opened it, hastily paging through the book until she could read the last page with writing on it.

Dropping the book into her lap, she leaned back and laughed. And laughed and laughed.

Jonathon stood and stared at her. "Dee?"

Finally forcing her laughter away, Dee called.

Winala and Tiela walked into the room and looked from

Jonathon to her.

"Mother?" asked Tiela.

Dee stood, set the book on a table, walked over and kissed her on the forehead. Then did the same to Winala. She stepped back and called again.

Ar walked into the bedroom. "Princess?"

She handed him the volume. "Stick this thing in the library. The search is over. Tiela and Winala have the touch. They can read everything in there." She smiled at Ar, and then at her daughters. "Everything in there except the Appendix. The skills in there will have to wait until they are very much more trained. Only I may read those pages for now."

Tiela frowned at her. Winala nodded.

Dee led them down the hall, down the stairs, and turned into a room.

After filling their cups, she sat and sampled a few of the things on a large platter. And questioned Ar about each of her daughter's studies.

Tiela frowned. Winala nodded.

Jonathon ate some of this and some of that and waited, calm as calm ever was.

Finally, Dee shooed two daughters from the room.

"O.K." She looked from face to face. "Either of you ever heard of the Great Straightening? Or the Dark Nine Cluster?"

"Ummm ah," said Jonathon. "I could research through our very oldest volumes."

Ar sighed.

"What?" snapped Dee. "Oh! Sorry, Ar."

He cleared his throat. "The Great Straightening happened not all that long past Darthar House separating into House Darthar and House Darthar Na." He cleared his throat. "The

Dark Nine Cluster, emmm, event, that happened not long after The Great Straightening."

Dee stood. "Thanks, Ar. Come on, Jonathon. I think that it time for a history lesson." She grumbled to herself as she headed back to the room where she had left Karanly and Andalur.

Anadalur jumped to his feet as soon as they entered and looked at Dee. "Word?"

Dee poured, refilled cups, and dropped back into her chair. "Sit, please?" And leaned back.

They did. Jonathon sipped. Andalur sat rigid, back straight and sipped whenever Dee did.

"Are there any written histories of The Fontala?"

"No, Word."

Dee sighed.

Andalur sat straighter. Or tried to, brows furrowing. "I could wake The One Who Remembers, if you wish?"

"What? Who?"

"The One Who Remembers. Of our Stand, The First Stand."

Dee stared at him.

"They are specially trained, the ones with the ability, to remember all that The Stand has ever done."

Jonathon nodded. "An oral tradition, is it?"

"Most so," murmured Andalur, nodding at him.

"Please bring that one to us," said Dee.

Andalur bounded to his feet. "As The Words says, so will the deed be done!" He touched the rose on his left breast pocket. And was gone.

"Ummmm ah," said Jonathon, taking a sip.

She looked at him. "How could they sleep that long?

Didn't they have anything to do since then?"

"Ummmmm." He held out his cup. She refilled it. He sipped.

Then he leaned toward her. "Dee, we need to know ever so much more. This all started because, I, ahh we, you and I, wanted to find out whether there were any of the people that had gathered anything from their mythology, or whatever, that might bring undo attention to us, The Hidden Ones." His eyes bored into hers. "Why now? Why this discovery now?"

Dee sighed.

Jonathon nodded. "Just so."

Karanly looked from one to the other.

Dee frowned darkly at something. "I thought that the search was to do something else. But there isn't anything else in that volume."

He nodded.

Andalur popped through the door followed by a tall, rather thin male. On his right cheek there was a great star burst of scar tissue. A jagged line ran from his hair line over his right eyebrow.

He bowed to her. "I am Farlon, House Faradon." His jacket had a broad red stripe around each cuff. "I am The One Who Remembers of The First Stand."

Dee waved at a chair. "Please sit." She waited until he did, then handed him a cup.

Farlon took a cautious sip after watching Andalur do the same. "Interesting," he murmured. "Does it have a name?"

"Coffee," said Dee, looking at him. "Can you tell me about the Great Straightening?"

"Most so, Word, most so." He took another sip. "Quite good, this liquid." He nodded at Dee. "But only from the perspective of The First Stand."

"Oh." She looked at Andalur. "How many Stands are there?"

Andalur stared at her then held out his hands. The fingers on his right hand splayed out. The left fist pointed one digit at Dee.

"Six?"

Andalur nodded and swallowed. "The Seventh Stand perished in the removal of The Dark Nine Cluster."

Dee leaned back and stared at the pair. She nodded. "Tell me of The Great Straightening, ummm ah, from your perspective."

Farlon looked puzzled and confused at Andalur, who nodded and said. "Tell The Word." He took a sip from his cup.

Dee leaned forward and filled all the cups.

Farlon sat straighter, cleared his throat, and began.

"It was a time of great confusion for all The Feyra."

Way Out West.

As it seemed warranted to them, Jeff and Randle took the next step. They began to poke at and harangue politicians. And as Jeff and Randle did make some goodly contributions, the politicians listened and then sent staff members to do research and talk with everyone before those politicians would do anything.

And then once they were satisfied, those politicians began to pull strings as only politicians knew how to do. They did this because they felt that something was going on that no one could explain to them and to these politicians this smelled of coverup, some agency out there was doing something that they didn't want anyone to know about. This idea was more than enough to get the blood boiling in the political mind, so to speak.

People settled down.
Other than telling each other monster stories.
For a few days.

Then he turned up. Mr. F.B.I.

Actually this was his first assignment. He was new to the job, having been posted way out here in this part of the country, just to see how he would do.

His boss had told him that this thing had political strings attached to it stretching all the way back to Washington, D.C. So his report had better be the best of the best, if he got the meaning.

He got the meaning, so here he was, investigating a monster story. But, he was determined that his report would be a model of thoroughness.

He talked to everyone. He talked to anyone that anyone said would have something to say on the matter under investigation. Pages of notes that covered everything from the local ranches to the state wildlife staff to the County Sheriff to the State Police. Every official report was copied and discussed, copies attached with photographs of the various sites previously investigated.

He walked and talked and noted and discussed and documented everything, even his excursion a short way up into the narrow canyon.

Finally, back in his office, after much editing on many a long evening, he dropped his volume on this Supervisor's desk with a loud 'thump.' It actually caused waves in the coffee cup sitting there.

He received a smile, a verbal pat on the back, and was sent back to the usual low level stuff.

The massive report with a note attached, complimenting the author, was sent upward, after having several copies made first, of course.

Maryland.

They were having a picnic. Of a sort. They were in the back yard. They couldn't picnic in a public park and talk about the things that they talked about. So there they were, sitting around a large ground cover, in the thick grass, eating and drinking the sorts of things one ate and drank when on a picnic.

The three men and the three women were part of a unique organization. That organization had a special assignment and had special powers in order to accomplish that special assignment. Just in case anyone ever happened to learn of their existence they had called themselves, the six of them, three couples all together, The Council. It was a rather innocuous term that could mean anything. Which was exactly the way they wanted it.

"Truly," said one of the men, "this is a joke!" He dropped his copy of the thick report on the grass behind himself. Each of the six had received a copy. "This isn't even close to Halloween!" he grumbled.

His wife handed him another beer.

The other man shook his head.

The last man set his mug on top of the volume laying near his side. It made a handy mini-table. "You are serious about this . . . joke?" He indicated the report.

"Yes. Some small bit."

"O.K.," said the man. "What is the problem."

"Our immediate boss thinks that we need to take a look at several factors." He held up one finger. "Someone is causing this commotion out there." A second finger rose. "There is a rather quietly secret Army installation not all that far away." A third finger joined its comrades. "And no one wants to talk about what they are doing." His fingers spread wide. "Research. Very secret research."

The speakers eye's coasted from face to face. "We are to find out what and why and if something they have, or had, escaped. If it is something that they did that is loose then the assumption given to me was that the events noted in this report might be a cause of concern in terms of National Security."

"Oh me, oh my," sighed one of the other men. "There are times when Hollywood movies are given much too much credence."

The speaker rose to his feet. "Make up a small team of crack research people. Then send a couple of very tough guys out there to take a look, properly equipped to camp here and there, and warn the locals of their presence."

The other nodded and reached for the apple pie. "It does sound like something the Army might be up to, troops that can get shot a whole bunch and still run away."

"Yep, but we have to see what we shall see."

The Great Straightening.

House Darthar Na.

"It was a time of great confusion for all The Feyra."

Farlon looked at them, nodded, and then began to relate all that he knew of the event.

Houses were organizing and reorganizing as The Feyra came to grips with the true understanding of who they were. The others, the people, were spreading and multiplying and gathering in ever larger clusters, organizing.

House Darthar, The Bringer of Order, had shown the way, arguing forcefully to all The Feyra that this was the wise path, the true path to survival. Cluster, or house, could no longer attack cluster, or house, else all would soon know that the very end of all was upon them, the Feyra would cease to exist.

The Head of House Darthar stormed across all the lands arguing, cajoling, demanding that Feyra whether cluster or house should listen, must listen, before the wildness caused all to disappear.

Some long time after long past, the Head returned to rest and heal, so battered in body and spirit that all feared his end.

As that one rested and healed and as the confusion and wildness flowed from here to there and back again, a great discussion grew among all of the family Darthar.

One among them, Zanta the Clever, had learned a very rare skill which she had practiced long and hard to master. Finally, after long past long, she took her eldest sister to a closed and protected room in the house and there she demonstrated that which she had perfected and those things that she had wrought.

The eldest sister took a new name, Daliera, a name which the two sisters had crafted.

Daliera put on the Armor Jacket of glistening purple scales calling it the Shield of Color. Then did Daliera snatch up the purple staff glistening with an internal purple light calling this thing The Flaming Sword. Throwing wide the door, Daliera strode purposeful steps throughout the halls of House Darthar, and then hurtled wide the doors to The Hall of Gathering and stomped to the front of wide eyes and startled expressions to bring the necessary arguments before all therein gathered.

Striding swiftly, she slammed the doors closed and told them locked. Then stepping once again to the central place in front of all those gathered and high upon the stone stairs before the High Throne of House Darthar where he sat, the Head of House Darthar, she began to speak to them.

Many days, many nights passed, with this one or that one adding this new thought or that new thought to the ever more twisting and intense argument and discussion while all those in the outside waited in confusion and indecision, in all the lands where there were Feyra.

Finally, after a many long time, it was agreed. Family Darthar would seemingly split into two, becoming House Darthar and House Darthar Na. Family members flowed to this side or that side with it being decided that The Head of House

Darthar would forever be the Lord of both houses.

Zanta the Clever joined her sister in House Darthar Na and there their plan became a reality, ever so slowly.

House Darthar Na, The Protector of The Innocent, and House Darthar, The Bringer of Order, crafted The Fontala.

A select few strolled out into the turmoil from cluster to cluster, from newly formed house to newly formed house, sending this one and that one to House Darthar Na.

Zanta the Clever worked long and hard and crafted new skills and trained those first few into becoming that new thing, The Fontala, who were named The Protectors of The Innocent.

And finally, after some time had passed, not a long time, not a short time, not too soon a time, after all the work and after all the effort and after all the training and after all the crafting and after all the learning of never before seen skills, it was over, it was done, it was complete.

The seven, the Hands of The Fontala, stood in The Throne Room of House Darthar Na and bowed deeply to Daliera, Head of House Darthar Na, and to Daliera, The Word of The Fontala, the Head of the Fontala. Close to the right side of Daliera stood Everill of House Handarill, The One of The All, the Voice of The Word.

The seven looked up and waited. The seven First Hand of the First Seven Stands of The Fontala waited for The One to speak the words. Ranks of The Stand stood waiting, wearing the Shield of Color, holding the soft glowing Flame Swords, waiting for each First Hand to receive the word. And, in each Stand, The One Who Remembers, waited and saw and listened and placed into firm memory all that occurred and readied themselves for all that would occur.

The Word spoke softly. The One of The All spoke the

words. The seven listened and bowed their heads. Then did they pour forth from House Darthar Na, the Seven Stands of The Fontala in seven directions to bring the words of House Darthar, The Bringer of Order, to all the Feyra, to every group, from the smallest clusters to the largest houses.

The First Stand flowed out and along the mountain range that held House Darthar Na, flowing in a soft wave of glittering purple. The Seeker, one of the rare few with that special skill, felt and guided The First Stand to each cluster no matter how small and to each house no matter how large. And to each and every Feyra they met the First Hand spoke the words to Bring Order to their fellows, spoke the words of the need to stop the destruction, the destruction that threatened to overwhelm all The Feyra, one by the other.

Cluster by cluster, house by house, the Words of Order were heard. Cluster by cluster, house by house, the Words of Order were believed. Most who heard understood, and then they knew that they were The Feyra. They were not wild and ravening beasts.

Some here, some there, this cluster or that house, refused to listen, refused to understand. These tried to destroy the bringers of the Word, the message of Order.

Flame Swords whirled through attacker and dwelling with the ease of leaves blowing on the faintest of breezes. No thing, neither Feyra nor beast, neither wood nor stone, could withstand the cutting ease of the tools crafted by Zanta the Clever. But still, some of The Fontala fell in battle.

The First Stand finally reached the great northern water and turned toward the place from which the sun rises, always seeking their own kind, The Feyra, always avoiding the others, the people and their places.

Finally, long time after long time ago, The First Stand of The Fontala returned to House Darthar Na. Among those lost was their Seeker.

There, before Daleira, The One Who Remembers spoke all the names, spoke all the names of each cluster no matter how small, spoke all the names of each house no matter how large, and told of all that had occurred.

Then, when the last Stand returned, and all told of all that had occurred there was held a great ceremony. All of House Darthar and all of House Darthar Na and all of The Fontala did celebrate the Bringing of Order to all of The Feyra and then they did mourn all who were no longer among them, The Feyra.

The work of the Seven Stands, the work of The Fontala, the Bringing of Order to all The Feyra was then called The Great Straightening.

Farlon stood and bowed deeply to Dee. "These are the words, these are the events, this is the memory of The One Who Remembers of The First Stand as true spoke to Daliera, The Word of The Fontala, to Daliera, Head of House Darthar Na."

Dee stood and bowed to him and then to Andalur. "Thank you both." She sat and waved them to also sit. And called.

Ar walked into the room. "Princess?"

She indicated Farlon. "This is The One Who Remembers of the First Stand. Is there any way to have written down all that he knows? If something ever happened to him the loss of knowledge would be a great disaster."

"We will begin."

"Ummmm ah, Ar?"

"Princess?"

"There are five others, one from each of the Stands."

"Six?"

"The Seventh Stand perished. We have lost one seventh of the history of The Fontala."

"Oh, my."

Dee looked at Andalur. "Can you waken the other First Hands and ask them to bring their memories to Ar? We have a great chore, one I would like to see finished as quickly as possible."

Andalur nodded.

"Afterwards I would like to speak with all the First Hands."

Andalur bounced to his feet. "As The Word says, so will the deed be done." He was gone.

"This way, please." Ar ushered Farlon from the room.

Jonathon stood. "Let's go eat."

As they ate, Jonathon cleared his throat.

"What?"

"All that history was not known. In all my previous research, in all my previous conversations, there was no mention of all that which we just heard."

He refilled their cups. "Some, as you may remember, called you Daliera of the Fontala when they heard your true name. But I do not believe that they truly understood what they meant. I think that only the form of the name was remembered. Nothing but that."

She nodded and munched on something. "Pretty over whelming, all right."

Karanly popped into the room. "What? Looks like the usual meal to me." She began to serve herself, stopped, and looked at Jonathon's expression. "Brother?"

He sipped. "Ummmm ah, we just heard a rather abbreviated history of The Great Straightening."

Karanly nodded, sat, and crunched on something.

"Almost lost history," explained Dee. "Almost lost history of The Feyra."

"Really?"

"Yes." Jonathon took a little from one of the serving bowls. "From our almost ever so long ago beginnings."

Karanly stared at him. As a part-time librarian her curiosity popped to the surface. "Where did you find that volume?"

"There is no volume," stated Jonathon.

"What? Then how could you know?"

"Oral history," explained Dee.

Dee and Jonathon began to explain what they knew to Karanly who stared at them throughout their presentation.

When they finished, she remembered to take something to eat, and then whispered to Dee, "What are you going to do? With them?"

Dee shrugged. "No idea. It is all a big surprise. Takes a lot of getting use to, knowing what we now know."

Someone knocked on their door, a very firm knock.

"Come in," said Dee.

Armilin stepped in and bowed to her. "Mother says to tell you that she is very proud and that she hoped to see the day when The Fontala were once again with us. Second sister Eagta will stand for me as House Head when the occasion arises."

Dee waved her to a chair and shoved a just filled cup in her direction and said to the others, "Armilin is The One of The All." She smiled at Armilin. "Boy, do I have a surprise for you!"

The four of them were lounging in a small comfortable room looking out the large window, watching dark settle over the nearby forest when Ar walked in. "Princess?"

"Ummmm?"

"They wait in The Throne Room."

"Be there in a little bit. Thanks, Ar."

Ar bowed and left.

Dee looked at Armilin. "Put on your jacket, ummmm, your Shield of Color, grab your staff, we have some people to meet."

Armilin stood, unwrapped a small bundle, shook out the jacket, and slipped it on over her glittering silver chain mail. Then she wrapped her hand around her staff.

"Let's go," said Dee, standing and heading for the door out. "You too, Karanly, Jonathon. I think that you need to be there also." She headed them down the hall and stopped outside the door to The Throne Room.

She reached for the door knob. "O.K., here we go. Oooops!" She explained to Armilin how she ought to behave based on what Farlon had said.

"Ready?"

Armilin nodded.

The group strolled into the room and up the central path of lighter stone. Twelve people standing there turned and stared at them. Especially at Armilin.

Dee climbed the stairs, turned, and sat down.

Armilin stood on her right side.

Karanly and Jonathon remained down on the floor, off to Dee's right as well, standing not too close, standing not too far away.

Dee leaned and spoke softly to Armilin who nodded and

looked at the twelve wearing purple, holding soft glowing staffs.

"I am Armilin, House Induna, Anointed One! I am Armilin, The One of The All." She bowed to them.

They all bowed.

Armilin indicated with one hand, "There stands Othara, Head of House Darthar and Lord of the Darthar family. There stands Karanalador, First Sister, House Darthar. Here sits Daliera, Head of House Darthar Na, The Word of The Fontala. Tell us who we see before us."

Dee shoved out her hand to stop them from replying and beckoned to Karanly who hurried up to her. Dee told her to make note of all the house names as they were given.

Karanly nodded and returned to the floor to stand next to Jonathon.

Dee smiled at the twelve.

Two stepped forward to announce themselves.

"Andalur, First Hand, First Stand, House Argonar." He bowed.

"Farlon, The One Who Remembers, First Stand, House Faralon."

They stepped back, another pair took their place.

"Meludo," she stated firmly. "First Hand, Second Stand, House Telat."

"Delat," he rasped all gravel throat. "The One Who Remembers, Second Stand, House Trillmar."

They were replaced by the next pair.

"Contala," said the short woman with a jagged scar down the left side of her face and neck. "First Hand, Third Stand, House Zbtan!"

The large man nodded to Dee. "Trakatar, The One Who Remembers, Third Stand, Sub-House Nerian, House Zbtan."

The fourth pair pushed past them as they stepped back.

"Stregt!" he announced. "First Hand, Fourth Stand! House Ovever."

"I do be Wisuot," she said, bowing deeply. "The One Who Remembers, Fourth Stand. From Zilan House."

Two tall and willowy women glided past them as they stepped back.

"Mensta," stated the taller one. "First Hand, Fifth Stand, House Head Darunat."

"Udoat," breathed the other, soft purr. "The One Who Remembers, Fifth Stand, House Hantaz, In-tied House Darunat."

The last pair stepped forward. He marched.

"Oatur!" he snapped. "First Hand! Sixth Stand! House Quarted-Vierda!"

She bowed to Dee. "Uztal, The One Who Remembers. Sixth Stand. House Abalam. Second Sister. Anointed One."

Dee stood and bowed to them, straightened up, and smiled at them. Then she pointed. "Farlon, take your colleagues to Ar please and explain what you all will be doing for some time."

She stepped down. "First Hands, Armilin, we have matters to discuss." She headed from The Throne Room beckoning Karanly and Jonathon to come along.

The First Hands followed and looked at each other and soft spoke one to the other. This Word was quite different.

After serving them all from the pastry tray, Dee sat and waited for them to settle down. Then she took a sip and began to talk and to explain all that she had done and had learned.

The Fontala had disappeared from the awareness of The

Feyra. At this time only a few even recognized the name as meaning something special but not why. For some unknown reason the Stands had slept for a very long time. She told them how she had come to be The Word and Armilin her voice as The One of The All. Finally she told them of the events leading up to the destruction of House Narkalar and the dark plans they had been involved in. Finished, she refilled cups, leaned back, and watched the puzzled expressions shifting with their emotions.

"This is true told?" asked Andalur.

"Just so," said Dee.

"All of The Stands must wake and be told all of this," stated Mensta.

"Not yet," replied Dee. "First, I need to know what you wish to do about The Seventh Stand."

Cantala leaned toward her. "They were destroyed, all died." A tear wandered down her face.

"I know," whispered Dee. "But what I want to know is this. Do we rebuild The Seventh Stand?" She looked from face to face. "The decision is up to you, for you to make."

She sat and watched them and waited and took a sip now and then. All of them were staring at long ago memories, not so long ago for them.

Then one, then another, turned in their chairs and looked at Andalur. One by one they nodded. He nodded back and turned to Dee.

After clearing his throat a few times, he said, "It is decided. We wish to rebuild The Seventh Stand."

Dee stood and bowed to each of them. "Then it shall be so. But first, you must listen carefully to what I have to say."

All eyes fastened upon her face, brows furrowing for some, eyebrows lifting for others.

"All the Stands have been asleep for a many great time and much, or little, has changed with The Feyra. Some Houses have grown, some Houses have shrunk, some Houses have merged together, some Houses have split apart. Some Houses are no more. Some Houses are newly created, or not so newly created long after you strode the world. To rebuild The Seventh we all must seek those best suited, best qualified to be members. Once awake, all members of all the Stands should visit their Houses and their relatives. But, as I said, much has changed and many of The Fontala may find that there is no longer something for them as it once was. Therefore, each and every member of the six Stands must know this as a true statement. House Darthar Na has room for any and all who herein wish to reside. This is true for House Darthar as well and all the sub-houses and cousin-houses associated with Family Darthar."

She sighed heavily. "Any who find that they can no longer be of The Fontala must return their armor and weapon with no exception, if they wish to withdraw. For this one summer all may do as they choose to do, to visit and seek out relatives, to travel where ever you might wish. But! And this will be so! By the Fall of this year as the people measure time, all will return here! No exceptions!"

She smiled at them. "With enough new members we will rebuild the Seventh Stand. And do remember, there is always a home for you here."

She bowed to them, deeply she bowed. "First Hands, see to your Stands." And laughed. "I will see you when ever you return. Ummm ah, before the Fall." She turned and walked quickly from the room giving them the privacy to talk and wondered to herself what would happen to them, to The Fontala. One way or the other it could be a great shock.

She strode down the hall to the correct room and wrapped her arms around Jonathon and leaned heavily against him. "Ohhhh, Jonathon, how could this happen. The Fontala have lost everything and all that time. Isn't there anything, anyway to . . . ahhhhhh, I know, I know." She leaned back and hiccuped. "Can you see what you can find out about all those houses the twelve named? I only recognized some of the names."

"Yes." He shoved her out at arms length. "Now we shall see exactly how sturdy these Fontala really are. Won't we?"

She nodded. "Let's go sit and look out one of the large windows."

Way Out West.

The two, very tough, very capable men arrived and told everyone that they would be in the area for awhile and would be looking around. Jeff guided their rig to the correct spot, wished them good luck, and drove away.

The pair stepped from their truck, hauled several large bags and containers from the bed of the pickup, made camp, and then dressed in clothes appropriate for nighttime work. They pulled various weapons from their containers, checked them, loaded them, checked them again, and laid down on the ground next to their rig to nap until the sun set.

A thin sliver of a moon rose above the mountain tops as one of the pair talked quietly with a higher up over their communications device.

Then the pair worked their way ever so slowly, ever so stealthily, toward the canyon's mouth.

If the Army thought that they could hide some local and secret operation in that narrow canyon then they were in for a surprise. Or maybe not. It would depend upon what the pair's ultimate bosses felt was best.

Two dark, very silent, shadows passed into the canyon.

Maryland.

He walked into their kitchen, interrupting their breakfast. It was two days later.

"Yes?" asked the man chewing on a piece of toast. "Awfully early." He shoved an empty plate at him. "Have some breakfast."

Their visitor sat, did, and gulped his coffee.

"Two guys," he told them. "Two guys who could sneak into anything have disappeared!"

The host nodded and poured more coffee. "How?"

He shrugged. "No evidence. They were just there and then they were not there. Doesn't make any sense. Anything unfriendly that they bumped into should have been scattered all over the landscape in small pieces."

"So, now what?"

"I am having aerial photos shot for that entire area. Teams will be in every town and hamlet within fifty miles. Even the military or otherwise installations. We are going to shoot some of that fancy see in the dark stuff for three nights just to see what we can see moving around."

"Sounds good."

"So, what do you think?"

"I think that we shall have to wait and see. First."

"Right!" He jumped to his feet. "Thanks for the eats." And charged for the front door.

As it slammed shut she looked at him. "Dear?"

He shrugged. "Pretty strange all right." He took some

more of the egg stuff. "I suppose it could be one of those survivalist groups tucked way up in that canyon, or somewhere nearby. Although it doesn't seem very likely. But they do pop up in some really strange places."

She smiled at him. "We will check on things like that."

"Good." He smiled. "I meant the eggs."

The Dark Nine Cluster

House Darthar Na.

It was halfway through Summer and Dee and Jonathon were sitting in a comfortable room eating a middle of the day meal accompanied by Tiela, Winala, and Karanly. The two Ice Cats were there as well, having a bit of a snack as Tiela and Winala slipped them a bit of this or a bit of that or a bit of some of that other stuff.

Both daughters had finished reading the purple volume, *The Fontalan*, now residing in the House library, and were very curious about The Fontala.

Winala was curious in a scholarly way and watched her sister as she pressed their mother to learn more. Tiela's interest was of a more practical nature. She had been studying The Way of The Staff with Armilin for some long time and now she thought that becoming one of The Fontala was a very fine thing to do, especially as her sister had agreed to become The Anointed One, the future House Head after their mother had relieved Tiela of that obligation.

Dee was only half-listening to her daughter plead her case. She was staring out the great window at the forest and something else that only she could see. She turned, refilled cups, and focused on his face.

"Jonathon, have you heard anything at all?

"No word has come. It seems that they are very good at

fading into the rest of us without causing excitement or concern."

She frowned vaguely in his direction. "Good. I suppose." And wondered how they could do that. She turned and stared out the window again.

"Dee?"

"Huh? What?" She looked back at him.

"Stop worrying so. I asked Hofga to listen well. There has not been a word. Even from those Houses whose names we recognized." He took a sip and then another. "Ah ummmm, with one exception."

"Oh?" She turned and watched his face and expression.

"Ummm ah." He took another sip. "House Zilan was part of that web, that Dark Plan, as plotted by House Narkalar."

She nodded. "I remember."

"Hofga told me that word has come that the Head of Zilan suddenly died and that the First Son is the new Head. He sent a very strong apology to Eltrill, Head of House Narkalar, for past behaviors." Jonathon took another sip. "Other than that word, it is very quiet out among The Feyra."

Dee nodded. Ar appeared. "Princess?"

"Call Wisuot, The One Who Remembers, Fourth Stand, to us, please."

"Of course."

Wisuot walked through the door, stopped, and bowed to Dee. "Word?"

"We have heard of a new House Head of Zilan."

Wisuot nodded. "Just so," she said. "It do be as it should be for House Zilan. Poor decisions threatening the existence of the house need remedy. It do be the way of House Zilan."

Dee looked at Ar.

"All six of them have been very busy creating many volumes of Fontala history for the library. I hired six fast scribe things from House Brockten. Hofga said that House Brockten has the fastest of the fast. All six have spent many hours narrating while the fast scribe things fill page after page." Ar cleared his throat. "In very clear script, of course."

Dee smiled and waggled a hand. "Sit, Wisuot, I wish to hear about something."

Wisuot pulled out a chair and sat. "As The Word says, so will the deed be done."

Dee looked at Tiela and then back to Wisuot. "Tell us of The Dark Nine Cluster."

Wisuot jerked. Dee shoved a filled cup across the table to her. Wisuot picked it up and took a careful sip. "Quite good. Does it have a name?"

Dee nodded. "Coffee."

Wisuot took another sip. "This is, of course, only what The Fourth Stand saw. And learned after."

Dee nodded.

Wisuot began.

House Energat.

They were having a quiet meal, just the two of them, House Head Angatak and First Brother, Daxata.

"It has been long some time since the great turmoil was ceased," observed Angatak.

"Just so," agreed Daxata. "The Great Straightening brought Feyra order to The Feyra."

"There are those no longer among us."

Daxata nodded. "There are always some who do not listen or do not wish to stop not nice behavior."

"Ummmm."

"Ah?"

"There is no organization for us."

"Just so. Most wish this to be so."

Angatak leaned both forearms on the table and looked across its shining surface at his First Brother. "I have been thinking and pondering on this matter for some not long time since The Great Straightening."

"On what matter, exactly?"

"We are strong, we are, The Feyra."

"Just so." Puzzled eyes looked across the table at the House Head.

"It has come to my mind, it has, that The Feyra require strong guidance and wise decisions. It has come to my mind, it has, that we require a new organization, a strong organization to proscribe those things."

Daxata sat back in his chair. "The Feyra, clusters and houses, do not take kindly to others interfering in their affairs."

"A strong organization, a strong and well planned new organization, would be able to tell them that it must be so."

"Great turmoil," suggested Daxata.

"Not if well planned and well executed." Angatak nodded and leaned back. "I mean to build that organization ever so quietly. Once it is done, it will have the strength. All will then see, ummm ah, the wisdom to do what we say is to be done."

"How?" whispered Daxata.

Angatak steepled his fingers in front of his face. "It has come to my mind, it has, that this organization must have nine very powerful houses in it. We are one of those." He set his fingers on the edge of the table. "I want you to talk to House Patha, a very strange house, a very strong house. I have some small feeling that they are of a similar thought."

House Patha.

He stood.

And stared at it.

The outer door.

It was a large door.

It was a large door constructed from heavy metal. It gleamed dark shine, almost black, it did, that door. Broad bands of a somewhat lighter metal crossed that door at odd angles, fastened with fist sized round-headed bolts.

Hanging from an out jutting hinge was a long rod with a round bronze ball, the door knocker.

He exhaled softly. To him that door said much about those who dwelled on the other side. Hard. Unbending.

One hand reached out, pulled, and let fall that thing.

A dull boom echoed outward as if the door was a thick hollow drum.

He waited. Polite as could be.

Slowly, ever so slowly, the door opened and swung in on silent hinges.

"Yes?" asked someone from the dark interior.

"Daxata. Come to talk."

"Ah. Do come in, Daxata." A large pale hand beckoned him into the dimness.

He walked in past a large shape who slowly closed the door behind him.

As the door latched, soft light glowed from a high ceiling. This interior space was as uninviting as the exterior had been. Dark walls, dark floor, an unadorned space with nothing to soften the hard nature of it.

"I am Zarga. This way." He turned and led Daxata down the long and wide corridor. The corridor twisted and turned and finally ended in a wide wall with three doors.

Zarga opened the middle door and led him into a room of great contrast to the hall and outer door. Warm wood clad walls glowed soft brown tones. Three large and comfortable chairs sat next to an ornately carved wooden table of pale blond wood.

The man seated there stood and bowed. "Most welcome, Daxata. I am Kontar, Head." He waggled one hand. "Please. Sit. What do you wish to talk about?"

Daxata sat and waited for the other to sit.

"I am Daxata of House Energat, sent by House Head Angatak."

"A strong house," murmured Zarga.

"Yes," agreed Kontar. "Ummmm."

"Head Angatak has had a thought, an idea for an organization, an organization unlike any yet to be seen among The Feyra."

Kontar leaned back. "An organization unlike any?"

"Just so. Head Angatak feels that it is time for The Feyra, all houses, all clusters, to be, ahhh, organized in a unified manner unlike any ever seen before."

Kontar tapped his teeth with both fingertips and hummed. "And what would this unlike any other ever seen organization be about doing."

"Leading!" stated Daxatar. "Leading The Feyra. A unified Feyra, under one leadership. This holds great promise, great reward to all."

"Sooooo," sighed Kontar. He nodded. "Do tell Head Angatak that we will soon visit."

Daxatar stood and bowed deeply.

House Energat.

Angatak nodded to Kontar, Head to Head.

This was the seventh meeting between the two. Sometimes they met in House Energat, sometimes in House Patha.

Daxata had traveled widely as the two House Heads drew up lists of suitable candidates, adding and deleting names each time Daxata returned and reported what this house or what that house had said to him, declining or accepting the invitation.

But now, finally, they had a list of the chosen seven, making their group nine strong houses.

Today the two House Heads were deep into ironing out the final details of this new things that they were ready to build, ever so quietly build. Not a word had leaked outward which is exactly what they made happen. Soon, they would be done. And then all would know.

Daxata kept careful records as he was directed to do. The prime pair felt that an accurate history should be compiled from the beginning so others, later in time, would be able to read and understand what they had created.

House Patha.

Some long time had passed and now were gathered the nine, to finalize the last detail and to prepare the announcement.

Angatak and Kontar sat side by side and looked around the table at the others and nodded. Every seat was occupied by The First Brother of each house from the seven select houses.

Angatak cleared his throat. "Welcome to House Nagaron, Patalar, Ra'am, Azala, Barzen, Guenda, and Omalop." He nodded at Kontar.

Kontar searched each face. "Let us begin."

And so it went.

On and off for many a day.

Discussion boiled forth and became heated argument to change into debates to become forged into a plan.

And so it went.

On and off for many a day.

Until the plan was bent and molded and formed into a new shape, the pieces placed into a new order.

And so it went.

On and off for many a day.

And finally the nine nodded agreement and leaned back in their chairs and nodded to each other. It was good. This plan. It was finalized. This plan. It was complete. This plan.

And then they stood. Seven bowed deeply to two.

A new thing existed. A new way of thinking for The Feyra.

Then they broke apart, each traveling to their own house to make the final preparations. Seven of them did. Two remained to ever so carefully craft the message that would be sent out into the realms of The Feyra, this new way of thinking.

House Darthar.

Othara, Head of House Darthar and Lord of Family

Darthar read, once again, the document, a very carefully worded document, describing the structure and the proposed duties of this new structure. The statement was signed by the Heads of the nine powerful houses calling themselves The Cluster. A number of other house names were listed as all supporting The Cluster.

He winced. The Feyra did not require someone, they did not need someone, deciding how they would live nor did they require some group to do their thinking for them.

He began to write. It was a carefully worded counter-declaration refuting the presentation, line by line, item by item. When he finished, he listed all those houses involved including those at the bottom who followed along. And then he sent his statement out and into the Feyra so all might see what he thought.

Done with all that, he leaned back in his chair and thought to himself that there would be a great disagreement even worse than that leading up to The Great Straightening. He stared into somewhere and thought to himself that there always seemed to be some group that felt that they had the right to decide how everyone else ought to behave regardless of what everyone else felt about being told how to behave.

This could get very messy, he thought.

Wisuot paused and looked from face to face, each staring into somewhere, somewhere that their thoughts had taken them during her telling of the long ago time.

Dee refilled cups and settled back in her chair.

Wisuot, sipped, and nodded to her and began to tell.

"Argument over argument flowed through The Feyra. Discussion and debate roiled in this area or in that area. Few of

The Feyra were excempt from this flow of words. And unknown to almost all, something else was building."

House Darthar.

"Do come in," said Othara to his unexpected visitor.

He led him down the hall to a comfortable room and waved the man to a comfortable chair before dropping into a similar one. He looked at his visitor and waited, calm as calm ever was.

"I have fled my house, House Energat. I am Daxata, First Brother. I seek safety here, if you will provide that."

Othara nodded. And waited, calm as calm ever was.

Daxata sighed heavily. "They have become dark in their zeal. House Energat Head Angatak and House Patha Head Kontar, drive the cluster of nine into not nice, dark not nice." He stared at the floor, then up into some far away place. "I can't do that," he mumbled, "I will not help!"

His eyes focused on Othara's. "That Dark Nine Cluster must not succeed. All the Feyra would suffer. All!"

"Ummmmm. You may stay here as long as you wish." Othara stood. "Let me show you to the rooms you may use."

Othara sat in the house library and read, again, the names of the lessor houses as listed in that document sent to him by the nine. He gathered paper and wrote a carefully worded message and had it sent to all but the nine hoping that if enough of the lessor supporters withdrew their support that the organization would collapse.

Some small time passed. Othara and his good friend Hofga sat in one the smaller rooms and discussed the problem as they saw it of The Dark Nine Cluster.

"They are prata!" growled Hofga. "Word has come that House Danadon, one of the smaller houses that withdrew from them is no more."

"Ummmm."

"Just so." Hofga glared at Othara. "It seems, it does to me, that they mean to force themselves into a role that many many do not wish them to have." He leaned forward, hands on knees, and glared even darker.

"Ummmmmm."

"And House Frantaln as well. They strike at all those that they know of that have supported your opposition to them."

"Ah ummmm." Othara sighed, soft gentle sigh.

Hofga nodded. "It will get very messy."

Othara looked at his friend, his long time friend. "The order is being disrupted, the order of The Feyra is being disrupted." He sighed again. "Deliberately. Just so some may tell others what to do."

"Just so." Hofga nodded.

"Stay here. For a few days."

Hofga surged to his feet. "Just so." And stomped from the room.

Othara nodded to himself, leaned over the material on the table, gathered together paper and began to write. He began to write an ever so carefully worded document.

Some time later, not all that much later, it was finished this document. He sent it to the Heads of the Nine houses.

House Energat.

Angatak, the Head, glowered at the document. Then he shifted his gaze up and glowered at the other eight sitting around the table.

"All the same?" he snarled.

Heads nodded.

"Exactly so," replied Kontar, Head of House Patha.

Angatak's fist thumped the table top. "House Darthar presumes to tell us what to do!"

"A suggestion," stated Kontar.

Angatak steepled his fingers under his chin and nodded. "I have a suggestion as well."

He leaned forward, hands flat on the table and began to explain, his eyes jumping from startled expression to startled expression.

"It will solidify our control," he snapped. "It will put an end to suggestions such as this!" He ripped and tore and shredded and scattered bits and pieces of the document over the table top. "And there will be no more of these!"

House Darthar Na.

They stood and looked out one of the large windows in one of the many outside rooms, Mondara, Head of House Darthar Na, and Zimil, his wife.

She leaned gently against him and murmured, "We are about to have a daughter."

He pulled her tight against his side. "At long last. It will be good to have a daughter." Fingers gently pinched her side. "Are you sure?"

Her laughter was soft and as gentle as her brushing against his side. "Of course." She tickled his ribs. "The rooms are already prepared."

"Ummmmm." He gave her an answering tickle. "Name?"

She kissed his cheek. "A good name."

"Ah."

"Daliera."

He twisted around and stared at her.

"Just so," she said. "Name linked to the Word of The Fontala. That one did agree. And?"

He wrapped her in his arms. "As do I. You are correct. A good name."

They turned back and watched them leave in seven directions. Then Zimil hurried away. A daughter was about to arrive and she needed to get to those two prepared rooms.

Wisuot paused in her narration and stared at Dee. Tears were running down Dee's cheeks.

She nodded and wiped her face with a sleeve. "I have almost no memory of my parents as Feyra."

Wisuot's eyes popped wide.

"Just talk to Ar," Dee whispered. "He can explain."

Wisuot nodded, cleared her throat and continued the tale.

House Darthar.

Othara had poured through many a library to construct his lists while Hofga had traveled far and wide. Between them they had prepared detailed maps and lists of all those associated with each of The Dark Nine Cluster.

Each of the Fontala Stands would find and visit the lessor houses of the lessor followers of one of the seven. Next they would visit the lessor seven organizers. Then the Stands would converge on House Kontar and finally House Angaret.

House Azala.

The Fourth Stand stood on the slopes of the small, the very small valley, and watched the house down below for any sign of aggression. A messenger had been sent down to talk with the House Head.

So they stood and watched and waited, a line of purple glittering in the early sunlight.

The outer door swung open and the messenger walked out accompanied by a young male. The pair strolled up the slope to speak with the First Hand, Stregt, and Wisuot, The One Who Remembers.

The young male, A'ata by name, was the new Head of House Azala. He told them that the house had severed all ties to The Dark Nine Cluster. Then, in the softest of voices, he told them what House Angatak, House Patha, and House Nagaron had done.

First Hand Segret gasped. A'ata ducked. But nothing had happened. Stregt sent fast messengers to the other six Stands, warning them of this dark thing that the three houses had brought into existence.

The First Hand told A'ata to stay safe and started the Stand toward House Nagaron planning on meeting the Seventh Stand there.

House Nagaron.

The Fourth Stand crested the ridge above House Nagaron and halted.

Flame and dark smoke poured into the sky above the remnants of the house. Survivors stood in small groups here and there, some wandered about on unsteady legs.

On all sides of the wreckage lay the dead and glaring up at them the survivors and the great black things called forth by House Nagaron.

The Fourth started down the slope in a tight wave of

purple.

The surviving house members attacked.

Flames Swords whirled in singing arcs. Bits and pieces of house members splattered everywhere, on combatants and the great dark things. Pieces of green armor flew, shattered from those things along with body parts and limbs.

Silence flew over the scene of carnage where just a moment ago war cries and screams of rage had soared above the clash of wild attack.

The Fourth Stand reformed and walked the field of carnage and the remains of House Nagaron. And then all knew that the Seventh Stand had stood and died to the last member. Lying alongside the body of Frantel, First Hand, they found the messenger that had been sent.

House Nagaron had ceased to exist along with the Seventh Stand.

First Hand Stegt sighed and reformed the Fourth into four columns with a great space between them and headed the Stand toward House Patha.

House Patha.

All the First Hands stood deep in the woods surrounding the looming structure that was House Patha. Then they were told of the events around House Nagaron and the Hands told their Stands.

The First and the Fifth left to mount a watch on House Energat. Word had come that House Energat had built or was building a great tower.

The Second, the Third, the Fourth, and the Sixth gathered together and formed a crescent inside the dense forest, just out of sight. Scouts lay immobile shadow in low foliage at the very edge of the trees and watched.

All waited for the sun to sail above the nearby ridge. As it did, an eagle screamed and all the Stands readied themselves.

The messenger who had been waiting, quiet as quiet, stood and rapped on the outside door. And waited. Then did it again. And waited.

The door opened and a face peered out through the narrow slit. The messenger banged into the door, grabbed someone and yanked them sprawling to one side of the opening. The scouts could see the rapid and very agitated conversation between the messenger, bending over this member of the house, and that house member.

Straightening up, the messenger waggled one hand and raced inside the structure followed by the Section of the Stand that had been standing tight against the wall.

The Stands slipped closer to the forest edge. Three of the scouts ran across the open ground to wait by the still open door. One danced sideways, staff whirling, and chopped the door from its hinges.

All waited. And wondered. In the early silence of morning all stood and watched and waited and wondered. Then a scout hurried a house member up the slope to speak with The First Hand of the Second Stand.

It was a young female, Second Daughter Taranal. She told them that the house was in the midst of a great argument. Word had come of the destruction of House Nagaron. Some within argued that House Energat would come to their aid. Others argued the House Energat had abandoned House Nagaron and looked what happened to them.

They waited in the stillness. The Fontala shifted from foot to foot as the tension began to build.

Down below someone in glowing purple stepped from the door and to one side. They watched folk stream out the door into the open meadow to stand in clusters of twos and threes.

Taranal told them that many of those she could see were members of the smaller houses allied with House Patha. And that those now exiting the structure were members of her family.

A lengthy discussion started between the members of the houses and the First Hands of the Stands. Finally all agree. House members and their allies returned to House Patha as the Stands gathered and prepared to advance on House Energat.

House Patha and their associated houses had agreed and promised that they were no longer a part of The Dark Nine Cluster. House Energat was now the solitary survivor of that organization.

The Stand streamed down the valley, four columns of purple gleaming in the bright sunlight, running in an easy lope that would carry them for mile after mile.

Long past high sun, close to darkening of twilight, they could see rising into the air, the top of the tower that marked House Energat.

House Energat.

The house and its great tower sat in the wide mouth of the valley offering a long view of the open plain stretching to the far horizon.

The Sixth Stand moved up the canyon and took a blocking position in a very narrow neck of the canyon. No one would be able to use this canyon for valley access.

The other five Stands formed an arc, each end of that arc anchored to the steep rock face of the canyon mouth and settled themselves in the gathering dark to wait for the light of the next day.

A select group formed a blocking force to prohibit anyone from the house leaving via the outside door.

Rations were handed around and eaten cold. Half settled to the ground to sleep while the other half watched carefully. At the midpoint of night they would switch. All would be up and ready as the first glow of the sun heralded the start of day.

The First Hands and The Ones Who Remember gathered and agreed.

If House Energat gave up their plan forever, all would be well. If, however, and especially if they released anything like the things that destroyed the Seventh Stand, it was decided that all The Fontala would be realized from their oaths to protect and all not Fantala would not see the rise of another day. This decision was told to all. And all were told that if they disagreed they might leave. None disagreed and all, remembering The Seventh Stand, readied themselves.

As the sun rose, Flame Swords crackled soft songs of destruction.

A messenger volunteered and strolled across the open grass and knocked on the outside door. And waited. And knocked again.

Great dark things clad in green armor poured from the top of the tower.

The messenger hurtled up toward the waiting Stands and into a pocket of glistening purple clad Fontala and spun to face the charging great dark things who were swallowed up in a sea of whirling Flame Blades. Dark things died, dark things flew in parts and pieces, shattered armor flew green segments to all sides.

The outer door was chopped free as Fontala poured into

the interior, slicing great holes in the exterior walls as more poured into the house, down hallways and up staircases, bursting into every room.

Finally all returned to the outside silence.

The house was torn to pieces and the remains burned in place. But they left the tower. It would remind all who saw it of the folly of House Energat and it allies to attempt to impose their idea of order on all The Feyra.

House Darthar Na.

Wisuot sat back, she had been leaning more and more forward during her narration, wiped the sweat from her face, and nodded at Dee.

"Most of those originally involved," she continued, "pulled out with little problem. Afterwards word spread rapidly and widely of all that had happened. Many of the folk nodded at the wisdom of quitting such a thing."

She sipped. "Then the Stands came here, to their chambers, rested, healed, and slept. We didn't realize for how long that would actually be."

Wisuot smiled, a soft gentle smile. "Apparently The Feyra learned from those times."

Dee shook her head. "Not entirely. But not as bad."

"So," sighed Wisuot. "Now you know all that I can speak of those events known as The Dark Nine Cluster."

She stood and bowed deeply to Dee. "Those do be the words, those do be the events, this do be the memory of The One Who Remembers of The Fourth Stand, as true spoke to Daliera, The Word of The Fontala, to Daliera, Head of House Darthar Na."

Dee stood and returned her bow. "Thank you."

Wisuot nodded. "I will return to the library. There do be much yet to do." She spun and walked from the room.

Dee sat and looked at Jonathon and then at Karanly. "So, you two want to explain?"

"Ummmm," said Jonathon.

Karanly sat quiet.

"Othara," growled Dee, "the Head of House Darthar and family Darthar knew all this. "And," she hissed, "Daliera was the First Sister, and apparently Zanta the Clever, the Second Sister."

"Oh," gasped Karanly.

Dee glared at them both.

"Farlon told all that he knew," stated Jonathon. "Of The Great Straightening." He held out his cup. Dee poured.

He took a sip. "Wisuot told all that she knew of The Dark Nine Cluster." His eyes fastened on Dee's. "But neither knew everything."

He sat straighter. "Emerill of House Hondarill, The One of The All, was with the Seventh Stand as were First Sister, Handarl, now named Daleira, and Second Sister Zanta, called by all The Clever." He sighed. "They were at that great carnage."

Jonathon looked sideways. Karanly was weeping silent tears and wiping at her eyes. "Karanly became the First Sister." His eyes shifted. "Dee," he whispered, "your parents named you after her, our First Sister, the first Word of The Fontala, a name that now belongs only in House Darthar Na."

He sighed, and slumped in his chair. "I had no idea of what you had learned, or of what you knew, as you grew and lived here. But, as you know, all that was lost when your parents fled out into the people replacing your Feyra memories with the people thoughts."

He sipped. "So, how could I tell you? You had no memory of The Feyra ways or history. That purple clad book was thought lost long ago time past."

Jonathon shook his head. "I have no idea why all this is happening as it is happening at this time."

Dee stood. "Let's go get something to eat. I need to think about, ummm, everything."

He nodded and stood. "Just so."

Way Out West.

Teams swarmed throughout the target area.

Cars of many makes, styles, and conditions disgorged visitors of many shapes, forms, and ages, wearing all manner of clothes.

They were as a group in no rush, creating no bother, creating no fuss as a bunch of visitors, just staying long enough to satisfy their mission goals. Or, sometimes, a little longer if some member felt the need for just a little more time.

And so it went as they slowly but ever so carefully covered the target area.

Maryland.

He took a big bite of his dessert, refilled his glass from a handy bottle, and leaned back

"Yes," said the host.

"A goose egg, a big nothing. No one found anything that we would be interested in, especially for this strange matter that we have been handed. But!"

He sat up and looked around the table. "There is something up that canyon."

"Ah," said the host.

"Nope," he replied. "We found no trace of any survivalist group, no frothing at the mouth militia types, no paranoid group of folk expecting the government to swoop down in black helicopters and jump on their butts. Lots of ranches, lots of open space, a number of small towns, some of them fading into the environment."

"So?"

"Night time aerial photos identify movement way up in that canyon. Our geologist helpers told us that a large earthquake jerked that canyon around not too long ago with lots of vertical displacement and lots of rock fall. Something is alive and moving around way up there. Soooooooo, perhaps, this is our mysterious cattle and sheep rustler."

"Ah, a few people as well?"

"Could be. Whoever they are, there was no indication of anyone up there before and we found no indication that anyone knew of anyone being tucked up in there."

"A very secret group, it seems."

"Yep."

"We need a very detailed and very accurate map of the area, all that acreage around that canyon and every possible way to walk into and out of it. Then we will decide what comes next."

Way Out West.

Combined teams of specialists and combat elite were set down by helicopters and trudged to each selected surveillance point. The combat elite formed a wide parameter around the specialists as they set their devices in all the best places, carefully eliminating any trace of their existence, devices and people, and hurried away, often jogging to get to their pickup points while there was still daylight.

Back in their large vans many miles away they settled in, to wait and to watch and to record anything that moved. Certain pieces of very specialized equipment only turned on when the light had faded to a point where the other equipment could no longer see.

The operators worked two hours on and two hours off with pairs rotating in and out.

It was truly very dull work, waiting for something to appear. But they and their equipment were very good at it, waiting and watching.

And so it went.

For a number of days and nights.

Maryland.

"Any ideas? Anyone?"

The host looked at the others. A few shrugs, nothing else.

"O.K., who are they?"

"Don't have the foggiest idea," replied one of the group. "Four days. It took them four days. And suddenly they knew. And busted all of our stuff. The good thing is this. They didn't seem to know what it was. We got lots of good images. Our analysts say that they are big, for the most part. Big in like pro-football players big, quarterback big. Some larger."

"Are they local?"

"Don't think so. We have a group trying to figure out who they are based on facial structure, what part of the world they are from. Slow going. But once we pin that down, to some location or other, then we will know how to proceed."

"So some group from somewhere outside the country has slipped in?"

"Looks like it."

"And?"

"Well, from some of the images it appears some of them show bullet wounds, healed bullet wounds."

"So, who are they arguing with?"

"Recent bullet wounds, not old ones. They were shot recently but appear to be healed up."

One of the men shook his head.

"Yep," said another. "Me too."

The host leaned back and sipped his red wine. "Give me a folder with the best photographs, the best head shots of these people."

"I will have it together tomorrow."

They met again, the six of them, three weeks later.

Over cheesecake and coffee, one of the men looked around the table, and popped the last piece of cheesecake on his plate into his mouth.

"O.K., here's what we know."

All eyes looked in his direction.

"Nothing!" He laughed. "Yep, just that. We know nothing."

Five varieties of frowns formed.

"No one can identify them by their facial features. Not for sure. Even the wizards at the Smithsonian can't. Lots of suggestions. All over the map literally. The one feature that puzzles them all are their eyes. They appear to be larger than any group that they have any record for."

Other man waggled a hand. "Not only that, we haven't seen anyone for almost two weeks. It is like they decamped and slipped away somehow."

"And?" asked the host.

He smiled. "I had some of those Tiger Teams, that we don't talk about publically, sent in to search that canyon and see if they can find anything useful, helpful, or whatever."

"Two," added the man responsible for those teams. "One from the mouth of the canyon, the other from topside."

"Well, let's hope that we can solve this puzzle soon. We are getting strong pressure from you know whom."

They talked about the cheesecake and other delights for awhile, then scattered to their various organizations to push ever harder for a solution to this problem.

Summer Into Fall

House Darthar Na.

Sitting in one of the small rooms, Dee was enjoying having breakfast with her two daughters, Tiela and Winala. It was one of the many since she had heard the stories of The Great Straightening and The Dark Nine Cluster. Since then she had been relaxing and pondering everything that she had been told about The Fontala.

Jonathon and Karanly had popped in and out at random. He had been wondering why it was that the Fontala had been reawakened at this time and had been visiting libraries far and wide "doing research."

Dee had long conversations with Armilin, now Head of House Induna, as her mother had died after slowly fading away. Induna was one of Dee's cousin-houses and she had learned over time that this house was a remnant of what had once been a very large house in the many long ago time, a house which had helped develop and hone the martial skill of the staff, The Fontala's Flame Swords.

Armilin was a Master of that skill and was teaching Tiela, bringing her to a higher and higher level. Dee also had Armilin working with Ar to see that an appropriate manual was written so that all she knew could not be lost.

Dee had come to realize that being The Word of The Fontala was like being a five-star general among the people.

Armilin, The One of The All, was essentially her Chief of Staff.

So, during all her conversations with Armilin one of the recurring topics was the rebuilding of The Seventh Stand.

Dee had accepted Armilin's recommendation that Armilin's Third Sister, Kitea, was of a high enough level of skill to be The First Hand of The Seventh Stand. And Dee had begrudgingly agree that Tiela could join that organization if she was accepted. Kitea and Armilin had both tested Tiela's skill and decided that they were acceptable. However, Tiela had yet to try on one of the purple jackets of armor, known among The Fontala as The Shield of Color. These jackets, in some manner unknown to anyone, were the final judge. If the rose insignia did not appear soon after the garment was put on, it meant that the individual would not be accepted into The Fontala.

Armilin had told Tiela, often, that many were not accepted. No one knew why, it was just what happened.

Tiela emptied her cup, sat as straight as she could, and announced that she was ready. "Now or never," she said, before her carefully build up courage slipped away. Armilin and Tiela left the room headed for the appropriate Fontala room.

Winala looked at Dee. "She will be accepted, Mother."

"Ummmmm."

Winala nodded. "She will." She petted both Ice Cats. Tiela's had to stay behind and was making unhappy sounds.

"Don't worry, Mother."

Dee smiled at her. "I am not. I have been thinking and have decided that The Seventh ought to have a special skill. So, how are your studies going?"

They were deep into a discussion of some complicated behavior that a House Head ought to know that Winala was explaining ever so carefully to her Mother when her sister and

Armilin walked into the room.

Tiela was grinning and wiping tears from her face with one purple sleeve. The red rose on the jacket glowed soft scarlet. She carried one of the long purple Flame Swords.

"Congratulations, Daughter."

"See," said Winala, jumping up and hugging her sister. "I knew that you would be accepted."

Dee nodded.

Ar entered carrying in a large tray with fancy pastries. "To celebrate," he said.

Some time later, Dee sat in one of the small comfortable rooms with Armilin and Ar, and explained what she wished to do with The Seventh Stand. Armilin stared at her. Ar's mouth dropped open.

"Well?" Dee looked at him.

"Most unusual."

"Ummmmm."

"Ah eh ummm. You are the Head of House Darthar Na and The Fontala as well, so, ummm eh ah, I suppose." He sighed. "It could be done. Most unusual!"

Dee grinned at them all. "Then Ar will start training members of The Seventh as they are selected. And that means that you will have to start right away." She rose to her feet. "I am going to be gone for awhile. Winala will take care of any matters that come up." She strolled from the room.

The Wild Garden. House Hinterane.

Janice, Dee, and Jonathon sat in a comfortable room with House Head Helsing. All sipped from their cups and waited for Dee to explain why they were gathering here.

Finally she decided all were ready.

She began. She started with the freeing of the young Ice Cat from the zoo and all that entailed. Then she explained the worry that Jonathon had expressed that there might be records in one or more the people's libraries that might make the people aware of them, The Hidden Ones, The Feyra. She outlined how that had brought them here, to this house. She nodded at Janice.

"So," she said to Helsing. "I now have a concern where I did not have one before."

Helsing watched her carefully.

Dee looked into his eyes. "I followed what that volume said in order to pass on to my daughters a thing that I felt was their birthright and played all the dumb games that were in that book." Her frown darkened, if darker was possible. "Now, because of that volume The Fontala are awake. And I have learned of their very beginnings."

She stood and stalked back and forth, grumbling to herself. Jonathon edged forward in his chair, watching her very carefully. He hoped that she wasn't about to do something violent, or worse.

Dee stopped, spun around, and leaned toward the House Head. "Why at this time? What is this house up to?" She stepped close, leaned, and hissed, "I want an answer!"

Janice gasped. Dee seemed to be getting blurry.

"Dee!" snapped Jonathon.

She jerked and straightened up. "OH!" Spinning away, she walked over and dropped into her chair. "Not in the mood for more manipulative games."

Helsing stood and walked around filling their cups. Then he sat and took a sip. "I did know your parents as very good friends. I did meet their very young daughter. This house did guard that purple volume well." He sipped. "This house has a rare skill. It is more a feeling than a skill, I suppose. Janice and I discussed this for some time before doing anything, anything at all."

He smiled at his daughter. "We both agreed. It was time for all that you did to happen."

He held up one hand to stop Dee's comments from gushing forth. "But we do not know why. We only felt that it was time for such an event." He nodded at Dee. "You are Daliera Fontala, Head of House Darthar Na, Word of The Fontala." He sighed, heavily he sighed. "For us there is no why! We do not know the why of anything, only that this thing had to happen, all that you did should be done. No more, no less, no why."

Janice stood and dragged her chair close to Dee's and sat. "What?"

Janice looked at her father who nodded.

"Ummmm," said Helsing.

"Oh, oh," sighed Dee.

"Dee!" snapped Janice. She paused. "Ummmmm. We did not know when you first came and when we gave you that purple clad volume what would happen, only that you needed to pass on the touch to your daughters. We had no idea of all the things that you would make happen, we only knew that somehow that you should use that book."

Janice sighed and slumped in her chair. "But now there is something else that you need to know."

Dee stared at her and the anxiety that she saw there.

"We think that there is someone, or some group, that has, ummmm, suspicions or feelings or hunches that we, The Hidden Ones, The Feyra, exist as a group. A group, or someone, of the people are being as careful The Feyra. And that is very bothering as the people are hardly ever that careful about anything."

Jonathon had been glaring at a wall, now he twisted in his chair and glared at Helsing. "Nothing?"

Helsing shook his head. "So far, only the very faintest of feelings. A very wealthy one of the people has been spending much to buy scraps and pieces and fragments of the very old, as the people measure time. Documents, small parts of documents that have survived. These are mostly strange tales, unusual sightings, folk tales, and mythology. These are being bought very secretly with the buyer hidden many layers deep in the background."

Janice looked at Jonathon. "It is hard to watch this person. This male person lives in secluded isolation of his own choosing, in a place of his own choosing. He is many guarded by his own, all dressed in soft gray garments of the same design."

"They buy much of the people's technology," added Helsing.

"Ummmmm ah," said Jonathon. "I feel the need to leave. I have research to do, deep research."

Dee stood. "Come with us, Janice. This feels most bothering."

Helsing stood. "Go, daughter. I would feel better if you did."

Janice jumped to her feet, ran over, and hugged her father. "Careful cautious!"

"Just so."

House Darthar Na.

It was summer here, high in the mountain range, but

tending toward fall. It seemed to Dee that most of the Fontala had returned to gather together once again.

Many had returned smiling after meeting with members of their families and learning about all that had transpired for all since that long ago past time. Some had wandered in with stricken faces, seeking a family and having found only empty space where once their house or cluster had been.

The Fontala now occupied portions of two floors and were arranging themselves as they felt was best.

A few brought new members with them, folk who wanted to be part of the newly reborn Seventh Stand or to fill small gaps in the membership of the other Stands. Some of these left dejected as the jackets had refused them.

Dee sat in a small room watching the sunlight beginning to flood the meadow below and sipping from her cup.

She turned her head as Kitea walked into the room accompanied with a slender young woman whose eyes seemed to see everything and whose face and stance had a soft confidence as she stopped and waited.

Kitea bowed deeply. "Daliera Word, this one is Anagon, Second Daughter, House Naztan, The One Who Remembers, Seventh Stand."

Anagon bowed deeply to Dee. "As the Word says, so will the deed be done."

Dee bowed to them both. "Welcome, Anagon. Welcome to the new Seventh Stand." She poured and handed each a cup. Then she gestured from them to sit and did after they did.

Dee sipped, and then began to explain to them what she had planned for The Seventh.

When she finished, she smiled at their expressions. Both look startled, shocked, and stunned, as each expression flitted across their faces. Dee filled their cups and called Ar.

He stepped into the room, frowned at the pair, and nodded to Dee. "Princess?"

She waved him into a chair and explained, the new idea, a bit of a change to what she had told him before.

Then she sighed. Ar looked startled, shocked, stunned, as each expression flitted across his face.

"Well?"

He nodded, slowly he nodded to her. And cleared this throat. "I think that I can do that." His eyes held her's. "Most different, Princess, most different."

"Ar?"

"It can be done."

"Ar?"

"Princess?"

"Can you make it happen with Tiela?"

"OH! MY!" He struggled to his feet. "I have never been asked to do something like this, something like that. Ever! Before!"

"Ummmmm."

"I can try. It will be hard work for both of us."

Ar stood and left, headed for The Practice Hall.

Dee sipped and looked from Kitea to Anagon. "Problem?"

Both jumped to their feet and bowed deeply.

"As the Word says, so will the deed be done," they intoned in unison.

Dee nodded. "Better go explain what is happening to your members. Then take them to The Practice Hall. They have a lot of work and Ar knows what to do."

They spun and ran from the room.

Dee sat and thought to herself, it will be interesting.

The door banged open, snapping Dee from her deep thought, as Tiela hurtled inside, frowning darkly. "MOTHER!"

"Sit."

She dropped into a chair.

"Ar talked to you?"

Tiela nodded.

"Do you wish to leave them?"

One quick shake of her head.

"Then?"

Tiela lurched to her feet and grumbled deep in her throat, "As the Word says, Mother, so will the deed be done."

"You have more experience in this. Go help your comrades."

Tiela managed a weak smile, nodded, bowed, and hurried away.

It was some days later.

Dee and Karanly were relaxing after a mid-day meal.

Karanly was telling Dee how Jonathon was still visiting library after library, searching deeper and deeper, slowly gathering one piece of information here, another bit of information there. Each time he returned to House Darthar to leave his notes, he looked more upset. Hofga was now traveling with him and looking even more unhappy.

"They say nothing?"

"Not a word. But Hofga mumbled to me, messy, now and then."

"Oh, oh."

"Just so."

Someone gentle knocked on the door to the room.

"Do come in," said Dee.

Kitea entered trailed by a rather tall, slim male.

They bowed to Dee and Karanly.

"This," said Kitea, "is Yallan, Second Son, House Farback. He is a Seeker, a very rare skill. The jacket has selected him into The Seventh."

Dee stood and bowed to him. "Welcome, Yallan." Then she looked at Kitea. "How builds The Seventh?"

Kitea smiled. "It does seem that word has spread of the Seventh rising again. Numbers come. Some go home sad. Soon we will be at full strength as well as all of the Stands. All practice long and hard." She hesitated.

"Ummmmmm."

"Ar and Tiela demand much, train much and hard." Her smile widened. "The Seventh is proud to do so."

Dee laughed. "Glad to hear it. I was, ummm ah, worried."

Kitea tapped her shirt with the first two fingers of her right hand. "Proud to be, happy to be." She bowed. The pair left.

"My," said Karanly. "A Seeker! Very rare. Just so." She took another slice of toast. "House Farback is true named. It is deep deep in a great mountain range. Few know of them, fewer ever hear that name." She winked at Dee. "Nice looking."

They were deep in a discussion about House Beasts when someone knocked ever so gently on the door.

Karanly jumped up, opened it, and stepped back.

Janice walked in followed by a small group.

Janice bowed to Dee. "This is House Hinterane. Our Father is still there but ordered all else to come here. For safety. He did not explain."

"Safety?" Dee stared at her friend.

Janice nodded. "He would not say. We brought the entire house library with us. It clutters your hallway near the outside door."

Ar walked in. "I asked them in. And will see that a room is set up for their library and use separate from the house libraries."

"Most kind," said Janice. Then she introduced her brothers and sisters.

Dee welcomed them all, Ar led them away, up to their rooms and began to settle them in. Dee held Janice back.

"Do you know?"

Janice shook her head. "Our Father only said that he was preparing the house and the grounds. He looked very worried." She dropped into a chair.

"Anything that I can do?"

"No." Janice took a just filled cup and sipped. "He said to wait and to see. So we are here."

"As long as you wish."

New York City.

Jonathon had worked his way from obscure library to obscure library slowly, ever so slowly, ferreting out more bits and pieces of information. He was following those bits and pieces of information that Helsing had gathered and was fitting them into the puzzle they were trying to solve.

It had become apparent that there were many layers hiding this one from others of the people and, perhaps, from The Feyra. It was this later thought that was most bothering. Why would this one so worry about us, The Hidden Ones?

Jonathon knew that he would find out, sooner or later. Now he approached the reference desk and began to explain what he was looking for, pointing out all the areas already explored.

"Well, you have certainly covered a lot of what I would have suggested," said the woman nodding more to herself than to him. She looked up from the page he had handed her. "Let me check a few things. Only take a minute or two." She spun around and began to rapidly type, watching the screen before her. Now and then she wrote a note on his page, then tapped away some more.

And, in the promised minute or two, she spun back and handed him his page and tapped a finger on her notes written at the bottom, telling him where he could find each of the volumes noted. "Hope this helps. Interesting search."

He nodded, and smiled at her. "Most helpful."

He spun away and headed in the right direction, headed for the first item on his new list. Hofga trailed along behind him watching everyone. Neither he nor Jonathon were comfortable surrounded by such a large number of the people.

Way Out West.

People calmed down.

But there were lots of conversations and speculation.

For weeks.

Large helicopters settled here and there. The teams exited and gathered together for final discussion and a radio check.

Team One waited until Team Two started down from their starting point before heading for the mouth of the canyon.

Each team was twelve plus two. The two were medically trained, trained much higher than the usual combat medic. All members of the teams knew that some people had disappeared. Every member was determined that whoever was responsible for that would either wind up securely bound or would occupy a body bag.

As the sun crept up, the teams walked carefully into that canyon.

Team One approached the great debris pile where the slope on one side of the canyon had split away, sliding into the bottom of the canyon, blocking it. A small pond was beginning to form on the upstream side.

Standing on top of the pile they waited for Team Two to arrive.

Two members of Team One worked their way up to the opening and waited on either side of it, yelling down to the Team One Leader that there was a path the led up to this opening from the canyon below.

Finally Team One slipped through the wide mouth of the opening and carefully made there way deeper inside. Team Two set up a blocking position around the entrance. Nothing would be able to leave or enter from the canyon side.

A hour later a runner from Team One appeared and told Team Two to follow to where Team One waited.

House Darthar Na.

Janice tapped a spot on a large map spread across the top of their table.

"Somewhere in all this apparently roadless, or unroaded, area as far as Father could determine. He only saw that one in one of the big cities with three of those grey clad guards of his. No one may approach close or enter any building that one owns. But he had a large home built somewhere in this area.

Everything flies in and out."

"Ummmm." Dee stared at the map. "Think that we might find out anything useful if we were on a book tour through that area?"

Janice laughed. "I'll go and set it up."

Montana.

They had flown to Missoula, spent two days there doing their usual book tour thing, hired a car and wandered up to Butte. From there they traveled to Helena and on for another two days to Great Falls.

There they had changed from car to truck rental, a pickup with a canopy over the rear. Inside they piled an ice chest and all their camping gear.

As long as they were here, Dee and Janice decided they might as well camp and enjoy the outdoors, more or less by themselves.

They drifted down the two lane road and through the Lewis and Clark National Forest, camping at several of the small campgrounds, enjoying the mountains and the forest, and the relative lack of other folk.

Dee inhaled the cool mountain air laced with the smell of the pine and laughed. This was so enjoyable. Janice looked up from the small camp stove. "It won't be all that good."

"Just enjoying the setting." Dee walked over and joined her.

Finally they stopped in Lewistown to take a room and a shower and to sit and relax and eat in a restaurant.

From there they wandered along the narrow road.

Every bookstore that they saw they stopped and visited and spent the day there much to the surprise of owners and browsers alike. Authors just did not do that, visit and spend time in very small towns and very small book stores.

But finally, many days later they wound up in the small town of Jordan, population around 350, more or less, noted all the closed businesses and took rooms in The Garfield Hotel and Motel. They sat in the coffee shop enjoying a leisurely breakfast and talked about this and that with the waitress, especially about the local area, especially that open space to the south and a little west of town.

Then, a few days later, having walked around town a few times, visiting the park, idly talking with whoever they met, they heard repeated stories of the wealthy Easterner who had build some sort of elaborate place "out there" with high fences, keep out signs, and guards "all over the place" wearing grey uniforms.

Dee and Janice checked out and spent a slow two days wandering their way back to Billings, got rid of the truck, took all their camping gear and flew out on the first flight that was going where they wanted to go.

New York City.

Three days were spent cycling between new questions for folk at the Reference Desk and taking notes from various of the volumes they were directed to.

"Getting lots of exercise," rumbled Hofga as they headed back down the stairs to the main floor and finally outside.

"Just so." Jonathon nodded and led his companion over to Central Park and spot deep inside a clump of shrubbery.

House Darthar Na.

Ar welcomed them inside and walked with them to a

small comfortable room and waved a hand at the food laid out on the table. "She hasn't returned yet."

Jonathon frowned, Hofga stared.

Ar cleared his throat. "They are on a Book Tour in the people state place named Montana, I think."

Jonathon nodded. "I will wait."

Hofga grumbled deep in his chest. "Home! Send word, as you need." He stomped for the outside door.

Maryland. Somewhere.

It was nice house, one among many located in this rather exclusive housing development. It was no bigger or any smaller than any of its neighbors, near and far.

Two automobiles were parked in the street in front of it. Another was parked in the short driveway, nose close to the garage door. All very normal.

The neighbors saw those cars every so often. The couple who lived there often had these small dinner parties for a few friends, as they had found out, at somewhat random times.

This was one of those times.

Light from the dining room windows spilled across the neatly mown lawn in the dark dusk of early evening. Six people sat around the table that was just the right size for the three couples. They talked freely among themselves knowing that no one could overhear their conversations. The walls, the windows, the building itself were so constructed that eavesdropping was impossible. This house was unique in its construction.

"Any idea what he is up to?"

All knew who this he was.

"Very little," replied one of the women. "He closed his New York offices and pulled everything to the enclave he built in Montana."

Another man nodded. "He also emptied his main house as well."

One of the women refilled their glasses and served dessert, a decadently rich, multi-layered chocolate cake.

"My mole has been silent since that relocation. Being very cautious, I hope." She had planted her spy a few years ago when they had first began to get suspicious about that person and began to suspect that their quarry might lead to some interesting knowledge.

Their host looked at the others. "Still no idea as to what he is looking for, no better idea?"

"Nope," answered the up to this point silent other man. "But he is pouring tons of money into the venture. Much more than he has ever done with any other venture he has been interested in." He smiled as he cut a small piece from his cake serving with his fork and beamed at their hostess. "Delicious. I have a number of staff combing backward through everything that we can get our hands on, searching for links and patterns."

The woman sitting next to him took a sip from her wine glass. "We know that he had a finger in the fiasco at that zoo. Those researchers were claiming that they had captured an alien beast of some sort. Still, he is not known to pour money into things that he can't get a whole of money from in return. Too bad that building and everything else was lost."

The man across the table nodded. "To me that is the most interesting aspect of that event. There was not a trace, not a scrap of anything to be found. It does feel to me as if everything was removed before that disaster occurred, doesn't it?"

Several around the table nodded. Two smiled.

Dinner soon ended. They group headed into the living

room and settled in their usual places, chairs or couch, with their usual beverages.

"So?" said one of the men. "Our old business."

"It just gets better and better." One of the men handed around folders containing numbers of photographs and detailed drawings. "There is quite a honeycomb of rooms in there. Bedrooms, storage rooms, that is we assume they are storage rooms, dining room from the plates, etc., that we found." He took a swallow from his glass of dark red wine. "And surprise, surprise, a back door. A back door that is a heck of a long way, a heck of a very, very, very long way behind anything that we had put in place. It appears that the group slipped out through that exit and off to somewhere unknown."

He handed around another set of folders. "These are photos and drawings, both in color, of their art work. They decorated some of the walls in some of the rooms. We are having various art-wise people trying to place it, style, locale, etc. Maybe they will come up with something useful. Others are inspecting the pottery and other artifacts. So, we get to wait for another couple weeks or so, just to see whether anything comes from that."

"It is amazing," said one of the men.

"What?" asked the previous speaker.

"That nothing that we can find, so far, leads us to whoever these people are."

"Aliens," whispered, the other man. "Ooooooooo!" He refilled his cup. "So we have finally found some. Now all we need to do is find their space ship." He laughed and slumped in his chair. "You all know that if any of this gets out that this is the kind of thing that will flood the media. And all the true believers will go bug-nuts."

"Well then," said their host. "We will have to make sure that nothing gets out, right?"

The man that handed out the folders laughed. "These are the only folders in existence, six copies. All originals I have locked away, somewhere, someplace."

After they had finished their dessert and coffee, the host walked them to the door. "Well, keep sharp. And let's hope that our mole will let us know something. Soon."

He and his wife stood in the doorway and waved as their guests drove away. Then they shut the door and walked to the living room.

"SO," he said as she sat in his lap.

"So," she replied, getting comfortable. "I think that he has found something."

"You do?"

"Certainly do. I have read copies of everything that we have that we know he bought for the fifth time."

"And?"

"Strange stuff, as in fairy tale strange stuff."

"Fairy tale stuff?"

"Manner of speaking. Something else. In all that stuff, all that strange stuff, there is a feel of something real, deeply hidden inside all those documents and what they say in those stories and accounts."

"Like that happening at the zoo?"

"Yes. Like that event. Only there was no fairy tale stuff there."

"Alien creature. Modern times." He gasped. She had thumped his chest with a knuckle. Hard.

She laughed into his frown. "Exactly. That is the key that we didn't see."

He grunted at her and rubbed his chest with his free hand. "Key?"

She lurched up and off and stood. "Right! I need to read through everything again this evening. What time it was that event occurred and how people saw things at that point in time." She hurried away. "Put some coffee on," she called back over her shoulder. "Then go to bed. This is going to be an all-nighter."

"I will make breakfast," he called at her back as she hurried down a hall.

It was week later and they were in the middle of eating their breakfast.

"Surprise." One of the men strolled into their kitchen. He stopped and inspected the contents of the several pots on the stove.

"Help yourself," said the woman.

"Doesn't your wife feed you?" asked the man.

"Sure," came the mumbled reply as something was sampled. "She went in early today." He sat at the table, plate heaped full.

The woman filled his cup.

"Well," he said between bites as he dumped hot sauce over everything. "Those characters we photographed are certainly different all right. A search for some distance all around their back door found all the weapons just dumped in a heap."

The host of this small breakfast party spread jelly on his toast. "Different all right."

"Yep," said their guest. "Most folk that hide themselves that well are usually pretty cash strapped. Lots of money just tossed on the ground. Could have sold those things for a bunch.

Any ideas?"

The host shook his head. "Their behavior is certainly different that any group that we have seen. They could have held out an army from that place if they had decided to fight."

The other man nodded and stood and served himself. "I should do this more often." And laughed.

Montana.

He sat in the communications room and frowned at the several men and one woman standing here and there.

"The team is in place?" he asked.

The woman looked at the clock, waited, and said, "Just about now."

A radio crackled, was silenced as the operator slipped on a headset and spoke softly into the mike poking in front of his mouth. He spun in his chair. "In place, sir."

The man wearing casual clothes nodded. "Proceed." He kept a carefully held bland expression on his face. But this time he was finding it hard to do. His staff had all agreed that this mission had a very high probability of success. They had argued that this was so even if they knew nothing, really, about the inhabitants of the target dwelling other than what the local folk would tell them, which was not much.

He rose to his feet. "I will be in the front room." He strolled out.

As soon as the door shut behind him one of the staff turned to another one. "Wonder what The Frog is up to, this time?"

The Frog was the name that the staff used for their employer whenever he wasn't around to hear. He had a round face, a wide mouth, and eyes that seemed to protrude. They never used this term if they thought that he could hear them. None of them knew, of course, that their employer could hear anything anyone said anywhere inside the entire complex. But he wasn't really bothered by their usage of this term, he thought that it probably helped build cohesion among his staff.

And none of them knew that he knew all about them. That expansive, and expensive, knowledge, had been why each and everyone of them had been hired.

The woman laughed. "I have no idea but he has that dollar sign look in his eyes. Whatever it is, he probably expects to make a ton or two of money." She listened carefully to the voice in her headset and took careful and precise notes.

House Darthar Na.

Dee and Janice walked into the small room, smiled at Jonathon, poured themselves coffee, and dropped into comfortable chairs.

"Ummmmmm," said Dee.

Jonathon nodded. "A strange person, even for one of the people."

"Ah," said Janice, looking at him over the top of her cup, steaming curling up and around her face. The air temperature in this room was on the cool side.

Jonathon pulled his sheaf of notes from somewhere, scanned the top page, and looked at them. Then he began to tell them all that he had found out.

This person was an extremely wealthy person as the people reckoned wealth. His family had passed it on from father to eldest son. This person is named William Williams, the Third, apparently a family naming custom of some sort. By all the accounts that Jonathon had found, this person was well educated as the people understand education and was understood to be very clever. He had added greatly to the family wealth and from these same accounts it seemed that he was interested in many things some of which others had made not nice remarks about.

Williams Three had for a good number of years been gathering stories of the unusual from as far back as he could find pieces of the people's writing. It was this activity that House Head Helsing had been watching as he felt that this person might be beginning to suspect the existence of The Feyra.

In the research that Jonathon had done and from what Helsing had already found out, it appeared that this person, Williams Three, was not above using not nice ways of acquiring whatever he wished to acquire. But in terms of the people laws, he had never been talked to about that as no other person had seemed to have what the people called proof.

Jonathon shook his head.

There had been nothing that he could find that had any information as to why this person might be gathering bits and pieces of accounts that touched upon them, The Hidden Ones.

What was interesting was that this Williams Three had closed all his offices and relocated to a place that he called The Island. Nothing indicated where this island might be.

Dee started to say something when the door flew open and Hofga stomped into the room, all dark frown and glower. "Ar let me in," he boomed and stopped in front of Jonathon.

"Ummmmm," said Jonathon.

"Word has come that House Antarax, a very small house, has been attacked and burned to the ground.

Dee stared at him. Jonathon stood. "Do you know where this house is located?"

"Most so," grumbled Hofga.

"Where?" asked Dee.

Hofga dropped into a chair as Dee shoved a full cup toward him. He took a sip. "It is, was, tucked into the forest, soft hidden not all that far from a small cabin people named Lee's Camp Store. It is some distance west from that people place named Portland. This store thing is on a narrow road and has a few other people houses set into the trees just to one side."

Jonathon looked at Dee. She stood and walked over, to stand close to him.

"Take us," said Jonathon to Hofga.

Lee's Camp Store.

The trio stood, not far down a narrow two lane road across the road from that store building, a small single story wooden cabin that had the appearance of having once been a house now turned into a store, and looked at the thin column still rising into the air from somewhere deep in the forest from where they stood.

Two firemen were rolling up their hoses and getting ready to return to their station.

One looked up at them. "Not much to see in there."

"You the press?" asked the other.

"Yes," said Dee. "Is it safe to go in there?"

"Oh sure," said the first. He pointed. "What you see is mostly steam. Just be careful where you walk when you get there."

Dee nodded and headed into the forest following a narrow trail.

Finally, they stood, staring at the debris.

"Who could, or would, do something like this?"

Hofga grumbled and stomped into the woods behind the remains of the cabin.

"Ummmm," said Jonathon. "What could a very small house so isolated have been doing to bring this about?" He began to wander about the collapsed and burned structure.

Dee cautiously stepped into the mess, nose wrinkling at the pungent odor of burned wood and water logged ash. Here and there she could see broken ceramics that appeared to have once been bowls, plates, cups, and platters.

So they wandered from here to there did Dee and Jonathon searching for some explanation but finding only the aftermath of a bad fire.

Nothing they saw offered an explanation. There was no apparent reason for all this mess. Suddenly, in the distance they heard deep grumbling coming closer. Under their feet the ground moved.

"Hofga is unhappy," said Jonathon, looking across the rubble in the direction that his friend had headed.

They waited as the deep voice came closer.

Hofga stomped into view, frowning darkly, choice words stirred the vegetation. Every footfall was accompanied by an undulation of the earth.

"CALM, CALM," called Jonathon.

"Parta!" growled Hofga, stepping lightly into the burned over area and around the remains of the cabin. He was followed by a young man and a young woman.

The three of them stopped in front of Jonathon.

Hofga waved his hand. "This is First Son, now House Antarax Head Dontilax, and Third Sister, perhaps now Second or First Sister, Fontellan. Let's leave this place!" He introduced the others.

"This is Jonathon, House Head Darthar, and Dee, House Head Darthar Na."

The pair stared from one to the other and hastily bowed.

Jonathon nodded and beckoned everyone to stand close.

House Darthar Na.

Dee climbed the wide stairs, pushed open the outside door, and turned. "Do come in. All."

Then she led the small group down the hall and into a room with a right-sized table, poured cups full and handed them to all. She dropped into a chair and looked from the still rumbling Hofga to the stunned looking pair. "What happened?"

Fontellan shoved her chair close to Dontilax's as he began to tell them.

House Antarax.

The family had just returned from one of the several small markets that they frequented in that large people cluster to the east. It was called Portland.

House Antarax was a Crafter House. One of their skills was pottery. The house had been in the area for some long time ago. The area where they had their structure had always had few people in it.

Their pottery, a stunning, thin-walled design of deep luminescent soft green had great appeal to the people. The house always made a small number of pieces, all utilitarian. Cups, bowls, platters, dishes were snapped up whenever they displayed their wares at the several small markets they visited.

All through the region the people appreciated artisans of all varieties. Thus the house felt little concern to be located in a very rural section or to journey to the large people cluster to sell their products or to buy those few supplies they required that were not easily otherwise available to them.

None of the people had ever seen the house or even seemed to know where these potters, as the people labeled them, lived.

And so it went for a many long time.

One day past, the family was outside clearing the small brush away from the open space around their dwelling, an annual event. The sun was well past its high point when it happened.

A large group of grey clad men ran into the clearing from all sides, shouting and yelling, and waving ugly people things at them.

Four of them tried to grab family members as they ran for the outside door. House Head Donidex leaped in front of these ugly folk and shoved them back. Four of the grey men shot him and grabbed First Sister Zarpon before she could get inside.

Various family members ran toward the escape way.

Dontilax stared at the table, then at Dee and Jonathon. "I met Fontellan deep in the forest. We saw no-one else. We were slowly edging toward the house when we saw the smoke billowing upward. So we ran deeper and deeper. And waited. We were drifting silent this way when we met Hofga."

Dee stared at Jonathon. "Grey clad men."

"Ummmm ah," he said. "Not nice, not good."

The Island. Montana.

The Frog glared at the Head of the detail just returned after a non-stop drive from the west coast. They had put their captive in a locked room and then he come to make his report.

Now the Head of the detail was being glared at by his

red-faced employer.

"Who told you to shoot anyone? IDIOT! Is that supposed to make that young woman want to talk to us? DOUBLE DIM-WIT!"

"He attacked us."

"With what? Dishes?"

"Ah, no."

"It was supposed to be a quick in-and-out, was it not?"

"Yes."

"So, please explain to me, very carefully and very clearly, how a bunch of potters could resist your group? Then very clearly explain the shooting of one of them? Then very carefully explain the burning of their dwelling? To the ground!"

The Head of the detail did. In a manner of speaking.

In the general chaos of everyone running every which way the shots were fired. Some had apparently left the building without being seen. And he didn't know how the fire started. Not at all.

William Williams the Third leaned to one side and punched at button.

"Yes?" said his Number One.

"That entire crew is now unemployed!"

"Yes."

"Immediately!"

"Understood."

He pointed at the door. "OUT! Back to your quarters. And stay there."

The Head of the detail spun and hurried from the room, pale faced and shaking.

Another button was pushed.

"Yes?" purred the velvet soft female voice.

"Go see if that woman will talk to you."

"Sure."

He sighed. This was not going the way he had wanted it to go. He had been sure that those potters were what he had thought that they were. Or at least could tell him what he wanted to know. That heavy-handed Head of the detail had certainly made a mess of everything. Now one of his people watching the place had see the firemen talking with three visitors, assumed reporters, visiting the scene. Reporters were not good to have nosing around.

His phone rang, his ever so secure phone line. What he heard ruined the rest of his day and the rest of the week as well.

The team he had sent to visit that collector of the rare and antique had all died in a series of explosions on the grounds and in the building as well. The inside of the house was gone, so was most of the house.

Maryland.

The man stared at his wife. She had just hung up the phone and had told him what she had been told. Their watchers on the east coast had told her of the explosions and those on the west coast had relayed the information about the burned down home of some potters.

He sagged in his chair. "Still no idea what he is up to?"

She shook her head. "Only that he is holding some young woman."

"Kidnaping would give us an excuse to go in."

"Of that we are not sure."

"A collector of the rare and the old and a bunch of grey clad, heavily armed men all blown up on the east coast. A potter's house burned to the ground on the west coast. Does anyone see anything to tie these two events together other than that his gangs were there?"

She bent and kissed his cheek. "Not yet, Dear, not yet."

"Anyone else I would drag in right now!"

"I know. Too much money, too many bought politicians."

He nodded. "Let's eat out tonight."

"Good idea."

The Island. Montana.

He looked at the woman with the soft and gentle voice. "Well?"

She took a seat and looked totally relaxed.

"Learn anything?"

She nodded. "Her name is Zarpon. As far as I can tell, she is perfectly healthy and somewhere around twenty-six years old. And she is very angry about everything that happened. She speaks with a strange accent that I cannot place and at times has a strange manner of speaking."

"How so?"

The woman smiled at him. "She said that what had happened was not nice. Very not nice."

"Very not nice?"

"Yes."

"That all?"

"Almost."

"And?" He glared at her. He hated to have to pry answers from her. But she was the best for what she did, the best he had ever met.

"She said that she hoped that one of her family told what happened to the Protectors of The Innocent."

"Any idea what that might be or mean?"

"No. Some very strange belief in what ever it might be."
He sighed. "We are a very long way from Oregon."

House Darthar Na.

Ar settled their new guests in comfortable rooms, saw that they had a good meal, and returned to see what else Dee might wish.

She looked at him over the rim of her cup.

"Oh my," he said.

"Ask Kitea, Anagon, and Yallan to come, please."

Ar headed up to The Training Hall.

Jonathon looked at her.

Dee took another sip. "I am going to find out whether this Williams person is holding one of us."

Jonathon nodded. And sat, quiet as quiet ever could be. Kitea, Anagon, and Yallan walked in and bowed to Dee.

"Word?" asked Kitea.

"Is The Seventh ready?"

Kitea bowed deeply. "Well trained. Is there a need?"

Dee nodded at Kitea and looked at Jonathon.

"Do you know of a house not too far from a large people place in the western part of the United States?"

He called Hofga, who in a moment or two stepped into the room. "Jonathon?" Jonathon told him and waited.

Hofga nodded after a bit. "House Monigan. It is not far from a people place called Booze Min."

Dee laughed. "Sorry Hof, that place is pronounced Bozeman." She looked at Jonathon. "Big college there. I want to move The Seventh Stand to House Monigan. And you, and Hofga, and myself."

He nodded. "First Hofga. He can prepare them to have

visitors. How many?"

"Two double hands and three," stated Kitea. "We are still building."

"Take jackets and staffs," said Dee. "But packed."

"As the Word says, so will the deed be done."

The room emptied leaving only Dee and Jonathon.

"Dee?"

"We will be very careful, very, very careful."

Maryland.

They were sitting around the dining room table, relaxing over coffee, having just finished an elegant and multi-layered cake.

One of the women looked at her associates. "Do any of you know of the author D. Grant?"

Their hostess nodded. "Yes. She is the one whose house burned to the ground some while back while she was on some sort of a retreat in the Himalayas. Right?"

"That is the one."

"Have you started reading novels of that genre?"

"They are fun, but that is not what is interesting."

All eyes focused on her with various expressions of interest on the five faces.

She nodded and smiled. "She was on a Book Tour and spent a few days in Jordan, Montana."

One of the men smiled. "Authors do that all the time."

"But do they also turn up visiting a burned down building in Oregon posing as a reporter?"

Their host sat up. "You are sure of this?"

"Certainly."

He poured more wine into his glass and took a sip. "Now

that is interesting. But why would she be doing that?"

A man patted the hand of his wife, the one who had raised this issue. "Perhaps she is doing research for a new book?"

The third man frowned. "A research project that just happens to intersect with some matters in which we are deeply interested?"

Their host stood. "Perhaps we have some additional research to do as well?"

All stood, thanked their hosts for another great meal, and hurried away.

The man threw his arm around his wife's shoulder's. "What do you think?"

She tickled his ribs. "I think that we need to know much more, a whole lot more."

Jordan, Montana.

The bus pulled up, parked, and disgorged its passengers, who all crowded into the Garfield Hotel and Motel, a two-story rectangular building on one side of the road at an intersection.

They crowded inside to organize themselves and to receive their room keys. Their accommodations had been arranged over the phone a few days earlier. So here they were, all wearing name tags with the main label and logo over their names telling one and all that this was a group being handled by an organization that called itself *The Best Tour Company*.

After all had a meal in the coffee shop the tour members scattered in groups of twos and threes to wander in every direction around the town, such as it was.

Dee strolled along with Kitea, Yallan, and Dee's daughter, Tiela.

Tiela was taking pictures with her brand new camera, purchased by Dee who was giving her detailed instructions on how it worked and all its features.

As they strolled along, Kitea indicated the direction that Yallan would head, he and Tiela, once it was dark enough.

And soon, in the gathering dark the tour members wandered back to their rooms and then into the coffee shop to have their evening meal.

The Island. Montana.

He congratulated the new Head of The Strike Force teams. "One of the first items on your agenda is to recruit. We have, ah, lost quite a rather large number of personnel in only two operations. Apparently neither of those two groups had sufficient pre-planning. That is your second agenda item. You need to gather sufficient talented staff to handle these matters."

He nodded. "That's it! You have sufficient funds to do whatever is required." One hand waggled the man from the room.

As the new Head of the Strike Force headed out, she strolled in and sat in a chair and waited for the door to close.

He waited, knowing that she could not be hurried any more than she was willing to be hurried, which was not very much, if ever at all.

She looked at him and waited until he looked in her direction. "Have you ever heard of a group of people anywhere that call themselves The Feyra?"

"No."

"So, maybe some sort of gypsy group?"

"No idea."

"That young woman stated that she was Feyra and that

we ought to release her before The Protectors of The Innocent heard she was being held here."

He nodded, and smiled. "Just another fringe religion of some sort. Some groups, some self-isolating groups often create their own systems of beliefs, their own mythologies. It sounds to me like certain Christian beliefs in Avenging Angels, something like that." He stared at her, brow wrinkling in a slight frown. "Anything else?"

"No. Just that this is not nice behavior on our part."

"I will have some of the staff research that word usage as well as feyra and this Protector of The Innocent thing. Maybe that will help us."

She shrugged, and smiled. "One other thing."

His stare turned into deep frown and glower. "What?" he snapped.

"She has eyes of the most clear green that I have ever seen." She stood and strolled from the room, gently closing the door, humming quietly to herself.

Maryland.

The woman walked across the room and pushed down the newspaper that he was reading.

He looked up. "What?"

"Dear, I think that you should invite The Council to our house for dinner for a change. Tonight! I will order in as it is too late for anything else."

He frowned the question at her.

"I have heard from my mole."

He set his newspaper down and walked across the room to the correct phone, the heavily guarded and safe one.

The Garfield Hotel and Motel. Montana.

It was mid-morning and Dee sat at a table in her room with a number of photographs on it. She had organized everything needed for this job when they were in Bozeman. While she had been doing that she had explained the people technology to Jonathon and how it could be quite useful at times.

The photographs were of Williams Three self-styled Island. They had been taken last night and were just close enough to see the necessary details illuminated by the various flood lights that were mounted on tall stanchions in various places around that compound.

"You did well," she said to her daughter Tiela.

Yallan tapped a finger on one of the buildings. "I could feel her in there." It was a Seeker's skill. He could always tell where one of them was, one of The Feyra. If he wished. He had accompanied Tiela.

Dee nodded and sipped from her cup. "We will have to watch them for several evenings to know what they do at night, which way they keep watch, and how many of them are out at night and exactly where they stand or move."

Two days later the group filed back on board their bus, name tags in place, all their gear stored in the lower storage areas.

Dee tipped the staff of the hotel motel and boarded last.

The sun was setting as they drove west on the narrow two lane road.

Dee leaned close to Jonathon. "We will be very careful. All know exactly how to proceed. That place is way out in the middle of nowhere. I don't think they expect anyone to come visiting, especially at night."

He nodded. "No one is bullet proof."

"We know, we know."

Maryland.

Over after dinner drinks, their hostess tapped the side of her wine glass gently with her fork.

All eyes stared at her.

"You have all restrained your curiosity quite well and quite long enough." She smiled at them and received polite laughs in return.

Taking a sip from her glass, she nodded at them. "My, our, mole has finally managed to communicate. It seems that she got deathly ill and had to go to the closest clinic. Our people there admitted her for a few days observation and will release her when she is well enough to return to her job."

"Well done," muttered one of the men, loud enough for her to hear.

She tilted her head at him. "We don't know much but neither does anyone else. The young woman that they snatched speaks in a strange dialect of English. That is, at time she uses different phrases when she talks about things."

"Such as?"

The hostess smiled. "She refers to herself being taken by them as being not nice. This term also describes her feelings about her captivity. She stated that she was Feyra, apparently some small ethnic group that no-one has ever heard of before or has any record on. This group also seems to have their own unique religious beliefs about something that she calls The Protectors of The Innocent."

"The Protectors of The Innocent?" asked one of the men.

She nodded. "Yes. She has said this on several occasions. She stated that it would be best for them if they released her before these protectors found out about her captivity."

Another of the men stated, "Everyone will do their own search on this small amount of data. Nothing that we know to date about our person of interest interest's has any mention of those terms or beliefs."

The woman laughed. "Our mole states that she is as puzzled as we are at this moment as to what that young woman is talking about."

And soon, after a few more samples of various of the beverages, all left to make phone calls or to talk with selected staff.

The Island. Montana.

The moon had set. The sky was black scattered with the bright pin pricks of near and distant stars on this clear night.

The four guards strolled casually along their required routes on one more long night of total boredom. None bothered to look up. None noticed that something high in the blackness of the night sky was passing across all those bright pin pricks of star light. Or heard them falling.

House Darthar Na.

Dee sat in one of the small comfortable rooms with Jonathon as they sipped coffee.

"That went well," she said. "Good to be home after all that traveling."

He nodded. "Just so. Ummmmm."

"Yes?"

"When did you decide that The Seventh Stand should

have a House Darthar Na skill?"

"Wings?"

"Dark wings."

"Ah, that."

"Ah ummmmm." He sipped.

"Well." She sipped. "After hearing their history I thought that as long as we were recreating The Seventh Stand that they ought to be given some, ah ummmm, new skills. I talked with Ar and he figured out how to change things. I thought of flying at night and decided that glaring white wings might be a little obvious."

He sighed, a very quite sigh. "It must be all that living among the people that makes you think that way."

"Good thing too," she replied. "Otherwise we might never have been able to get her back. Who knows what that slug would have done to her."

He looked at her.

"And it was very nice of you to give them that house you owned near the ocean for their new House. Hofga said that you had found all the rest of the members of that family."

He shoved his cup at her and waited for her to refill it. "I added your property to mine. Now their nearest neighbor is much further away from any other houses than mine was."

She smiled at him. "Hopefully they will have no more problems." She sighed. "We have an awfully large amount of stuff to look through."

He shook his head. "I will take care of that. Janice will help. She was well trained by her father."

"Ahhhh. O.K., ummmm, good." She stood. "Then I think that I will take a nap. That was really tiring."

"It always is, Dee." He stood and left.

A Puzzle. A Mystery.

Maryland.

They hastily gathered. Three couples and one more.

The single woman looked around the room, told them that what she was going to tell might be hard to accept, maybe, and to hold their questions until she finished.

First she explained how they had worked ever so slowly to get her hired by their target of interest. It had taken some time and a great amount of supporting documentation, references, etc. She smiled at them. All here knew how that sort of thing went.

Heads nodded.

She took a sip from her wine glass, gathered herself, and began.

She had driven back to The Island after three days of "being sick and recovering." As she approached the only gate, the only entrance to the sprawling establishment, she became aware, slowly, of something different. Then it dawned of her. All the light standards were missing. She couldn't see one standing. The next surprise was the lack of people. No one was walking around. No grey clad guards wandering here and there. She drove through the gate, she had to open it herself, and parked next to the main building, got out of her car, and stared at it, turned and slowly scanned the entire complex, all that she could see from where she stood. And stared, not really understanding what she saw.

All the light standards that she could see were laying on the ground just like so many trees that had been cut down. As she looked here and there it dawned on her that things were really not right anywhere. A door lay in the street. She walked over and looked at it. The hinges had been sheared from the wall. Another door lay nearby with a piece of the wall still attached by the hinges.

Stone walls had large pieces missing, the chunks lying in the street. The stone, the wood, the metal all seemed to have been cut with something that left very smooth surfaces, almost like a laser had been used.

Someone at the table gasped. She nodded.

Slowly, carefully she crept into the main building and made her cautious way to his office stepping over the bodies that lay everywhere. From the injuries it appeared that the same weapon had been used on them that had cut up everything that she had inspected outside.

Bodies, rifles, doors, and apparently anything in the way of whoever had done this had been cut into one or more pieces. It looked to her as if whoever it was had been in a hurry, maybe even running.

His office was a shambles. Every cabinet was open. Every lock cut off. Every wall had great slash marks in them as if someone was searching for hidden spaces.

Not one piece of paper remained. Everything was gone, including the hard drives from every computer, their cases sliced open for easy access, and then smashed.

Her employer lay slumped in his chair, his head in his lap.

She wandered from room to room, from building to building. What she had seen in the main building was repeated over and over and over. Whoever, whatever, had taken everything that might have information on it. The entire complex had been emptied.

Every piece of equipment had been sliced into pieces so that they were beyond repair. Radios, vehicles, towers, generators, and on and on and on.

She emptied her glass.

"And I am certainly glad that I was not there when whatever happened, happened."

One of the men reached over and refilled her glass.

"No one," he stated, "that we have heard about has a laser weapon of that capability, that powerful, at least not anything that one could carry about." He looked around the table.

All shook their heads.

"This," said the man who headed The Council, "is going to take a real effort to clean up. Good thing that he wanted to be so isolated. Get moving people, we have a real mess to clean up and a real mystery to solve, if we can." He smiled at them. "Let's hope that the woman they captured religious beliefs have no reality behind them." He sighed. "And for our sakes, let's hope that we are faster than the reporters this time."

The small group met three weeks later.

Everyone had been to the site at one time or another. The compound had been heavily guarded and no visitors other than those who needed to visit were allowed in. The media had been told a very carefully crafted story of mistakes made during what turned out to be a fatal test of a new design for an advanced piece of unspecified technology.

"So," said their host. "Nothing?"

Everyone around the table nodded.

"As far as we were able to find out, and that is very far indeed, nobody has a piece of gear that can do what we all saw the results of with our own eyes. Nobody, absolutely nobody!" He smiled. "And yet someone obviously has." He leaned back and refilled his wine glass and took an appreciative sip.

"A complete dead end?" asked one of the women.

All nodded at the one who had just spoken.

"Yes?" asked their host watching her face.

"That author was in the vicinity."

"That . . . author?"

"D. Grant. She was visiting that nearby town as part of some sort of tour group. In a bus. We are searching for that bus. It has to have been rented somewhere, someplace."

"Her? Again?"

She smiled at him. "Interesting, isn't it?"

"And?" he prompted. He knew she enjoyed being prompted. Her agency was like that.

"We contacted her publisher to, ah, arrange an interview by one of the more trendy magazines." She laughed. "She doesn't do interviews. No one knows how to contact her. No one knows where she lives. There is absolutely no record of any kind. No airplane tickets, no passport trace, no credit card records, no property title or deed in effect. Her only property was bought by a neighbor after the house there had burned to the ground. No telephone of any kind. It appears that she doesn't exist, in a manner of speaking."

He nodded. "Yet she does."

"Certainly does. She walks into their main office and has her assistant set up book tours, who by the way is another blank. If she has a manuscript, she dumps the finished project on her editor." The woman laughed. "She is a perfect example of don't call me, I will call you." She laughed and waggled a hand. "Already did. We will know the instant she walks into that place and whatever she is about."

He smiled.

She refilled her wine glass, took a sip, and smiled broadly at him.

He winked. "O.K., spill it."

"Her latest book, fiction by the way, is about a group of hidden folk who call themselves The Feyra."

"Like this prisoner?"

"Seems so."

"So we wait and watch? And wonder why some small group would call themselves that."

Everyone nodded. And then talked about the dessert and other innocent things. Their agencies were very good at watching and waiting, if they had to be.

Well, This Is A Fine How-De-Doo!

House Darthar Na.

A few weeks had passed since the rescue of Zarpon, First Daughter, House Antarax.

The seven Stands had mingled and discussed the new skills that the Seventh Stand had been given, given to them by House Darthar Na, a unique skill, unique to House Darthar Na. In the Training Hall various members of The Seventh Stand demonstrated to others, newly joined, soaring around The Training Hall on their great dark wings. Then dropping to the floor, the wings disappearing as they landed.

Several members of The Seventh limped, injured during the rescue of Zarpon, one had been shot. But luckily, the assault had been so fast in those dark hours of the night that few defenders could react in time.

Dee had spent her free time talking with her two daughters, Tiela and Winala, about their studies and training.

Deep in the Fall, almost Winter, here in their mountainous area, Jonathon and Karanly popped in and out, just to visit.

Jonathon walked into the room, arms holding a very large box. Karanly carried a large flat portfolio.

Dee filled cups and handed them around.

"Zapon, House Antarax, sent these gifts," explained Jonathon, setting the box on a table next to Dee.

Dee stood, opened the box, and began to take out and set on a large table the dishes and cups. "They are beautiful. No wonder they do so well at markets."

"They are being ever so much more careful," he said.

Karanly handed her the flat file. "Here."

Dee opened it and slid out the portrait. "She is very pretty. Who is she?"

"Zapon said that this is the woman who questioned her while she was being held captive."

"Oh." Dee looked up. "She wasn't there when we went in." She sipped from her cup. "She was lucky to be absent."

Janice walked in, took a filled cup, and sat.

Dee explained the gifts to her.

Janice nodded and looked at her.

"Yes," said Dee. "Jonathon, Janice and I need to go to the publisher's office. I promised him a new book and he is probably getting very nervous from not hearing anything from me. We will probably be gone for a few days. I'll give a call."

He nodded. "When?"

"Now is as good a time as any. The world as we know it is pretty quiet and calm." She looked at Janice.

Janice nodded and stood. "While we are there I would like to go see how the rebuilding of our house is coming along."

The Big City. The Main Office.

Dee and Janice sat in the guest chairs and waited for the usual storm of grumbling and mumbling to blow itself out as it always did.

Dee had explained, very carefully, how slow the writing was going this time.

He stared at her as she did, convinced that authors were a strange, if not peculiar, but a necessary part of life, especially his life. Finally, he nodded, winced a smile into place, and agreed to whatever they wished, and watched two smiling characters leave his office.

As they stood and waited for the elevator to arrive, having decided to have a meal in the restaurant in this building, Dee looked up and down the hall, then leaned close to Janice. "Did you notice?" she whispered.

"What?"

"The woman that Zarpon drew the portrait of is working in our office."

"You sure?"

"Absolutely. I have always been good at remembering faces. Not names, but faces."

"What do you think we ought to do?"

Dee smiled. "Have a good meal."

"Then?"

"We bug out. She can just sit there and twiddle her thumbs."

"What?" Janice looked at her. There were times when Dee's people infected language dialect didn't make sense. Why would that woman be interested in insects?

Dee laughed at her friend's puzzled expression. "Wasting her time. We will just have a very good meal, go meet Jonathon in the park, and go home, ummmm, after we visit your house and see how things are going. As far as I am concerned that woman can sit there and wait as long as she wishes. It won't do her any good."

A soft ping announced the arrival of the elevator.

She dialed the telephone on her desk and waited for the complicated connection to complete. It took a few moments.

"She just left the office with her helper. I heard them say

they were going downstairs to the restaurant here in the building. Yep, her and her assistant. You probably have an hour or less before they are done."

She hung up and went back to her paper shuffling as a low level clerk.

Athen's Best.

Dee and Janice ordered one of the special offerings on the menu and sipped Greek wine while they waited for the main dishes to arrive, munching on the appetizers. They were not in a hurry and discussed which of the desserts they ought to try this time.

Halfway through their dessert Dee looked up. A well dressed man and a well dressed woman had stopped at their table.

"D. Grant?" asked the man.

She nodded and looked for the book to sign.

"May we sit?" asked the woman.

"Sure," said Dee. They must be a pair of reporters or perhaps book reviewers.

"Will it be all right if we talk?" asked the man, indicating their dessert.

Dee nodded. Her mouth was full.

He looked at the woman.

She leaned slightly forward. "Tell us about that mess in Montana. Please?"

Janice stared at them and wondered what they were talking about.

Dee swallowed and snorted. "What mess?"

The woman looked at the man.

"We know," he said, "that you were in Jordan."

Dee nodded and shrugged, casting a glance at Janice who nodded and said, "Book tour."

"And," added the woman. "In Oregon visiting a burned down structure."

"And," he continued, "near a zoo that had a disaster."

"Book tours." Dee smiled. "I have been to many places, at many times. It is what authors do, trying to sell their books, or at least, generate some interest in their books. It is a very bothersome part of the job any more."

The waiter came by and Dee ordered two more coffees. He hurried away.

The woman watched Dee's face. "What can you tell us about The Feyra or the Protectors of The Innocent."

"I write fiction. The Feyra were mentioned in my last book, fictional characters. The who of what?"

The man smiled. "We do not know. But we think that you do and would like you to come with us." He cleared his throat and flopped open a small leather case. "We have lots of questions."

"Guess what?" asked Dee, after looking at his credentials.

"What?"

"Nope."

"Huh?"

"Nope. We are not going anywhere with you two, fancy badge and I.D. or not. I am not interested in playing question and answer with you, whoever you might be, not even a little bit." She stood. "Enjoy your coffee. It is on my bill." She smiled at them. "You really ought to order some of that dessert."

The man touched something on this collar and sighed.

The woman touched his arm. He nodded.

Dee and Janice walked over to the waiter, handed him the

correct amount plus a generous tip and walked out the door into the street and strolled toward the park.

Two large men stepped from the hotel and followed them.

"Dee?"

"Whoever they are, they can't really follow us, can they?"

"I wanted to see how the construction was going."

"So, let's rent a car and go out there and see."

They turned back to the hotel to do that.

The man looked at his wife as he drank his coffee and frowned.

"It appears," she said, "that they are renting a car. What do you think?"

"I think that we had better be very careful. Everything she said is true. And she didn't blink at our credentials."

"Does she have political connections that are that deep? Certainly acts like it."

"Nothing that we have been able to find."

"Then?"

"No idea at all."

"She is very confident, Dear."

He nodded. "Yes, she certainly is."

The Wild Gardens.

The gate was open. The gate and the supporting structure, the very high walls appeared the same as the last time they had visited.

Janice headed the rental car up the long drive to where the house had been standing. Workmen of various types were hard at it, planting new shrubs and some very large trees.

Carpenters were everywhere building the new structure inside what little of the shattered structure that still stood.

A man hobbled from a group of other men where he had been gesturing a various plans on a large table using a cane for this purpose.

Janice ran over to him and wrapped him in her arms, sobbing. And, after some time, they parted and walked over to Dee.

He nodded. "Welcome, Daliera Fontala. You and my Third Daughter look well, healthy in fact."

Dee laughed. "We are, we are." And frowned at him. "And how are you?"

He grinned at her. "As well as can be expected. The cane helps." He waved it. "Things are being restored. Are the rest behaving?"

Janice frowned a not very serious frown at her Father. "They are, as you expect them to be, perfect guests." She waggled one hand at all the activity. "Is this wise?"

Helsing shrugged. "Maybe yes, maybe no. Word has come that a certain individual and all of his no longer will kill or kidnap any on our folk. True?"

Dee bowed to him. "Just so." As she straightened up, she said, "We have things to say of a private nature." She looked around. "Is there someplace?"

He pointed at a large trailer. "I rented one of those people things. Come." He headed that way.

Inside the trailer he filled cups and handed them around and carefully eased himself into a chair.

Dee and Janice sat.

Dee sipped, waited, and then began to tell Helsing of their encounter with the people while they had been eating a meal.

"One of those people government groups?"

Dee nodded.

"They do seem to have a lot of them."

"I think that they are the ones that questioned Zarpon of House Antarax. The questioner was a woman who currently resides in my publishers office, I presume waiting for us to appear. I assume that she must be working with or for the pair that came bothering us."

Helsing nodded. "The people do that often. Boxes inside boxes inside boxes."

"Do these know anything?" asked Dee.

Helsing shrugged. "They tend to be a suspicious lot. But most likely they know only what those not nice people knew. I think that it will make no sense to them at all. But careful cautious, Dee and daughter." He nodded. "They have probably followed you to here and know that the not nice one sent those gray clad ones here. I am a well established dealer in very old documents. This is something any people can find out. My Third Daughter is your assistant. But D. Grant must be careful. It appears to me that you have pulled their eyes toward you."

Dee nodded.

Jonathon opened the door and stepped inside.

"Let's go home," she said to him.

"I will return your rental car," said Helsing to the empty air.

Maryland.

The man closed the folder and looked at his wife.

"A ruptured gas main did all that damage?"

She nodded. "Every team of investigators came to the same conclusion. That old man is known everywhere among collectors and traders of the best of the best ancient documents. For many years. It is a rather small number of people who can afford to do that so they all know about each other."

"And our quarry and his daughter left their rental car there and slipped past our watchers?"

"Poof!" said his wife. "Gone like a puff of smoke."

He gurgled deep in his throat.

She stood and tugged him toward the kitchen. "I bought a sinfully delicious cheesecake to calm irritated husbands with."

He sighed as he was towed to a small table where they sat and she served them large slices and a very dark coffee.

And while they ate, he pondered how they were going to trap their quarry.

The Gray House.

It wasn't totally gray or a house. It was a large wooden building tucked deep into a heavy patch of forest at the end of a twisting and narrow road.

Sensors of many varieties and capabilities were thick in the growth over a wide patch around the structure. The structure itself was heavily shielded from everything imaginable. The people who worked there were very much concerned with their privacy. It was the nature of what they did.

In a good sized conference room in the center of the building they sat around the table sipping coffee or tea, some even had wine.

The conversation had been loose and free-floating. It had been learned long ago that this was the best way to generate new ideas and approaches to whatever problem they were interested in at the moment.

"So," summarized one of the men. "We know almost

nothing. Useful. Or otherwise."

Some shrugged. Some nodded. No one disagreed.

"That, in and of itself, is very interesting," said one of the women.

He smiled. "Very interesting."

"Very interesting, indeed," added one of the other men. "We have a moderately well known, moderately successful individual about which we actually know nothing at all."

"Almost a paradox," suggested another of the women.

"Well," suggested the third man, "certainly a puzzle."

The third woman sat up and looked around the table. "I, for one, would certainly like to know how that is possible. She pays all her taxes via a tax preparer who claims that she always pays him in cash. Anything else she either buys or rents, always paid for in cash. There is no bank account. There is no phone of any make or model. There are no credit cards. She only accepts cash from her publisher whenever she has a need which does not appear to be very often. He suggests that authors are strange anyway. Her parents are dead and equally as untraceable. Her house burned to the ground. So, can anyone tell me how she survives, where she lives, where she buys her clothes, food, etc., anything at all? None of us could find out anything and none of us could do something like this. What organization could? Yet she does. Sooooo, there is an organization out there of some kind, isn't there?" She sat back and refilled her wine glass.

"I have a suggestion," said the first man. "But I will need full agreement if we are to proceed."

House Darthar Na.

Dee, Janice, and Jonathon sat in one of the small rooms, chairs facing the large outside window, watching the snow fall, sipping coffee from their cups, a portion of the gift from Zarpon, House Antarax.

"Hofga dropped off the coffee," explained Dee.

They had been discussing those people that had spoken to Dee and that woman working in her publisher's office.

"They are connected," said Jonathon.

Dee nodded. "I think so too."

"Do you think that their credentials were real?" asked Janice.

Dee shrugged. "They were probably watching that Williams Three person for some reason. That is how they knew that I had been in Jorden and out on the west coast. But why?"

Jonathon sipped. "People organizations are strange, very strange. They are always so busy poking their noses into everyone's business. They are like young children that haven't learned proper manners. Must be because of their short life spans."

Dee laughed. "Everything that I ever heard when I was living as one of them suggests that they are worse than that!"

"The people are often hard to understand." Jonathon refilled all their cups and winked at Dee. It was always the house host who was supposed to do that. But Dee was more relaxed about things like that, not as prickly proper as some.

"I think," said Dee, looking out the large window at the forest beyond the meadow. "That I shall have a large Christmas tree in the main entry area."

Then she had to explain this people thing to Jonathon. Janice had seen much of this behavior as her house was located close to where many of the people lived.

Karanly popped in and filled a cup. "Do they really give each other gifts that are all decorated?"

So Dee explained that as well.

Jonathon nodded. "Strange."

Dee laughed. "It is fun." Then she looked out the window again remembering just those few bits and pieces about her parents and their enjoyment when her family was hiding out among the people doing all that people behavior.

Dee called Ar and explained to him what she would like done. Ar stared at her, jerked, then nodded. He assured her that the house sprites would began immediately. He hurried from the room, she was the most different House Head that House Darthar Na had ever had. She was ever so much different than he could have ever imagined.

But soon enough, all the hallways were decorated with the people stuff of Christmas.

Jonathon strode down the hall and frowned, just a little.

Karanly laughed and hugged Dee as they walked along with him. "I like it. There are some things that the people do that are nice."

They stopped to look at a large tree.

"Yes." Jonathon nodded. House Darthar Na was certainly bringing changes into the world of The Feyra. But nothing harmful.

All through the snow time Dee had Kitea, First Hand, Seventh Stand, exercising the flyers and herself and Anagon and Yallan in The Training Hall. All soared and swooped around and around until using their great dark wings, a House Darthar Na special skill, unique to that house, given to them by Ar as directed by Dee, until flying was as familiar to them as walking down the hallway. Dee retained her white feather covered wings. She was a flash of white among all that dark.

Finally late in the year as the people marked time, Dee

gathered all the Stands into a great new hall, Fontala Hall, for a feast of celebration, with all the foods that she remembered. The Stands were all now fully staffed, Thirty Fingers to a Stand, plus two, with the exception of the Seventh which had plus three.

Jonathon and Karanly came from House Darthar and Hofga from his house. Dee had Ar prepare gifts for everyone, an activity that took a number of days. Ar had watched all the Fontala members and with Dee's prodding had prepared something that had special meaning for each one.

Foods was eaten, then gifts were opened to the great surprise of all those there. Dee hugged her daughters and watched all the activity and beamed happily, and decided that it was the best Christmas she had ever had, even if it was far removed from the intent of the people celebration.

Then she wandered the halls talking and laughing with this one or that one until she suddenly realized what had happened. The Fontala were once again, a single cohesive organization and that they had taken over all the rooms on the fourth floor.

A number of days later Dee sat in one of the small comfortable rooms talking quietly with Jonathon and Ar about something that she though needed to be done.

Jonathon stared at her, Ar's mouth fell open.

"Princess?" gasped Ar.

"Is it possible?"

Ar hissed softly to himself and looked at Jonathon who shrugged.

Dura walked into the room. She was the equivalent of Ar in House Darthar Na, the one who knew the ways of all her house skills.

"Jonathon?" She bowed to him and smiled at Ar. Then

she looked puzzled at the group. Beings of her special skills resided in every house, large or small, high or low, even in the clusters. But they rarely visited outside their house and were very, very guarded with their knowledge, extremely protective of that knowledge.

Ar stood and bowed to her. "Most welcome to House Darthar Na."

She nodded, sat, and sipped from her cup, just handed to her by Ar.

Then Ar explained, slowly, carefully, the several things that Dee had asked to be done, if possible.

Dura nodded, set her cup down and walked from the room beckoning Ar to come. In the hall, she slipped her arm under one of his. "Your Princess wants change, great change. Is this nice?"

Ar shrugged. "We have to decide that, I believe."

The pair walked slowly down the hall speaking softly to each other.

Inside the room, Dee sipped and then nodded.

Armilin walked in and bowed to Dee. "Word?"

Dee told her.

Armilin nodded and bowed deeply. "As the Word says, so will the deed be done." She spun around and hurried from the room, sending a call to all The First Hands to meet her in the appropriate room.

"Dee?"

She refilled his cup. "Jonathon?"

"Regular staffs? You want them to be able to change those Flame Blades into regular staff as well? As they wish?"

She nodded. "Yes. I think that in many cases a good thumping rather than chopping folk into pieces should be sufficient."

"Ah ummmm." He took a sip. Then nodded.

Karanly nudged him with her elbow. "I think that all Dee has done and wished to have done will be all to the good of The Feyra."

"Ummm ah." He nodded at Dee. "I do agree. Most folk will stop not nice as soon as they see them. And many will do that after a good thumping. A few will have to die."

Dee grinned at him, reached under the table, and handed each of them a very decorated small box. And laughed at their expressions. "A very merry people Christmas."

They carefully undid the wrappings and even more carefully opened their box. Each lifted out a cup.

"For when you visit here. I asked Zarpon to make something special, just for you."

"Beautiful," gurgled Karanly.

"Umm," said Jonathon, holding out his cup.

Dee filled it, then Karanly's, and then her own.

"Have either of you ever had eggnog?"

Both frowned and shook their heads. Both wondered what sort of animal or plant that was.

Dee smiled at them. "We will have some later. I asked Ar to put a large fireplace in one of the rooms. We can sit in front of the fire, listen to music, and sip eggnog. It is a people custom. I don't see why we can't borrow some of their customs as long as they sorta fit into Feyra culture. After all we have already borrowed a few things." She held up her coffee cup.

Jonathon sipped, and smiled. "Hofga's choice?"

Dee nodded. "Yes. He said that it was your favorite."

Maryland.

He stood next to the tree and looked out the living room window at the blowing snow. Roads were closing and drifts were building. His wife handed him a tall mug.

"Merry Christmas," she said. "I put some brandy in the eggnog."

He took a swallow. "Always a good idea."

"Anything?"

He shook his head. "Not a trace."

"Think that you frightened her into hiding?"

"Did she look frightened to you?"

"No." She took a swallow from her own tall mug. "Actually she looked and sounded more like a CEO of one of the large corporations, or like a Four Star General. Unruffled by most anything."

He nodded. "Used to giving orders, not worried about pestering, and very comfortable in her position. Do you think that she works somewhere in The White House? Has the attitude for it."

"No. There is absolutely nothing to suggest that. But if she does, it is so deep cover than even we will not be able to pry away all the layers."

He nodded and took another swallow. "A worrisome thought, anyone with that kind of political clout."

She nodded.

"Perhaps," he suggested. "She has just holed up for the winter?"

She nudged his elbow. "Then we shall just have to wait and watch."

He watched the snow blast past the house. "Wait and watch it is."

Spring Has Sprung.
As It Always Does.

House Darthar Na.

Feyra everywhere had celebrated what the people called The Winter Solstice and what they called The Approach of Warmth. With a few exceptions The Hidden Ones much preferred warm weather over cold.

And the warmth was approaching, the air temperature was rising, the snow was mostly gone from the large meadow below the house.

Dee was sitting on the bottom of the entry stairs watching her daughters soar around the great open space, one set of dark wings, one set of white wings. They were playing with their Ice Cats, now fully grown. The Ice Cats leaped to touch them with soft paws as each zipped over their pet's head, then up and around.

Janice joined her of the lower step. "Looks like they are having a great time."

Dee smiled. "All four of them."

"That people female is still sitting in your editor's office, doing low level clerical work."

"Ummmm."

"I asked Second Sister Togala to visit and check and see. I showed her that picture."

"Who ever they are, they are quite patient."

Janice nodded.

"Ummmm ah."

"Yes. I think that we ought to have a very private talk with that one."

Dee nodded. "I will talk with Jonathon, ask him to take us there."

The Big City. The Main Office.

Dee and Janice strolled in and stopped at one of the desks.

"Come into my office," ordered Dee, setting her hand on a shoulder.

Janice watched carefully.

The woman nodded and stood. They led her into Dee's office. Janice closed the door and stood in front of it.

Dee pointed at a chair. "Sit!" Then walked around her desk, sat, and waited for her to do so.

Dee picked up the phone and asked for a large pot of coffee and three cups. "Now! I would like to know your name, who you work for, and why are they so interested in me!"

They sat in silence until the coffee servings arrived. Dee filled three cups and pushed one across her desk and handed one to Janice. Then she leaned back and took a sip.

The woman looked at her cup and took a sip. "I am Dot," she said in a soft and gentle voice. "Short for Dorothy. I am Dorothy Jant. I work for a very special group inside the government. That group, often called The Council, is very curious about you."

"Why?"

"Because you have turned up or near to places that they were watching. They are curious how a moderately successful author could treat them so casually. Most people would go pale in the face and get very nervous if they saw those credentials. They are very curious how someone that writes fiction of the sort that you do could just walk away and disappear from very highly trained agents. They are very curious how you can be totally untraceable."

She took a sip from her cup and shrugged. "That is all that I know."

"Oh!" She smiled at Dee. "And they are very curious about whatever destroyed the compound build by William Williams the Third and freed that woman that they were holding."

Dee nodded and took a sip. "A very curious group."

Dot sipped. "That they are. It is their assignment. You are an unknown. With the resources that they have and can call upon such an unknown makes them very nervous as well."

"I am a very private person," stated Dee. "That group ought to have better things to be nervous about or curious about than an author such as I am."

Dot smiled. "Oh, they do, they really do."

Dee waggled her hand at Dot. "I really do not want to be bothered by them for any reason that they might think is valid. Their curiosity and their bother is not my problem." She smiled. "You may tell them that."

Dot finished her coffee. "I will. May I leave?"

"Of course." They watched Dot walk through the door, over to her desk, and pick up the phone.

Dee stood. "Let's go downstairs and get a snack at one of the street venders."

Maryland.

The phone rang and he answered it.

"What? She did what? Where is she? O.K., good job."

Snatching up another phone he spoke to the person at the other end and told him to move. Now!

The Big City.

Dee and Janice strolled along carefully eating their snack, polish sausage covered in sauerkraut inside a long bun. Their free hands held wads of paper napkins which they used often.

"Pretty good," said Dee. "Think that the house sprites could do something like this?"

Janice nodded as she chewed and swallowed the last portion. "Just explain it and it will be done."

Dee smiled. "It will be a surprise for Jonathon and Karanly." She laughed. "And everyone else."

"OH!" Janice gasped, eyes flying wide.

Dee's head snapped around. "What? OUCH!"

Maryland.

Her eyes fluttered open, focused, and stared at the ceiling. This was not a room that she recognized. She rolled off the bed and to her feet.

"It will wear off very quickly now that you are awake," said the man sitting in the chair set into one corner of the room.

She spun toward that calm voice. "What do you think that you are doing?" she rasped.

"Trying to solve a problem. Your friend is quite safe and unharmed. In a room just down the hall from here." He stood. "Please come with me. Everyone is very anxious to meet you. Please? All will be shortly explained." He swung wide the door to the hall.

"Am I a prisoner?"

"Oh, no. A guest."

Dee laughed.

He nodded. "Does sound odd, I suppose." He stepped into the hall. "Please?" And swept his arm in the right direction.

Dee shrugged and stepped out into a rather plain hallway that could be anyplace.

He started walking. "Just two doors this way."

Two doors down the hall, he pushed open a door and gestured for her to go in. "Please?"

Dee stepped in, stopped, and stared.

Five people sat around a table and stared back at her. The table had seven place settings. A number of steaming platters and bowls were scattered around the table top.

Her stomach rumbled. She was very hungry so she assumed that she had been asleep or drugged for sometime.

The man pulled out a chair for her. "Please." And sat in the chair next to her's as she sat.

The woman on Dee's other side touched Dee's arm gently. "Sorry for the rough treatment. We will tell you everything while we eat." She poured wine into Dee's glass and then her's and took a sip. "Not too bad."

So they ate with each of them taking turns speaking. Dee ate and listened.

The three couples explained who they were and what agencies they represented. Then the woman told Dee that they had been watching William Williams the Third's activities as close as they could and had been trying to figure out what he was up to. Dot had been planted inside the Williams organization with the hope of finding out. Williams had been in touch with a number of foreign countries and had received rather large sums of money from them.

So they worried about what Williams was up to and whether he was developing something that could, or would, eventually threaten the security of the country.

But, added one of the men, someone, or some group, had eliminated the Williams operation and had taken away everything that contained information as to what Williams had been doing as well as liberating the woman that Williams had been holding hostage.

Over dessert they explained their concern with Dee and her potential link to these worrisome activities.

Dee laughed. "I am an author not a member of some group threatening anyone or anything."

The third man filled his coffee cup. "I suppose. But!"

"What?" she snapped.

He sighed. "We," he waggled one hand at the others seated around the table, "can find out almost anything about anyone when we really try hard. But, for all practical purposes, you are invisible."

"So what?"

"Makes you unique."

"Perhaps. But, so what?"

They all stared at her.

Dee laughed. "What?"

The man seated on her left sighed. "We are not getting anywhere."

Dee looked at him. "Perhaps that is because your basic assumptions are wrong. You are all so wrapped up in searching for bad guys, as you define them, that you see them when they really aren't there."

He sighed again.

"Well?" She nudged him. And stood. "I would like to

leave now, with my friend and associate, and with your apology. Your behavior is very not nice!"

"Wait!" he snapped.

"Now what?" she grumbled looking down at him.

"What did you say we were? Not nice?"

"Just so. Grabbing us off the street."

He nodded. "Better sit down. I have a few more questions first. Please?"

Dee frowned at him but dropped into her seat. "Any more coffee?"

The woman on her right filled a cup and pushed it over to her. "Here, Dear."

He looked at her. "You said that we were not nice, right?"

She sipped. "Certainly are."

"That is the way that the woman Williams kidnaped talked. She said that he was not nice to hold her so. As far as I know and our language specialists know, no one in the nation uses those terms that way."

Dee shrugged. "So what?"

"She said that she was Feyra. We could find out nothing on any group claiming that name."

Dee sipped. "Did you read my latest book?"

"Your birth certificate from a hospital that no longer exists says that your name is Daliera Fontala."

"I prefer Dee."

"A unique name."

She shrugged. "So what?"

"Your parents died in a fire at their house while you were on a book tour."

She nodded slowly.

"Your own house burned down while you were out of the

country."

She nodded again.

"Neither event was really explained to our satisfaction. We think that someone, or some group, was responsible."

Dee held out her cup for a refill. And shrugged.

"Why would some group, or someone, be so determined to do that to some mere author of fantasy fiction?"

"Hard to say," grumbled Dee, taking a sip.

The man touched his ear. Then she noticed that he was wearing some tiny thing there. He refilled his wine glass and took a swallow. Then he shoved his chair back and turned it so he could look into her eyes.

"Ms. Grant, what are you hiding from us? For you most certainly are. And we know it. We could keep you locked up for a very long time."

"No, you really are not able do that." Dee shrugged, picked up her cup, took a sip, and stared back at him. "Bring my friend here! Now!"

He nodded. The others were staring at Dee. How could anyone say that with such confidence, or give them orders like that?

Shortly thereafter the door opened and Janice walked in, stopped, and looked around the room. "Dee?"

Someone grabbed a chair and made room for Janice at the table.

"It is all right," said Dee. "Have something to eat." She waved a hand at the others in the room. "This is The Council that Dot mentioned."

"Very clever," said the woman sitting to her right.

Dee nodded and looked from face to face. "I am going to tell you something that you are going to find hard to believe so you had better hope that whoever is listening on that ear piece understands that I am telling truth."

A few smiled at the man on her left.

He smiled back.

"First!" she stated. "Leave me alone, leave us alone!. No more fancy drugs and snatching us from the street. I will not stand for that ever happening again!"

A large and muscular man across the table from her stood and stared at her.

"Better believe her," said Janice to him.

"And what will you do if we decide to do that?" challenged the standing man.

Dee took a sip, and looked at him. "I will kill you."

He laughed. She was short and weighed maybe a hundred pounds.

"True," said the man on her left, lightly touching his ear.

"Nonsense!" The man started around the table, glowering at Dee.

Janice looked at her. "Don't hurt him, Dee."

Everyone stared at Janice.

Dee nodded, stood, and thrust her palm at the man as soon as he got very close, as he reached for her, her hand almost touching him.

He flew backwards, and up, and bounced off the wall and crashed in a heap on the floor.

The only doors to the room flew open and two large men ran in, guns in hand.

The man on her left snapped, "OUT! NOW!"

They left.

He turned in his chair. "Charles?"

Charles lurched to his feet. "Like being tackled by a pro

footballer, Ralph." He stared at Dee and walked back to his chair. The rest calmed down, taking their cue from Ralph's behavior.

The man on her left looked at Dee. "I am Ralph. I lead this group. Where did you learn to do something like that?"

She shook her head.

"O.K. Now what?"

"Does this group know how to keep a secret?"

Ralph laughed. "From everyone in the world." Then he looked at her again, his expression changing.

He smiled at her. "Ahhhhhhhhhhhhhh. You are what Williams was trying to find with all that research into old bits and pieces." He nodded. "That is it, isn't it? Now I understand the few things that the captive said." He leaned back in his chair. "Oh, my."

Dee watched him carefully.

The woman on her left gently touched Dee's arm. "I am Sandra, his wife. We had copies of everything that Williams ever bought or acquired and studied them carefully, trying to figure out what he was up to and why other, ahh, agencies would give him so much money. We thought that he was trying to build some new kind of terrible weapon, some new terrorist thing. We were very worried about that."

She refilled Dee's cup. "I think that my brilliant husband just figured it out." She smiled at Dee. "He is, you know, quite brilliant."

Ralph winked at his wife. Then he looked back at Dee.

"Dee?"

"Yes?"

"This is a promise, an absolutely binding promise, and a very, very serious one. If anything you say in this room ever escapes, I will personally kill whoever is responsible." He looked at the others. "Any doubts?"

Everyone shook their heads.

Ralph tapped his ear. "Everything off! Now! Instantly!" He nodded.

The doors locked.

"Just us six and you two. No one else can hear anything that we say or do. No recordings, no notes, only memory. And no one will violate that."

Dee nodded.

"So, may I ask some questions? And get answers?"

Dee nodded. "Perhaps." Janice sighed.

Dee looked at her. "It will be all right." Her eyes shifted to Ralph's. "It had better be."

Ralph looked around the table. "It will." Every head nodded agreement.

Dee sipped from her cup. "My friend will probably be getting very nervous and terribly angry that we didn't meet him in the park."

Ralph looked around the table. "Apparently no one knew that there was someone else. Would you like to place a phone call and tell him, or her, you are O.K.?"

"No need." Dee nodded.

Jonathon stepped from a dark corner. "Dee?"

Someone popped up from their chair, and dropped down, then up again, and pulled another chair to the table. They all stared at him and then at her. There was no door over there.

Once they were all settled, Dee explained to Jonathon about The Council and what she felt would be best.

Jonathon looked around the table. "Are you sure?"

She nodded. "Only if you agree, Lord."

Six pair of eyes snapped from Dee to Jonathon.

"Will they behave themselves, Princess?"

Six pair of eyes snapped from Jonathon to Dee.

"I think they will."

"Ah ummmmm." Jonathon took a sip from his cup. Someone had just filled it.

Ralph stared at Jonathon. "How did he do that? Just walk into this room?"

"Shhhh," said Dee.

Then she looked around the table. "You six know all about my life and wonder what that Williams Three person was up to. But," she held up her hand, "you actually know very little, if anything at all."

Various frowns and puzzled looks stared at her.

"My name is Daliera Fontala, as you know. I am Head of House Darthar Na. Jonathon is Head of House Darthar and Lord of the Darthar family. Janice is Third Sister, House Hinterane. House is a synonym for family."

She grinned at them. "None of the houses appear on any tax roll or map." She took a deep breath and looked at Jonathon.

He nodded and took a sip.

"We," she indicated Janice and Jonathon," are The Feyra, The Hidden Ones. You have probably already heard that name." She waited for a moment. "We are not people." And laughed. "Nor are we fiction."

She smiled at them. "I know. We look like you, ah, more or less. But we are not you. We are a sub-species that split away millions of years ago as the people measure time. We have worked hard ever since to remain hidden." She sighed. "Compared to the vast numbers of people, we are very few. And we are worried about your behavior. Much more than you should be about our's. Your technology is frightening to us. In many ways we live much simper lives, more quiet lives, more private lives, than you people do."

She refilled her cup and took a sip. "We were watching Williams because we felt he might be about to realize that we existed and we weren't sure what to do about that. Then he had his people kill one of our's and kidnap another."

Jonathon stood. "We are not interested in the affairs of the people, we are not interested in interfering in the affairs of the people, we just wish to live our lives. It is a rare thing for any of the people to know one of us. But," his eyes scanned the faces of the six watching him, "now you know some of us."

He sat and refilled his cup. And took a sip.

Janice sat slumped in her chair, staring at nothing at all.

Dee sighed and wondered whether she had done the right thing or not.

"Hard to believe," mumbled Charles, rubbing his chest.

Dee looked at Ralph. "Now what?"

He shook his head, then straightened up. "A hidden folk that no one knows of or about?"

"Just so," said Jonathon. "Only in your folk tales and mythology."

"One of the woman looked at Dee. "I am Anabelle. Do you have any children?"

"Two daughters."

"And you are some sort of sub-species of humanity?"

Dee nodded.

"Easy to say." She frowned at Dee.

Dee stared at her and pulled a short rod from her shirt pocket and tossed it to her.

Anabelle caught it. The rod was a soft purple color.

"Pretty color."

"Stick in into the table top!"

"What?"

"Do it!"

Anabelle stabbed. The rod bounced back. She looked puzzled at Dee.

"Toss it back," Dee said to Anabelle. "New idea," she explained to Jonathon.

Dee caught the rod and looked at Ralph. Then she gently pushed it into the table top and pulled it up and out, leaving a neat smooth walled hole in the wood. "It works for me." She dragged it across her plate and watched the two pieces fall apart.

Ralph picked up one of the pieces and ran his finger over the cut edge. "Smooth." He stared at Dee, hard, leaned close, and whispered ever so softly, "The Protectors of The Innocent?"

He held out his hand. "May I look at that?"

Dee handed the rod to him.

Ralph ran his fingers over it and carefully inspected it. "Looks and feels like a piece of wood." He tapped it on the surface of the table and bent close to inspect the spot. "No mark." He handed the rod back to her.

"Touch me with it." He gritted his teeth.

She did. He grunted.

"Nothing happened," he said to his worried looking wife.

Dee smiled at him. "Of course not." She pushed the rod back into her pocket, stood and walked over to Jonathon beckoning Janice to join them.

She looked at Ralph. "Please leave us alone. We are leaving now."

Ralph jumped to his feet. "May I ask for a, ah, favor?"

Dee and his wife stared at him.

"Please?"

"What?" asked Dee.

"May I visit? You? At home? In your house?"

"When?"

"Now."

Charles lunged to his feet. "Ralph!"

Ralph looked at Dee. "I will be safe, won't I? If I visit? Now?"

Dee looked at Jonathon, who said, "He may."

Dee nodded and said to Ralph, "Perfectly safe." And looked at Ralph, now standing with his arm over his wife's shoulders. "The rest," he said, "will do nothing even if they don't understand."

Heads nodded.

Charles looked at Ralph. "We will wait. How long?"

Ralph looked at Dee. "How about two weeks?"

Dee laughed. "It could be a very boring two weeks as you measure time. Stand close, very close to us."

Ralph set his cell phone on the table, and his watch and several other things from his pockets. "Two weeks, Charles, two week."

The five stepped out into the hall, gently closing the door behind themselves.

Charles ran after them, opened the door, run into the hall, and looked up and down.

He walked back into the room and over to a cabinet. "I think that I will have some of that strong brandy. The hall was empty."

Almost Never Heard Of!

House Darthar Na.

Dee laughed happily and bounded up the stairs to the outer door and shoved it open. Then she spun to look down at the others.

"Do come in, Jonathon, Janice."

Ar walked from the main hall to stand by her side. "Princess?"

Ralph and Sandra walked up the stairs to join the others standing just inside the doorway. And suddenly stopped.

Sandra gasped. Ralph reached out a careful hand.

"There is something in the way," he said.

"Interesting," observed Jonathon. He was surprised. It had worked on . . . people.

"Do come in, Sandra and Ralph," said Dee.

They stepped inside.

Ar gasped. "Princess!"

"Ummmm."

"Oh! Humble pardon, Princess, but those two are . . . are people! Here!"

She smiled. "Certainly are. Ah ummm, Ar?"

"Princess?"

"They are my guests. Please show them to a nice bedroom and then bring them back to me. They are restricted to this floor and the next one up."

Ar bowed, straightened up, and beckoned Ralph and

Sandra to follow him. They did, staring at Ar and at one another. Sandra clenched her husband's hand tightly.

"A rare thing, Princess," said Jonathon as the three of them walked down the hallway and into one of the smaller comfortable rooms with a great window that looked out at the meadow and forest.

Dee poured and handed Jonathon and Janice cups, then took the third and sat in one of the large, comfortable chairs. "Ar told me that we had met with them a few times in the past."

"Ummm ah." Jonathon sipped.

Janice sipped and stared at her.

"I think," explained Dee, "that group, The Council, was working their way through everything that they could find and would have realized that we are out there, scattered around the world, out of sight. They were getting very worried that a hidden folk might be a threat to them. So, before they understood and reacted violently, it seemed best to me, to let them understand some very small amount about the secret they have now vowed to keep."

"Ah ummmmm." Jonathon looked at her and took a sip.

Janice turned and looked at him. "I think that if they had known earlier then maybe they could have prevented that Williams Three person from doing not nice to House Antarax."

Jonathon nodded and looked at Dee. "Careful cautious. Think deep. Use all your people knowledge and experience. You are the only one of us that has ever been raised and lived among them like you have."

She nodded and refilled his cup. "They will come to understand that as long as they keep our secret that we will continue to talk to them. They are very important and powerful people in the people government of that area they call The

United States which is very large, powerful organization of the people's."

He sipped.

Ar opened the door and Ralph and Sandra walked into the room.

"Where are we?" he asked, looking out the window.

"In my house," replied Dee.

"Ah, O.K., I understand." Ralph smiled at her, and sighed. "This is going to be hard. May I ask about, eh, things?"

"Of course. But I may not answer." Dee smiled at him.

Ralph laughed. "Fair enough."

His wife patted his arm.

The door to the room banged open as Tiela and Winala charged into the room followed by their Ice Cats.

"Mother!" gasped Tiela. "Ar said that there are two people in the house!"

"Oh," said Winala, looking at Ralph and Sandra who were frozen in place, eyes wide, staring at the Ice Cats, who were sitting and staring at them.

"They are guests," said Dee, calmly filling two cups and handing one to each daughter. She gestured. "Tiela and Winala, this is Ralph and Sandra. They are the people." She smiled, a rather wry smile. "It is a sort of an experiment."

The Ice Cats had moved forward and were starting to gurgle deep in their throats.

Both daughters spoke to their pets. The Ice Cats walked over and sat at the side of their daughter and looked hungry eyes at the food sitting on the table.

"These are your daughters?" Sandra looked at Tiela and Winala and then at Dee, a slight frown creasing her forehead. Dee didn't look old enough to have daughters as old as this pair appeared to be.

"Just so." Dee smiled. "They tend to be impulsive, at times."

Sandra smiled. "That is what I have heard people say about daughters."

"Dee?" Ralph cleared his throat.

"Ummmmmm."

He nodded at one of the large white animals now sitting very close to him.

"They are called Hamel, often referred to as Ice Cats. The pair of them were given as gifts to my daughters, when all were quite small, girls and kittens, by House Milaton. They are the only ones that raise them."

Ralph nodded. "Then those fellows at the zoo were correct."

Dee smiled at him.

Ralph reached a very careful hand out and gently scratched the Ice Cat behind the ear. Its head was almost even with his shoulder. "Dee, may my wife and I talk with you privately?"

She nodded.

The rest left the room.

Dee slouched in her chair after refilling her cup.

He watched as she took a sip. "I noticed that everyone drinks a lot of coffee."

Holding her cup on her stomach with both hands, Dee nodded. "It has been a favorite beverage ever since it was discovered by the people. The caffeine has no effect on us."

"When we came from our rooms with Ar, I noticed a lot of people, ah, folk, walking here and there. They all stared at us intensely."

"Yes. We do not interact with the people. The people's beliefs tend to make the people unstable and violent."

She stood. "I am tired." She pointed. "Third door on the right hand side. A dining room." She grinned. "Just say out loud what you would like to eat just before you enter." She headed for the hall. "See you in the morning."

Ralph and Sandra walked into the hall in the correct direction.

"Who or what are they?" Sandra slipped her arm under one of his. "Really?"

"She said that they were a hidden folk that has been around as long as humanity has been, maybe even longer. An idea like that is gonna be hard to grasp all at once. I think that two weeks may be a much too short a period of time to learn much of anything."

"Let's eat," she said.

"Sure." They were standing in front of the door that Dee said was the dining room.

She nudged him. "So what do you want to eat, Dear?"

"Wife's choice."

She laughed and rattled off her choices. "For two," she added.

He pushed open the door and followed her inside.

It was a small room with a small table set for two. Serving bowls were scattered around the table top. With everything that she had named.

He sat and began to serve her and then himself. "Now this is truly amazing."

"Think hard, Dear."

He poured dressing on his salad. "About?"

She chewed slowly. "A great salad."

"About that?" He poured her wine glass full.

"Not at all. You are going to figure how you, my most clever husband, are going to make the others believe that you haven't suffered some strange sort of mental breakdown."

He laughed and clinked his glass against her's. "I will be very careful and very selective and tell them nothing too far from the ordinary."

She nodded. "So no descriptions about a dining room, strange looking advisors, and pets?"

"Absolutely not!"

"While we are here we are going to be very careful, aren't we, Dear?"

"Absolutely." He leaned back and smiled broadly at his wife. "Absolutely."

Maryland.

"It has been two weeks to the day!"

Charles, Ralph's Number Two in the Council, looked at the other three and glowered.

No one looked very bothered. They were used to his glower.

"And what do you suggest that we do about it?" asked Randy. "We have no idea of where they are."

"We just have to wait," said Charles' wife, Prentice.

Charles sat and sighed. "Right," he grumbled.

The door opened and they walked into the room.

Ralph looked at the faces and laughed. "Such a dark and dower expression. Who died?"

The pair sat in their usual chairs.

"I, we, all of us, were worried," explained Charles.

Ralph stood, leaned forward, and snatched a wine bottle

from the cluster in the middle of the table, sat and filled his glass and then Sandra's. "I suppose that you all want a report of some kind?" He took a sip and looked around the table at all the expectant faces. Everyone nodded.

He cleared his throat. "Well, they are very nice. They, as a culture, are quite shy and very carefully guarded about what they will talk about. I believe, I truly believe, as much as I have ever believed anything, that The Council has some new friends that no one else knows anything about."

He held up his hands to stop the outburst of questions that he could see forming. "Let me just tell you about our vacation as that is what it was, more or less. Then we, Sandra and I, will attempt to answer questions, bearing in mind that we really know very little about them."

House Darthar Na.

Dee sat in one of the small comfortable rooms looking out the large window at the meadow and the forest, sipping coffee. Jonathon and Karanly sat in comfortable chairs as well.

"Those two people seemed to be nice," she said.

"Ummmm." Jonathon took a sip.

Karanly sat up. "The people do have terribly complicated multi-layered ways of organizing themselves."

Dee nodded. "They do that. But I think that Council thing will hold to their promise to us."

"Ah ummmm," said Jonathon.

"Why?" asked Karanly.

"They, that Council thing, represent organizations in their people system that are dedicated to protecting their political entity from other people who would do not nice to them. I think that they would like to be the only ones to know of us. Those six people are very intelligent, are very clever, and are very mindful of having friends that no one else knows about."

Jonathon sat up and stared at her. "Friends?"

Dee nodded. "I think that they would like to be."

"Ummm ah." He sat back. He wasn't convinced that people could really understand that.

Dee twisted in her chair and looked at him. "It apparently happen in the long ago. Can you tell me as much as you know of those occurrences?"

"Hofga can." Jonathon nodded.

The door to the room banged open and Hofga thumped into the room. He always thumped.

Dee stood, filled a cup, and handed it to him. "Special blend." And grinned. It was his gift of coffee that they were drinking.

Hofga dropped into a chair, took a sip, winked at Dee, and looked at Jonathon.

Jonathon nodded at his friend. "Dee wants to know all that there is to know about the few times that we had people friends."

"Ahhhhh, kopta!"

"I do," said Dee. "Please?"

Hofga nodded. "Princess." He took a sip. "I have knowledge of two times. There may have been more, but if there were, nothing was written down or survived for me to find."

"Very rare, then?"

"Just so." His eyes jumped from Jonathon's to Karanly's and back to Dee's. "We are The Hidden Ones. And the people seem to be the ever busy, ever agitated ones."

"Tell me all you know."

Hofga nodded.

"The oldest, the most long ago, was around 400 A.D. as the people measure time. Perhaps older, perhaps younger."

It happened, he explained, late in their Fall season just on the edge of the dark and the cold.

Thran, although his name may have been something totally different, was hunting. This male of the people lived in his home at the edge of the forest some distance from where the rest of people houses huddled together, six, maybe eight, dwellings in all.

So, on that day, he was moving as quietly as he could along a game trail deep in the forest, some distance from his dwelling. He was very nervous to be this deep inside the forest.

He had grown up hearing the stories of the forest spirits and other creatures that lived hidden here, this deep inside the forest. Everyone knew that these beings were not to be bothered. But the summer had been cooler and shorter than usual. With what food he had stored and preserved he would not survive the coming cold time that all the elders said was going to be worse than ever.

He intended to survive. So he pushed ever deeper into the forest forbidden territory. All he wanted was sufficient food to survive, nothing more. Surely even the forest spirits and the other creatures would understand that. But maybe not. The tales were unclear as to whether such beings actually cared whether he starved or not.

Suddenly he jerked to a halt, one foot still in the air, standing as still as still could be. Something was coming his way, from in front of him, on this very same game trail.

Slowly, ever so carefully and quietly, he slipped into a thick brush cluster, his green and brown clothes merging with the green and brown of all that growth. Then he waited, breathing as softly as he was capable of doing.

Slowly, slowly, it came. The creature was making a soft sound, a soft moan it seemed to him. Carefully he checked the game trail and pondered the wisdom of bolting for his life back down the narrow meandering path as fast as he could run, back the way he had come.

Then he gasped in surprise and stared, mouth hanging open.

It was a tall woman that was making the soft moaning sound. She was staggering his way, using a long staff for support as she dragged one leg and hobbled as fast as she seemed to be able to go. As she came closer he could see an arrow protruding through her right thigh, her pant leg heavily stained, deep dark red on dark brown.

She stopped and looked right at him, wobbling from side to side. One of her eyes was puffy, a trickle of blood wandered from the corner of her mouth and over her chin. Her upper garment was torn. Her clothes were dirty, her one open eye wild and staring here and there and back at him.

"Help," she gasped. "Me." And collapsed into the brush screen that he was using for cover.

Thran, or whatever his name really was, was a large man. He carefully gathered her into his arms, snatched up her staff in one hand, and started out of the forest, moving as fast as he could, headed for his dwelling.

He was staggering badly by the time he kicked his door open and lurched into his small house. Carefully he laid his burden on the narrow bed on her side, the injured leg free.

Taking his knife from his belt he cut the shaft in half and threw that piece on the nearby table. Then he sucked in a deep breath and yanked the rest of the shaft free and pitched the barbed arrow and shaft piece onto the table next to the other part.

He checked her face and leaned very close. He could feel the soft breath against his cheek. Her eyes popped open.

"Shhhh," he said straightening up. "You are safe. But your wounds need tending."

Swiftly he cut her pant leg further open exposing the bleeding wounds. Spinning away, he gathered the appropriate plant materials and started. He had done this same thing many times before for hunters and others of his clan.

Then he gently washed the dirt from her face and was surprised. No one that he knew had features like her's. He had not met anyone in the few other clans that he had visited that looked as she did.

So while he worried about who she might be, he worked swiftly and gently. Finished, he draped a cover, one of his two, over her, built up the fire, and began to heat water to make something to eat. He was really hungry and she required food to heal. And to sleep as well.

Several days passed. Thran slept on the floor. It wasn't all that much different that sleeping in the forest on the ground which he had done many a time. The days passed mostly in silence. She seemed content to not engage in conversation. Of course, he was not one who talked very much anyway so it was no bother to him.

Then one day she surprised him.

"Help me. I must return to my house. They will be worried."

He nodded, helped her stand, and walked with her deep into the forest, down the same game trail that he been following.

She used the staff. They walked slowly.

Deeper. And deeper they walked. Well beyond any distance that he had ever come.

Into a small meadow.

She pointed at another trail. "They ran from there."

He nodded and studied the ground. Even after this much time he could see where she had struggled and fought.

He looked down that trail and wondered what clan lived that way and why they would attack her. It was not the way of his clan to attack strangers. Perhaps they were marauders?

Then she led him to a spot and stepped past the growth onto a narrow trail he would never have seen.

She led him deeper and deeper.

Into another small meadow and over to a building that seemed to blend into and merge with the thick surrounding vegetation.

Opening a door in what had appeared to be a blank wall, she stepped inside and turned. "Do come in."

Inside, he stared. It was the largest dwelling that he had ever been inside.

Others came running. She explained to these excited folk what had happened. Then she led him to a room and fed him all that he could eat.

These must be some of the chieftains that he had heard about. They asked him a few questions and he explained why he had been walking down that trail and how he had first met her.

Then they told him that he could have all the food that he could carry and that he would ever be in need of again.

And it was true.

He always had sufficient. Never too much, never enough to make others of his clan suspicious. He was just considered lucky.

And so it went.

Year. After year. After year.

He aged, grew older.

She visited him often. And never seemed to age.

So then he knew who she was. She was one of the forest spirits.

And so, one day, he told a nephew his tale. And that tale was passed on and eventually written down somewhat altered with the passage of time.

It was a tale about a brave hunter that had once met a forest spirit.

"That house," said Hofga, "eventually merged with another house. The written people account was found when the two house libraries were merged. It was set aside and noted as a rare happening for The Feyra."

Dee refilled his cup.

He took a sip and settled back in his chair.

"The second account happened much more recently. It was in the middle of the 1700's as the people measure time."

He was a very successful painter of portraits in the area where he lived. One of the few. They were in high demand by those who could afford such. He was one of the very skilled, one within the few that were sought out.

Each of the skilled carefully guarded how they made the particular shades of color that marked their work as much as their signature did in one of the corners.

He was also the one that accepted students, never more than three at a time.

Potential students had to show their work to him and to discuss how they painted and why they painted and what they thought he could teach them.

Most who walked into his studio seeking training were refused. He never explained why. They knew better than to ask.

Then, one sunny day, she walked into his studio, portfolio held under her left arm. She walked in with a confident stride, a determined look on her face.

He waved her to a stool while he carefully finished a tiny bit of the portrait that he was working on.

At the moment he had no students so he could spend all his time on his own work. Finally he turned on his stool and smiled at her.

"I wish to learn," she said.

He nodded and wondered from what part of the county she had come from. Her accent had something strange about it.

"It is expensive," he said.

She shrugged.

Well, he thought to himself, she has an interesting self confidence that you don't often see in a student. Maybe she even has talent?

"Show me your work. Please?

She handed him her portfolio.

"Ask when you are done." She wandered around his studio, apparently unconcerned, while he opened and began to slowly leaf through her work. Some of her work was in black and white, some in color. The bulk were portraits, interesting portraits. He could almost feel the presence of the face, of the individuals she had drawn.

Well, well, well, he thought, she does have talent.

He looked up. "You wish me to each you?"

"Just so." She sat on the stool near him.

"What can I teach you?"

"Color."

"Color?"

"Just so."

"Explain."

She did. In very precise terms, pointing to places on the portrait that he had been working on, discussing the interplay of color and light and shadow. Then she leaned back and waited, still as still ever could be.

For a moment he sat and stared at her. Then he nodded and smiled. "It will be my pleasure to do what I may."

She nodded, reached into a pocket, and pulled out her fist, and held it out to him. "Payment."

He held out his hand. She dropped the coins into his quickly cupped hands.

"Enough?" she asked.

He gulped and nodded. "Tomorrow? Will you be able to start tomorrow? Ah, afternoon?"

She nodded. And reached for her portfolio.

"Ah, may I look at these until tomorrow?"

She nodded, stood, and walked from his studio.

Every afternoon, exactly at the same time, six days a week, she walked into his studio. And they worked. He carefully made her do this or that bit of painting, demonstrating how to make things better. And every day she did. And got better.

So he wondered about his student. He had refused everyone else that had come looking to be a student. Now he had one student, only the one student. The interesting thing to him was the realization that his work was also getting better.

And not only was he getting better but that the very top tier of society and wealth were now bidding against each other for his work. His fame was spreading widely. But as his reputation grew so did the grumbling from those few painters that somehow felt they were being unfairly overshadowed by him and being under-appreciated by those that should be buying their work

Then one day, late in the summer, she walked in, ever so quiet as always, ever so self assured, sat on her stool, and pointed at one spot on his current project.

"Show me how to make a paint like that, that very bright white."

He shook his head. It was his secret, ever so carefully guarded. It was one of those things that made his work ever so unique.

She opened her portfolio, she always carried it, and handed him a small painting of a forest at the edge of a meadow.

"I will show you how to make this green if you will show me how to make your white." She pointed at an area that had immediately caught his eye.

He nodded, once again, or perhaps still, amazed that such a young woman could be so talented.

They spent the entire afternoon talking about and showing each other the manufacture of those certain pigments.

Monday morning and he groaned and pushed himself upright.

He had been taken from his house, beaten, and thrown into this small room yesterday, the day when he never had guests or visitors. Two of his competitors had pooled their resources and had hired those who did this sort of work, to remove their competition.

He had no idea of where he actually was or for how long he had to live.

For two days he sat on that dusty floor and ate the food that he wouldn't feed to a rat. He wondered when it would happen, when they would kill him, and where they would dump his body, far from where he had lived, he supposed.

It was in the middle of the night, some days later, when heavy thumping sounds came from over his head that startled him awake. It was this new noise, the new different noise that had pulled him from his troubled sleep.

Now what is it this time? Were his captors preparing to kill him?

Then it became quiet, very quiet, much more quiet than it had ever been. He sighed. So, he thought, here it comes.

The door to his room slammed open. Someone walked in, holding a lantern high, followed by several others holding heavy wooden staffs.

"What they did was not nice," said his student. "Come. You are not far from your house."

He lurched upright and stared at her and her companions. "Who are they?" He pointed.

"First, Second, and Third Brothers."

Once they stepped outside the building he saw that she was correct. His house was not very far from here.

Then, over the next week or two, he heard various stories of the mysterious disappearance of two well-known artists and of the fire that badly damaged a house not too far from where he lived.

When he asked her about these things, she merely shrugged, and said that those people were not nice.

And as time passed no one talked any longer about those happenings. Then one day she walked in and held out a closed fist and waited for him to hold out his hand. She dropped a fist full on gold coins into his open hand.

"I am done," she said. "Teacher." And started to turn to leave.

"WAIT!"

She turned back and looked at him, a slight frown creasing her brow. "Ummmm."

"I shouldn't accept this. You saved my life."

"I will see and admire more paintings, Teacher." She nodded. "Be calm. Paint beautiful. Worry not." She bowed to him, turned, and walked calmly away.

For the rest of his long career he found that, somehow, his life was calm in spite of sudden changes in his fortunes or political favor.

He told his son as he sat in a chair and spoke of his favorite student and showed his son, also a painter, how to mix certain pigments.

He no longer painted. His eyes only saw mostly blurry things and his hands refused to remain steady. Of course he had lived a long time and had done some truly beautiful work. And his son nodded as the tale was spun and worked on his own painting. And people marveled over his whites and greens.

"That house," said Hofga, "still exists and tells every new member that tale. They have one room with many paintings in it. His. And some of her's. She was very talented."

He waited until Dee refilled his cup. He took a sip and nodded. "Those are the only two happenings that I have found. In neither event did the people know who they had met."

"Unlike now," said Jonathon.

"Just so," agreed Hofga. "Careful cautious," he said to Dee.

She nodded. And wondered whether she had made a big mistake. Or not.

Maryland.

They had enjoyed a good dinner and were relaxing in the living room, sipping the beverage of their choice.

"So, now what?" asked Charles.

Each of their organizations had spent the last few weeks having certain of their staff pour through everything that they could think of or find. One group had read everything that Williams had collected, their copies, once again. Slowly carefully.

Ralph looked from face to face. "Anyone find anything new?"

All heads shook.

He laughed. "It is really interesting, you know. All of us have once again come up blank." He poked a finger at the hole in the table top. He had that table moved into this room. "And no one has any idea how anyone could do this either?"

"Ralph?"

"Charles?"

"Can you contact them?"

"Nope. No one can. But Dot is still in place."

Charles sighed.

Ralph smiled at his friend. "Frustrating, isn't it? This has got to be the most pure example of don't call me, I will call you, that I have ever heard of."

"Do you think that she will?"

"What?"

"Call you."

Ralph held out his glass. His wife filled it.

"No idea," he said, taking a swallow. "One can only hope, I suppose."

Randy, the third man in the room, and the most suspicious of everything, set his glass on the table next to his chair. "Are they are on our side?"

Ralph shrugged. "I don't know. Should they be?"

"Of course!" snapped Randy.

"Why?"

"Cause we are the good guys."

"Are we?"

"Certainly."

"How do they know that?"

Randy hissed and refilled his glass.

"Well?"

Randy frowned at him.

Ralph nodded. "Would you think that we are the good guys? Williams killed a young woman's father, kidnaped her, and burned down her home. We shot two young women with drugged darts and held them in separate rooms and demanded that they answer our questions. I wouldn't be very happy with me if I did those things to me, would you?"

Randy nodded. "O.K. Point well taken. So how do we convince them that what people like Williams was doing was not our doing and that the other thing was a really bad miscalculation, an unfortunate thing that we all regret?"

"So," Ralph scanned all the faces in the room. "How do we not make any more of those unfortunate miscalculations? We have all visited the Williams hideout in the wilds of Montana.

Whatever happened there I have no desire to come knocking on my door. Do any of you?"

Sandra lightly touched his shoulder. "Do you think that they could figure out where we live?"

"We could. Why not them? And don't forget that her friend just walked into that room with little apparent difficulty at all."

Someone knocked on the front door of the house.

Hands jumped inside jackets and into purses.

"Whoa!" snapped Ralph. "Are we nervous?" He stood and headed for the front door. He laughed back at them over his shoulder and opened the door. And stared.

"May I come in?"

He backed up. "Of course."

She waited.

"Oh!" He smiled at her. "Do come in, Dee."

She stepped inside. "Thank you."

He gestured her in the correct direction "We were just relaxing, more or less, after dinner. The same old group."

He walked in first and noted that everyone only held glasses filled with various liquids in their hands.

"You remember D. Grant," he said and led her to a chair next to the one he had been sitting in. "Coffee?" He indicated a large pot. It was there just in case someone ever wanted coffee instead of their usual after-dinner beverage.

She nodded and sat. "Thank you."

He filled and handed her a tall mug and sat. "So, you just came to visit?" His eyes jumped from surprised face to shocked expression.

"Ummmmm." She took a sip.

He nodded. And waited. The rest took their cue from

him. Glasses were refilled and sipped.

Dee looked at Ralph. "Do you have any pets?"

"No. My work often takes us, my wife and I, away from home for extended periods of time."

"Ummmmm." She sipped.

He wondered about that question.

"We were talking about your group," she waggled her free hand at the others, "not too many long ago."

Hands began a slow drift toward the insides of jackets and toward open purses.

"About?" Ralph lightly tapped the back of his wife's hand with one finger.

She winked at him. He felt it was safe, whatever was happening.

"We have no easy way to talk with you, or you with us," stated Dee.

Ralph nodded. "True."

"We have thought deep about this, many of us."

He refilled her mug.

"Do you have children?"

"No. Same problem as pets, I am afraid."

"Ummmmm." She sipped.

He waited. Thoroughly puzzled.

"I would like Sandra to come with me."

Charles started to stand and dropped back into his chair.

"To your house?" asked Sandra.

Dee nodded.

"As a hostage, Dee?"

Dee glared at her. "We do not do things like that! Those who would do that, die! We would like to give you a special skill, if we can. No one is sure that you will be able to learn this special skill." Dee smiled at her. "It is unheard of to do such a thing. There was a very long debate with much grumbling about what I suggested."

"What is this, ah, special skill?" Sandra's hands folded over her husband's.

"I would rather not say until we can see whether it is even possible for you to learn it."

"Take me, instead," said Ralph.

"No." Dee looked into his eyes. "There is no harm involved, just very, very hard work. With, perhaps, nothing to show for it."

Sandra smiled at her. "Fine. I don't mind hard work."

"Now?" asked Dee.

Sandra stood. "Do I need to pack anything?"

Dee shook her head. "No need. Whatever you might need can be provided."

Jonathon walked into the room, eyes rapidly noting everything.

Dee stood and took one of Sandra's hand in her's. "Ready?"

Sandra smiled at her husband. "As I ever will be." Dee nodded. They followed Jonathon to the outer door and stepped outside.

Ralph refilled his glass and looked at all the others staring at him. "That was interesting."

"What," grumbled Charles, "is going on?"

Ralph shook his head. "No idea. But she initiated the contact, not us. I think that means we didn't totally alienate them with our previous behavior." He smiled at them as he sat. "Sandra and I had a very nice time visiting with Dee and her family. Just have to see what Sandra says when she returns. And don't forget. Sandra is very capable of taking care of herself."

He stood. "I think that is enough for one evening. But!" He laughed. "I do have an assignment for the group."

"Yes?" asked Randy.

"It is tricky."

Charles laughed. "Oh, oh."

Wives smiled.

"I want each of you to think very hard. What can we offer Dee and the others. I think that she just ever so gently touched upon some sort of interaction between us. They appear to be totally self-sufficient and very shy about us. Look at it this way."

He waved his hand broadly. "Out there, somewhere, is an unknown country apparently making a very tenuous contact with us, no one else. I don't think that their trust level is very high with us at the moment. So, what do we do? The usual staff work isn't going to do the job. So, let's meet at Charles place in two weeks, shall we?"

Everyone stood, thanked him and Sandra for having them, and headed for their cars, already deep in thought. This was really something new for them to think about.

Something New, Unheard Of!

House Darthar Na.

They sat in one of the small rooms with a large window and looked out at the meadow and the forest, did Dee, Sandra, Ar, and Dura, sipping coffee.

Ar and Dura did it just to be polite.

The four of them had been discussing what Dee had suggested. Neither one, Ar or Dura, had a good idea. As far as they knew, what Dee was suggesting have never been done before, or had even been tried.

Sandra tried not to stare at them. She felt that it would probably not be considered polite to do that. She was really beginning to wonder why whatever it was that she was supposed to do was supposed to be such hard work. During her last visit she hadn't noticed anyone that seemed to be doing much of anything. Just lots of people walking here and there, in various sized groups, talking quietly. And nothing that they were saying was making any sense to her, not at all.

But she had noticed that everyone nodded to Dee. Then she remembered that Dee had been called 'Princess' every once in awhile. This must be some small kingdom that still had royalty and wondered how they had managed to remain so unknown all this time.

"In the morning," announced Dee. "Ar and Dura will start your training. Better get some sleep. Training is always hard work. Can you find your bedroom? It is the same one as before."

Sandra stood. "Yes. Well then, in the morning." She nodded to Dee, and looking carefully unconcerned, she strolled from the room.

Maryland.

Ralph had told his office that he wasn't to be disturbed unless his staff felt that it was absolutely necessary. The place pretty much ran itself anyway.

So, he stayed home and read and reread everything again. Everything. That included all they knew about whatever it was that Williams had been up to. A number of contacts in other countries had been pressed hard, very hard, for a few more bits and pieces of information. But still, there was very little useful information.

He sighed, looked at the calender, each day since his wife had left he had crossed off with a broad-tipped red felt tip pen marker.

Charles had phoned this morning and said that the group was preparing a report listing all their thoughts on the problem that he had posed. That report would be a single copy, carefully guarded. No one wanted any politician finding out that they were talking with an unknown foreign group, or government, or whatever they were, and trying to make a deal, or a treaty, or agreement, or some sort of trade pact, and then having those same politicians trying to drag in all those special interests that he, or she, might be entangled with. Or trying to remove the entire process from their hands.

He stood and slashed through yet another date with red.

"Honey," said a soft voice from behind him. "I'm home."

He jerked, gasped, spun around and grabbed her.

"OOOOOF! Not so hard, Dear." She smiled up at him as he set her on her feet. "Get out a bottle of that very good red wine. I have something amazing to tell you."

They sat in the living room, quiet in their company, and sipped and savored the wine. It was a bottle that he had bought and had stashed for a very special occasion, which she had insisted this was.

Finally, she tucked her legs up, and settled under his arm draped over her shoulders.

"The first day Dee sent me to bed early because she said that training was hard. And I thought that it couldn't be that hard."

She squirmed around, handed him her glass, stood and slowly turned around.

"WOW!" he said.

"Certainly did. Hard doesn't even come close to describing what training was. I lost a lot of weight even though I ate tons of food. And gained some muscle mass as well."

Then she told him all about that after sitting down and reclaiming her glass.

Sandra meandered down the stairs and turned into the room that she remembered from when she and her husband had ordered a meal.

Dee was already there. She served Sandra.

Sandra sat across the table from her. "The condemned eats their last meal?"

"Hope not." Dee dumped some of the dish on her own plate.

Sandra jerked and stared at her.

As they ate, Dee explained. Whatever Ar or Dura said to

do then Sandra had to put all her energies into doing it, regardless of how strange it might sound or feel like.

"I don't know how many days it will take. I spend weeks learning a new skill, ate lots and lots of food, and still lost weight. When I finished all I did was eat and sleep for some days time."

Sandra nodded and thought to herself that nothing could be that hard, and she had done some really hard stuff.

When they had finished eating and talking, Ar walked in and bowed to Dee. "We are ready, Princess. She will not be harmed. Tired and hungry, but not harmed. We will be very careful."

Sandra stood. And wondered what it was that they were really up to.

Ar started for the door. "The Training Hall is this way."

When they entered the hall, Sandra stopped and stared at it. It was huge, at least three stories high as far as she could judge.

Ar walked out to the very center of all that space and nodded as Dura joined him.

"I locked the doors," said Ar. "We do not want anyone walking in while we are working."

Dura handed her some garments. "Wear these."

Sandra looked around the hall as she took them. "Now?"

"Yes."

So she took off her clothes and dressed in the loose fitting but very comfortable garments. Undressing in front of two people that were vaguely blue and looked somewhat unhuman was different than standing in front of some leering male in a gym.

"Now," said Ar. "We will begin."

Nothing that they told her made any sense to her, nothing she tried to do made any sense to her. Nothing, nothing, nothing.

By the end of the day she was more tired than she thought that she had ever been. The doors unlocked and she staggered down the hall to eat and then headed up to her bedroom, a hot bath, and fell into bed.

Every day, over and over and over and over, she did what she was told to do, with slight variations as Ar and Dura made changes in her training.

Many days later, she had lost track of how many days had passed, panting and sweating, chest heaving, she suddenly felt something new. Ar nodded and Dura said to do it this way.

Many days passed, and they did it over and over and over and over, when suddenly it worked. A little.

Ar stared at her, Dura gasped.

"I did not think that it was possible," said Ar.

"Strange strange," agreed Dura.

"Tomorrow we will start the next step." Ar nodded to Sandra as she lurched for the door.

The next step? She almost cried. So all that she had done was take to one step? Sandra really began to wonder whether she would be able to last if many more steps were like this first one.

But, the next day she started. Again.

She nudged her husband. "Gimme some more of that."

He poured the last of the bottle into her glass. "Well, apparently you survived. Did you learn anything at all from all that training?"

She nodded. "Show you in a bit. I just want to sit and

enjoy being at home and finish my wine."

"Sounds good to me."

And after some time had passed, she stood. "Up, up, up! Take my hand."

Grinning broadly, he stood, and did.

House Darthar Na.

"Very good." Dee smiled at them.

Ralph stared at his wife. "You . . . did . . . that?"

"Yes, Dear, I did."

He looked up and down the long hall. "I need something strong. Nice wood work."

Dee pointed at a nearby door. "In there."

Inside the room she pulled the top off a bottle and poured two glasses half full. "Very old brandy." Then poured herself a cup of coffee.

Ralph grabbed the glass, took a swallow, coughed, and dropped into a chair. "Good stuff," he wheezed.

Sandra laughed and took a sip. "Very good."

He stared at his wife and then at Dee.

Dee nodded. "I thought that it was worth a try. People can't do things like that. I do not know what Ar and Dura did but I do know that Sandra will not be able to teach anyone else how to do that."

She looked at Ralph, a very hard look, a very stern look. "You now have a wife who is unique among the people. Guard her well. Tell no one."

He nodded, slowly realizing what had happened and what could happen if anyone knew.

Dee nodded to them both. "She will only be able to bring one other with her, perhaps, two or three. It was necessary to limit her ability to move people."

Ralph looked from his wife to Dee and nodded. He understood why.

"Ummmmm," said Dee. "When you two are here, she will not be able to bring anyone else." She looked at them, a very careful look. "It will only work with the clothes that you happen to be wearing, nothing else. Well, maybe a few other things you might be holding." She refilled her cup and took a sip.

"Ar told me that if you tried to carry anything like any kind of people technology, especially people technology, you would go somewhere else. He said that it would be a most not nice place, but wouldn't tell me what it was. Strange, strange. He said, and Dura agreed, that the protection of us took priority over any command that I might give him or her."

"We will be very careful," said Sandra. She nudged her husband

"Right!" He stared at both of them and asked as Ar and Dura entered the room, "Other than whatever it was that happened to her, is she still, ehh, the same?"

Ar and Dura bowed to Dee.

"Just so," said Ar.

"Mostly so," added Dura.

Dee, Sandra, and Ralph stared at her.

"It may have affected her taste buds," explained Dura. She shrugged. "She is of the people. The changes we made are of The Feyra. There will be something else, that is what we think."

"Ummmm," said Dee.

"Just so," said Ar.

"Dee, I would like to talk to you about a problem we have with some strange folk. Perhaps you could come and look at some photographs? But for now, let's go home." Ralph smiled at Dee and his wife. "This is going to take a lot of thought and getting used to."

Sandra stood and bowed to Dee. "Thank you, Princess. It was a great gift, or skill, or whatever it is. However things work out, thank you." She grabbed her husband's hand. They were gone.

"Her taste buds?" asked Dee.

Dura nodded. "She has Feyra now. I think so."

Dee smiled. "Hope that she didn't like chocolate really well."

Maryland.

Holding her hand, he towed her into the kitchen.

"Sit. I will make you a large mug of your favorite delight."

She sat and smiled at his back as he busied himself at the stove. Finally, he spun around and with a dramatic flourish presented her with a large white mug capped with white froth.

"Thank you, Dear." She took a careful sip of the hot liquid and retched.

"What?" He stared at her. "Is it?"

"This tastes absolutely awful. What did you put in it?"

He took the mug and took a careful sip. "Tastes just fine to me." He frowned at the drink and at her.

"Taste buds," they both said at the same time.

"Oh my," she said.

"We could ask them to undo it."

She shook her head. "Small thing."

"You sure?" He sat across from her, reached across the small space, and held her hand.

"Yes." She looked at the kitchen clock. "Let's make a many course dinner for tonight. You can tell The Council that we now have a way to contact Dee, but not now. Secret."

He ran a finger across his lips. "Sealed and zipped tight." And laughed.

She laughed with him. "You check the frig and I will check the pantry."

It was now evening and they were gathered around the dining room table, slumping, and feeling comfortably stuffed, sipping from the beverage of their choice.

Charles hoisted his glass in the air. "A toast!" And waited until all held their glasses high. "To Ralph and Sandra for solving one problem, one very touchy problem." They all smiled at their hosts and sipped and refilled glasses.

Ralph nodded. Sandra smiled.

Then Ralph looked around the table. "So, what can we offer them?" He saw lots of shoulder shrugs.

Anabelle nudged her husband.

"Go ahead," said Randy.

"We can offer them what everyone wants," she said, a sly smile curling her lips.

"Gold?" laughed Charles.

"Nope."

Each suggested something, some more outlandish than others.

At each offer, Anabelle's smile grew wider and wider.

"O.K.," said Ralph finally. "Spit it out!"

She slowly looked from expectant face to expectant face, sucked in a deep breath, and exhaled slowly. "Peace and quiet."

"Huh?" said Charles.

"Everyone wants that," explained Anabelle. "It doesn't matter what their politics might happen to be, or their form of government, or the amount of their wealth or lack of it."

"O.K." Charles nodded. "But don't they already have that?"

She nodded back. "Exactly. And they apparently wish to keep it that way and to not lose it."

"Ahhhhhhhh," sighed Charles.

Ralph nodded at her. "I think that is something Williams didn't consider."

"O.K., sure, all well and good." Charles held up his hand. "But!" One finger shot up. "But what do they offer us?"

Ralph laughed loudly. "I really have no idea." He waggled a hand at them. "But let us just suppose that there is something, all right?"

They sat quite, all eyes looking at him.

Ralph smiled a soft gentle smile at them. "Now, let us just suppose, for the sake of supposing, this! That what happened at that zoo and what happened to the Williams bunch and their ever so carefully guarded secret, is something that they did. Now what does that suggest? What sort of things ought we now consider?"

"Holy cow," gasped Charles.

Randy nudged his wife. She refilled his glass. He took a gulp and stared into space, lost in thought. Then he rapped a knuckle on the table top.

All side conversations stopped.

"It appears," he whispered, all harsh tones, "that if we suppose that then we have to suppose that they can do other things that we can not do." He leaned back and slumped in his chair. He knew everything that there was to know along those lines, what they could or could not do. He cleared his throat. "That supposition is, to say the least, bothering." He stared at Ralph. "Peace and quiet."

"Makes your skin tingle, doesn't it?" asked Ralph.

Charles cleared his throat loudly.

"Yes?" said Ralph.

"Do you think that Dee and her, ahhhh, friends would help us, erm, if we had a good, oh ah, reason for asking them for help?"

"I think," said Ralph very slowly, "that this is going to takes lots of very careful thought." He slowly scanned their faces. "I will need a free hand in this, no strings attached, no subtle attempts at manipulation, none of the usual things that we so often do. Remember, we have very little knowledge about this group, we can not even find them."

"Go for it," said Charles, rubbing his hands together. "I will agree, here and now, that whatever bargain, or deal, or agreement you can come up with, I will stick to it absolutely." He laughed. "Even if I don't like it all that much. Randy?"

Randy stood. "O.K." He winked at Ralph. "Do it! This is totally unknown territory for us. Go for broke!" He looked at his wife.

She nodded. "My crowd will do it. Even if I have to break some heads."

And all agreed.

"Uncharted waters, unknown seas, strange lands," chanted Charles. He grinned. "Don't let the natives take your head, Ralph." He laughed. "Shall I buy you a pith helmet?"

"Just a good bottle of wine. Or two."

"You got it." Charles stood and glared at the rest. "Just make some deals with that foreign government. But you know that if this gets out we will all wind up in the slammer for the rest of our lives."

"To say the least," said Randy. "To say the least."

House Darthar Na.

Dee was sitting on the bottom of the entry stairs watching her daughters once again entertaining the Ice Cats. It was a very nice day to be outside. The meadow was green. The sun was taking the chill from the air.

The girls swooped and soared, one set of white wings flashing in the sunlight, one set of dark wings making a shadow to them. The Ice Cats hurtled high in the air. And around and around and around the meadow they went.

Dee laughed at the shear joy of having two daughters who were as talented as they were and as happy.

Ar walked from the house. "Princess, those two . . . people are here."

"ON THE GROUND!" shouted Dee.

Tiela and Winala thumped to the ground, wings disappearing, running over to their mother, Ice Cats by their sides.

Ar opened the outside door. Ralph and Sandra walked out.

"Hello," said Sandra.

"Nice day," added Ralph. He watched the Ice Cats carefully, one of them was sniffing his pant leg.

"Takes some getting used to," he said. "A lion sized white cat looking you over."

Tiela and Winala headed up the stairs and inside. The Ice Cats trailing behind.

Sandra sat on the step next to Dee. "Chocolate tastes

simply awful. Now."

Dee nodded. "Sorry." And looked from face to face. "We, ummmm, like vanilla ice cream."

Ralph sat next to his wife. "I would like to tell you everything about our group so you may know who we really are and what we do, or have done."

Dee nodded.

Jonathon walked from the house.

"We will listen," said Dee.

Ralph leaned back, elbows on the step behind, and began.

The sun had moved a long way on its journey toward the far horizon before Ralph finished. He was now sitting, leaning forward, his arms folded over his knees.

"So now you know," said Ralph.

"Just so," said Jonathon.

Dee nodded. "No spy story even comes close."

Ralph grinned at her. "Just the way we like it."

Dee stood. "Let's go get something to eat." She headed up the stairs and then down the hall, headed for an appropriate room. "Will you be visiting?"

"A few days," said Sandra, wondering what Dee and the ever so quiet Jonathon were thinking, now that they knew all about The Council in detail, warts and all. Their faces never gave a hint of what they were thinking.

They entered a small room with a table set for six, food and platters sitting here and there on the table.

Dee poured four cups and handed them around. Then she sat down and served the food. The door opened and Tiela and Winala and the Ice cats joined them.

As they finished, Tiela stood and bowed to Sandra and

Ralph, and said to Dee, "Time for practice." She left the room, Ice Cat by her side.

Ralph sipped from his cup and looked at Dee.

"When will you be willing to tell us about your, eh, house?" he asked. "You know everything about us."

"Everything?"

He nodded. "Everything. You now know as much about us as we do. You are the only ones outside of The Council who do. We are unique in that aspect. We are a part of the system, but a very much separate and independent part of it. No oversight, no one looking over our shoulders. I am the only one who speaks to The President. I am the only one that he personally knows that is part of The Council. We keep no written records. We cannot be fired. It is frightening to have that kind of responsibility."

Dee nodded and refilled their cups, those that required refilling.

"I will tell some little."

Ralph and Sandra listened carefully. So did Jonathon.

We are a very small population, explained Dee. The houses are scattered, one far from the other, in many parts of the world. As far as she knew, the smallest state in their people system, in terms of population, probably contained more than all of them.

Because of cultural differences, among other things, The Feyra almost never interacted with the people. They felt that the people were much too quick to jump to bad conclusions. This was something that they had learned many a long time ago. The people believed too strongly in too many mythologies and acted as if those mythologies had some foundation in reality.

She sipped and continued her explanation. Her folk did not believe as the people did. They, The Feyra, had very strong systems to keep one house from interfering in the business of another as long as all behaved in a nice manner. This was also a result of a many long ago occurrence.

She had, by allowing two people to come to her house whenever they wished, put into action an idea and a happening so radical as to have never been done before. It was not knowledge that would escape her and Jonathon's houses as they knew it would cause a great disturbance among the Feyra.

We, she stated forcefully, do not wish to be like any of the people, anywhere. We are not interested in the people technology although they had used a few things recently.

We know who we are. We know our own history much better than most of the people know theirs. The people appear to have a problem understanding their own history.

"So," she concluded, "now you know something and I know something." She sipped. "One more thing. We are very nervous. The people keep growing and growing in numbers. Their technology is frightening. We worry much about that. The people are much too aggressive."

Dee stood and walked to the door. "Would you like some vanilla ice cream?"

Maryland.

"Dear," she said, just to get his attention.

They were sitting on the couch. Actually he was slumped on the couch, legs sticking straight out, cold beverage held in one hand on his stomach, staring at a football game on the wide screen.

She was sitting at the end of the couch watching him. He

wasn't watching that game, she could tell by the expression on his face. He was mulling something over in his mind.

His eyes refocused. "Yes?"

"We have to be very careful."

"About?" He straightened up and took a swallow from his bottle.

"Them. Dee and them."

"Sure." He nodded. "Why?"

"I did a little research."

"Uh huh?"

"There are no people anywhere in the world that look like Ar or Dura."

"O.K."

"Dee and the others that we met could walk down any street anywhere and no one would pay any attention to them."

"Uh huh."

"They have houses everywhere in the world."

"Ah."

"No one that we know of does. And they worry about our behavior."

"I see. Interesting, isn't it?"

"Only you would look at it that way."

He smiled. "As far as we have been able to tell nothing has ever happened anywhere in the world other than that stupid Williams behavior. He had too much money, too much ego, and too little sense."

She nodded. "His organization was eliminated. Every scrap of paper, every record of any kind is gone. And no one knows anything."

"And that is why we should be careful, right?"

She stood. "Would you like some ice cream?"

"Vanilla?"
She laughed.

Really And Truly?

House Darthar Na.

Dee handed a filled cup to Jonathon and waited for the proper amount of time to pass. It was the proper and polite thing to do among The Feyra.

Then she shoved the folder across the small table to him.

"Ummmm." Jonathon took a sip.

"Tell me if these are some of us."

Jonathon set down his cup, opened the folder, and began to study them, all the photographs, one by one by one. She explained what she had been told about them.

Then he stood, placed them all back into the folder, tucked the folder under one arm, and said, "I will have to visit Hongar. You remember him?"

Dee nodded. "Oh yes. He was the one with the white fangs poking down past his long snout looking at me with those yellow eyes who licked his lips at me."

Jonathon nodded. "Only for a moment."

Dee smiled.

"Hongar," stated Jonathon, "knows more about The Feyra and their families than anyone. He has been collecting information for a great many long time. Perhaps he can tell me something."

Jonathon stepped from the room.

A Very Large Place.

Jonathon stood for a moment and looked around.

He stood in front of a large, black stone, gloomy looking castle with pediments and towers all along the upper walls. He nodded to himself. Hongar had his own peculiar idea of a proper dwelling.

He walked to the small door and pushed it open. It was a small door in a very large door.

"May I visit?" he called into the dark interior.

"Jonathon," rumbled the large and thick in every dimension man that stood just inside the door looking down at him. "Do come in."

Hongor lumbered off and through a large archway. "This way." And then into a room and dropped into a large chair, one of many that were set around the table.

For once Hongar remembered his manners and served coffee, handing Jonathon a large green mug.

"I have heard," rumbled Hongar, "much of House Darthar Na since last you and she visited seeking information."

"Ummmmm." Jonathon took a sip.

"Word has come that she has raised from the depths of the many long ago The Fontala. It has truly been a very many long ago time since The Feyra have seen them. Is there now some great cause of worry?"

Jonathon shook his head and then he told Hongar all he knew about the events that had come about. This information would go into Hongar's extensive library of things dealing with The Feyra, all the houses and clusters that are and ever were.

Hongar refilled their cups when Jonathon finished.

He looked at Jonathon. "Something?"

"Just so." Jonathon opened the folder and handed him all

the photographs. "I would know if these are of the people. Do you have any idea?" He sipped. "These images were made not a very long ago time."

Hongar walked away, photographs in hand, and disappeared into another room.

From that room, Jonathon could hear the sound of books being dropped on a table. It went on for some time.

Then silence.

Hongar walked back into the room and dropped into his chair. And looked at Jonathon with a slight frown creasing his brow.

"What?"

"In the ever so many long ago time, not much time before The Great Straightening, a number of The Feyra faded into the unknown. I thought them forever gone for never has there ever been a word come to me since that ever so long ago time."

He held out the photographs.

"You said these were made not a very long ago time?"

"Just so," stated Jonathon. "Less than a year ago as the people measure time."

For just a moment Hongar shifted shape and then shifted back again. It was a sign of agitation that Jonathon recognized well.

"Tell me," said Jonathon softly.

"These are Feyra as are you and I. These are that small group that faded from our sight. But now they have been seen."

"Ummmmm." Jonathon took a sip.

"There is little known of them, these Feyra. In that ever so long ago time, they were called by some, The Dwellers of the Dark, for the dark part of the day was when they were active. They preferred that time for all their activities as we do not.

They are not of a dark intent. They just live with a different pattern. More shy than most. More isolated than most."

He leaned back and stared at Jonathon. "Where do they live now?"

Jonathon shrugged. "Seen and then not seen. Somewhere in the west areas of that place the people call The United States. It is an area of great open spaces."

Hongar leaned forward. "Will House Darthar find them and speak to them, these lost to us Feyra?"

"A difficult thing to do, Hongar, to avoid the people and to find those who are so well hidden."

Hongar nodded.

"It will take deep thought," said Jonathon. He stood.

Hongar nodded and returned all the photographs. "If I may aid, do send word."

Jonathon nodded. And was gone.

House Darthar Na.

Dee and Jonathon sat in one of the small dining rooms having a snack.

He handed the folder back to her.

"Ummmmm," she said.

"Hongar told that in the ever so long ago time they faded into the unknown."

"Wait here!" She left the room headed for the house library. And shortly returned with a purple clad volume.

Then she sat down and began to thumb through it.

"I think that I remember having seen a comment like that in here."

She held the book open and read the page that she was seeking. "Yep. Here it is. It says, *Great were our numbers. Greater was the carnage as cluster tore cluster. A small number faded into the darkness of night."*

Jonathon nodded. "Hongar told that at that many long ago time they became called by some, The Dwellers of the Dark. None really know what they called themselves. Ummmm."

"What?"

"Ah ummmmmm." Jonathon took a sip. "Hongar suggested that House Darthar ought to find them and speak with them. They are a small group of nocturnal Feyra it seems."

"Nocturnal Feyra?"

He tapped the photographs. "These are dark adapted, large eyes. We should ask those people that you choose to speak with to tell us all that they know."

Dee nodded. "Yes. I think that they ought to do that as well." She refilled their cups. "Have you ever heard of nocturnal Feyra before?"

"No." He took a sip.

"Are you going to look for them?"

"I will talk with Hofga."

"It could be very difficult."

"Just so." He nodded.

A Favor Asked.

House Darthar Na.

It was another fine warm day.

Dee sat on the bottom step watching the First and Third Stands practicing in the large meadow.

Staffs whirled, clattered, and banged in patterns hard for the eye to follow as the two Stands attacked one another

Armilin strolled in and out and among the combatants correcting this one or that one, pushing, pushing, pushing, demanding higher and higher and higher levels of skill.

The other Stands stood around the edge of the meadow watching, talking quietly, long staffs leaning against their shoulders, one end on the ground.

The Stands had been rotating in and out of the conflict. One Stand ran from the field while another ran in attacking the one still there.

Armilin had insisted that they had to do this. She wanted Dee to watch. Suddenly Armilin yelled something and all seven of the Stands were engaged in a great melee, two hundred and ten Fontala attacking two hundred and ten Fontala.

Dee ran up the stairs for a better view.

Armilin shouted something else. All the combatants froze in place, chests heaving. Then they began to stream up the stairs past Dee, headed for their dining hall, talking quietly. Some limped.

Armilin stopped next to Dee.

Dee smiled at her. "I have never seen anything like that."

Armilin bowed. "They are getting very, very good."

They walked up and into the great main hallway, wooden paneling gleaming soft golden light back from the sunlight streaming in from high windows here and there and stood and watched the Stands heading up the stairs.

Ralph and Sandra stepped from one of the rooms.

Armilin stared at them.

"They are guests," explained Dee.

Armilin bowed to them and hurtled past, yelling something. Everyone in sight charged up the stairs and disappeared.

Dee led the visiting pair into another room.

"I am having a mid-day meal. Join me?"

Ralph pulled out his wife's chair and sat in the one next to it. He really wanted to ask about that group that had hurried up the stairs, but he didn't.

Dee poured three cups full and handed them one.

Partway through the meal, Winala joined them.

"Tiela is eating with the others," she said as she served herself.

When they had finally finished their meal, Ralph cleared his throat. "Dee," he sighed. "I would like to ask for a favor."

"Oh?"

"Yes." He pulled out a map from an inside pocket of his jacket and unfolded it. There was a great red circle drawn on it.

He tapped the map and dragged his finger around the red circle. "This is all very heavy forest, more or less wilderness."

Dee nodded.

Ralph cleared his throat. "Charles' oldest daughter and her best friend went camping in there. They do that a lot, camping in various areas, and are very experienced campers. They are now three days over due to come out."

Dee nodded.

He pointed at a smaller black circle. "Right here there lives a group of very radical folk. We think that they took the girls, well, young women. But no one has received anything of any sort from them, no letters, no demands, none of the usual stuff. No communication of any kind. Charles is pretty well known is his, eh, normal job. Those type of people generally don't like him."

Sandra nudged him with her elbow. "Tell her the rest."

"We sent a small select team in there. We haven't heard from them either."

Dee nodded.

Ralph sipped and looked at her and then at the table top. "Can you give us any help?"

Dee stared at him. "Help? You? You want our help?"

He nodded and yanked a sheaf of photographs from another pocket. "High altitude stuff, taken at night. See those lights. That's the group."

"Do it yourself."

"Ah," he said, "that is the problem. We can't. At the moment no one knows about the lost girls or our lost team. No one! And we can't let anyone know. The media would have a field day. Other crazy groups would feel empowered to do things like that. And we are afraid that if we sent in a much larger team that the girls might not survive. And that bunch would probably send a video to the local stations showing how oppressed they are, from their own government."

Dee glowered at him. "And how am I supposed to do anything?" She leaned in his direction. "We do not, DO NOT, get involved in people things. It is not safe. For us!"

Ralph slumped in his chair and thumped his chest. "I know in here that you are somehow responsible for what happened to Williams and his enterprise. I can't prove it, but I do know it." He tapped his chest again.

She leaned back and shrugged.

Ralph stood and began to walk back and forth, frowning. Then he stopped and spun in her direction. "We can give you anything that you would want."

Dee nodded and frowned ever more darkly at him, the maps, and the photographs.

Jonathon walked into the room. Dee handed him a filled cup and explained.

"Prata!" he growled at Ralph.

Ralph jerked back and banged into the wall.

Sandra gasped, and blinked. For a moment there she was sure they were about to die.

Jonathon yanked the map over and looked at it closely, then the photographs. He tapped a symbol. "What is this?"

Ralph stepped closer and looked. "Landing strip. Abandoned."

"This?"

Ralph pulled another folded paper from his pocket, opened it and scanned the several columns. "Old government installation. Also abandoned."

Jonathon tapped the map. "Do those people watch this place?"

Ralph shook his head. "No. This listing says that we have a couple of people there. They watch and would know if anyone came close."

Dee looked at the map and pointed. "This is the closest

road?"

"Yes." Ralph draw a long black line with his pen. "The only access road into their place runs like this?"

Dee straightened up. "You will stay here. We will talk." She walked from the room followed by Jonathon.

Ralph dropped into his chair. "I thought that we were dead."

Sandra nodded. "That man is dangerous."

Dee and Jonathon sat in another of the small rooms. Dee served them coffee.

"We have never gotten involved with them and their happenings." He frowned darkly at the table top. "The people are always doing things like this."

She nodded. "I know."

Jonathon reached over and gently touched her shoulder. "Dee, I asked Helsing to research these six people. Everything that Ralph told us is so. There is no mention of this Council anywhere in that strange people government. It has been true for some time ago."

"Ummmmm."

"Just so."

She looked into his eyes. "I think that we can do this thing, help them with this thing." She nodded. "I have been thinking about those young girls. They are the problem. Not their captors."

"Ah ummmmm."

"They will talk about things."

Jonathon sipped and looked at her.

"Just so," she agreed. "I will talk with Ralph. Do you think that Hofga would help?"

"I will talk with him about that as well."

Maryland.

Ralph looked around the table. "Sandwiches and coffee. This is a early working session. Each of you has a paper in front of you. How soon can you supply or do those things."

Each couple looked at their papers. Soft comments started.

Charles stood. "Tomorrow." Prentice nodded. "Before noon," she said.

Anabelle stood, laying one hand of her husband's shoulder. "Tomorrow for both of us as well."

"Good." Ralph stood. "Charles, we leave in a couple of hours. Travel light."

Idaho.

They sent the two watchers home and began to straighten up the place, a little.

Ralph spread detailed maps on the table as well as a stack of high resolution aerial photos of the camp.

Charles turned from the small camp stove where the coffee pot was beginning to make soft gurgling noises as it started to perk.

"O.K., Ralph, what are we doing?"

"We are waiting here in order to get your daughter and her buddy back."

Charles stared at him. "Just you and me." He sat at the table and grinned at his friend and boss. "Tall order, but it might be fun. But between us, at the moment, all we have is one rifle and two handguns."

Ralph nodded. "We will get the young ladies. But you

and I will do whatever we are directed to do. No heroics. No shooting. We will just tag along and try not to get killed."

"No shooting?" Charles laughed. "So what did you get us into this time?"

Ralph picked up the pot and poured coffee into two thick walled white mugs. "I am not really sure."

"What!"

"Drink your coffee and wait. We can't do anything until it is dark."

Charles sipped noisily. Then he shoved the curtain aside and peered out the window. "Plenty dark out there. Now."

Ralph nodded, and blew on his cup. That stuff was really hot. He wondered how Charles could drink it that way and not burn his tongue.

The door opened. Both men jerked.

Dee and Armilin walked in.

Ralph stood. "Charles, this is Armilin. It is her show."

Armilin nodded at him. She wore a short purple jacket that gleamed soft shine and carried a long grey wood staff.

Charles looked at her, then at Ralph. "What are we going to do? Beat them up with wooden sticks?"

Armilin said something. The staff suddenly glowed with a soft purple light. With a flick of her wrist the staff flashed past Charles' nose and sliced the corner off the table. She turned and walked outside.

Charles knelt next to the table and inspected the cut. Then he looked up at Dee and Ralph, frowning.

"Ahhhhh," said Ralph.

Dee began to sort through the photographs and removed two portraits. "These?"

Charles stood and nodded. "The dark-haired one is my

daughter. The blond is her friend."

Dee nodded and walked outside into the dark night and became vague shadow in the blackness. Two lion-sized, cat like creatures flowed up to her. She showed them the pictures. The loped into the forest taking long elastic strides.

"Charles, whatever you see, it is secret," stated Ralph, squinting into the night. "Very, very secret. From everyone not here. Understand?"

Charles stared out the door and nodded. The moon was down but it seemed to him that there was a rather large number of figures standing around out there. They all seemed to carrying long staffs. Vaguely he see could another group walk to one side. And disappear.

"Ralph?"

"Not now."

They walked out and saw the rest split into two groups and run on silent feet into the forest.

Armilin strode up to them. "Follow me and be quiet."

Dee touched Ralph and spoke softly to him and Charles. "Remember, no guns, no shooting."

Ralph nodded. Charles grumbled and then nodded.

The three followed Armilin, the faint glow of her staff barely visible.

It was sometime later when they stopped and stood in deeper shadow among the trees and peered around them at the compound. A few figures could be seen walking here and there, obvious guards. A few of the windows in the buildings shown a dim yellow light, perhaps candle light.

They waited.

Figures dropped from the sky, staffs whirling. Soft liquid

sounds came from here and there as the guards disappeared. The waiting shadows poured into the compound from all sides as the fences toppled.

Charles started forward. Ralph grabbed his arm and hissed softly, "Whoa! Don't go in there!"

Charles jerked and stepped back.

Dee stood next to them and watched. Her staff suddenly glowed soft purple light. "Someone is running this way. Step back."

Ralph yanked Charles further back.

Dee stepped forward and waited, a silent figure standing in deep shadow holding a long faintly seen staff. Then she swung as the footsteps thumped close.

The large rifle thumped to the ground as the figure crumpled.

"Ralph!" hissed Charles, staring at the two body pieces.

"Later," hissed back Ralph.

They stood and waited as silence finally draped itself over the compound. No running feet. No sudden gasps.

Armilin slipped up to them from the dark. "This way," she said.

They followed her to a small structure.

The remains of the door to the small building were canted to one side. The large hasp was sliced away. A large piece of the door was lying on the ground, sliced cleanly from the still standing portion.

"In there," she said to Charles.

He carefully eased into the room.

"Daddy?"

"Mr. James?"

Charles laughed and hugged them both. "Boy, am I ever

glad to see you two."

Armilin took Dee's staff and slipped away. Tiela ran from somewhere. One of her Stand members ran with her, holding both staffs. "Follow me, Mother. Where are those . . . people?" Her fellow Stand member raced off into the dark.

Charles stepped from the building followed by two young women. "Shall we go?" he asked.

Tiela led them through the encampment and out one side. In the dark they could vaguely see shapes lying here and there on the ground. And finally, after a long hurried walk, near run, they stepped out near the tumble down shack.

Tiela kissed Dee on the cheek and raced into the darkness.

"We have to wait until it gets light," explained Charles. "And then we will get you home." He opened the door and shooed both the young women inside.

Dee shed her jacket and made a small bundle of it which she then fastened to the back of her belt. Then she stepped inside, followed by Ralph, her staff now soft grey wood.

"How did you find us?" asked Charles' daughter looking at her father.

"Oh," laughed Charles. "Ralph and I are just a pair of very clever fellows."

"Dad?"

"What?"

"There were monsters there, real monsters."

"Oh?"

The other young women nodded. "We saw them, Mr. James, we really did."

He grinned at her. "Hobgoblins and boogie-men."

"No!" snapped his daughter. "We saw clawed hands reach right from the wall and kill the guards."

"Sure," he said. "Think that I ought to go back there and thank them?"

"NO!" cried both.

"O.K." He sat. "Guess we will just leave them alone then." His eyes flicked to Ralph's. Ralph gave the slightest of nods.

They sat and waited. Finally, as the sun rose they could hear the thumping of a helicopter approaching.

"Our ride is here." Ralph walked outside.

Maryland.

One of the followup crew made his report.

"Transformers, batteries, generators, computers, cell phones, electric wires, recording equipment, tapes, DVD's, all sliced to ribbons. Perimeter fences likewise. No survivors. Found our first team in shallow graves, all shot in the back of the head. Something cut through all the walls and doors. Lots of foot prints, mostly all the same boot pattern. None matching anything we found on the remains. We also found what were identified as very large cat tracks of some sort, very large, like lion large."

Randy waved him from the room. "Well, there you have it. That is all that we found."

Ralph stood. "Good job. All that prep-work did the job." He sat down. "Smoothest operation that we have ever done."

Charles stood, eyes glistening. "Thank you, one and all." He dropped into his chair. His wife kissed his cheek.

Ralph nodded. "We will meet in a week. At Charles' house. He owes us a good meal."

House Darthar Na.

Dee and her two guests were sitting, sipping, looking out the large window at the meadow and the surrounding forest.

Dee turned her head. "I have an additional favor to ask."

"Anything within our capabilities," said Ralph.

"We are The Hidden Folk. We wish to remain so. That is the favor."

"Lips are sealed. No one will talk about that event. Two young ladies only think that they saw some B-grade movie monster attack those guards and are already beginning to think that it had to be something else they saw. All human remains have been removed. The forest will eventually reclaim that space. Charles and I are heros of some sort to those two for leading the troops to their rescue." He sipped. "Thanks Dee. Was anyone hurt?"

"Two sprained ankles and a twisted knee."

"Good." he nodded. "Any chance that I can meet your crew."

"One of these days. Perhaps."

Ralph smiled. "Good enough for government work." And laughed loudly.

Then he looked at her, carefully looked at her. "I have the other favor."

Tiela and Winala walked into the room accompanied by their Ice Cats.

Then Ar walked in carrying a large tray. "Pastries," he announced. "Jonathon bought them in the people place called France."

All sat around the table now set with plates.

"Thanks, Dee." Ralph took one from the platter as it was passed to him. The platter made its way around the table. The

Ice Cats eyed the platter as it passed their noses. One Ice Cat sat next to each daughter.

Winala laughed as she touched her Ice Cat on the tip of her nose. Leaving a spot of white frosting.

When all but a few crumbs were left, Dee nodded at Ralph. He nodded back and fished from a large brief case a thick volume. "Everything that we know is in this." He smiled.

She nodded and pulled the book over.

"Why?" he asked.

"Why do you care?"

"Huh?" He sat straighter.

"What is this group of, ah ummmm, strange folk to you?"

"Ah, yes. Good question. Partially because people are missing."

Dee thumbed through the volume. "It appears that some of the people were hunting them."

"And partially from curiosity."

Dee nodded. And sipped.

"What will you do to them, Ralph, assuming that you can find and contact them?"

Ralph leaned forward, forearms now on the table. "We need to know if this group is dangerous."

"Ummmmm." Dee looked at him, just looked long and hard at him. Then she shook her head. "For the people, different is always termed dangerous."

Sandra lightly touched her husband's arm.

He nodded.

She looked at Dee. "Dee, if this group can slip into the country and out again without anyone noticing, if this group can live in places for very long periods of time without anyone noticing, if this group tells others how to do this, then it is dangerous. To us. We already have enough people blowing up things elsewhere because they don't like us. Being able to do what this group apparently can do with great ease would be very bad for us. This is dangerous!"

Dee filled their cups. And took a sip from hers. Then she sighed, a soft gentle sigh. "I think that Jonathon thinks that we could look for them. What we find out, if and when we meet them, we will judge in our own terms as to what is dangerous or not. Depending on what we find, we may or may not tell you anything."

Ralph leaned back and sipped. "Fair enough."

Searching

Way Out West.

The small group stood in a loose cluster way up there, far out of sight of any people who might look in this direction.

Dee, Jonathon, Hofga, Kitea, Anagon, Yallan, and five additional members of the Seventh Stand, stood there and listened.

Dee pointed. "Just down there is the back door that they used to slip away from the people searching for them. No one has any idea of which way they went once they slipped out, not the direction or the distance."

Hofga nodded. "I will go look. Alone." He walked over the edge and headed down toward the small opening that was the exit, the back door.

Jonathon stepped over and watched him as Hofga walked back and forth down there, head bent, obviously searching the ground for some trace. "Hofga is very good at seeing tiny things, tiny traces. He has never said but I suspect that it is a skill of his house."

Finally Hofga stopped, looked up, and pointed. He started walking in that direction, headed toward a range of foothills in the far distance.

Jonathon nodded. "We will just follow along behind him, on foot."

As they walked Dee talked with The Fontala and explained what little that she knew. "When it is dark I want

Yallan and two others to fly in the direction Hofga suggests. Yallan is a Seeker so maybe he will be able to feel a trace of them. When he does, the two will land and wait on the ground for all to gather. No one knows anything about this cluster. So we will be careful cautious, very careful cautious."

And then they walked and walked and walked and walked and eventually assembled on top of one of the foothills and prepared to camp.

Everyone had carried sleeping gear and bits and pieces of the rest of their camping gear.

Jonathon said that he would go back and bring them their meal. Which he did.

After they finished eating, it was dark. So they settled down for the night.

Yallan said that he couldn't feel a trace anywhere around them.

Kitea assigned two pair to keep watch through the night changing at an agreed time.

Then all flopped down on top of their sleeping gear. It was a warm night.

In the early dawn light Hofga violently shook Dee awake.

"Huh? What?" She sat up and stared around the camp for whatever was causing this excitement. She couldn't see anything. So she glared at Hofga.

He stood and pointed, here, then there. "We had visitors. At night."

Those who were assigned to watch gasped and stared at the footprints on the ground. They hadn't heard or seen anything.

Yallan leaped to his feet and hurried over. "I didn't feel

them."

Jonathon popped in, holding a box of mugs and a large, steaming coffee pot.

"Ummmmm." He filled mugs and handed them out.

After a small time passed, he looked at Dee. "It seems that they know that we are here. They must have a unique house skill. That must explain why there are no records of their existence anywhere from that ever so long ago time. If none of us could sense their presence then they could stay hidden ever since."

Dee nodded. "O.K. So what do we do? Leave out cookies and milk?" Then she had to explain what she meant to all those puzzled expressions, what she had been alluding to.

Jonathon sighed, ever so softly. Her people upbringing certainly had lots of strange beliefs and behaviors.

Over the first meal of the day, fetched in by Jonathon, they discussed this new problem.

Dee looked at Hofga. "They must be around here somewhere to just come into camp and to wander around like that."

He nodded. "Just so."

Kitea sat next to Dee. "Now they must know that we are Feyra."

"Ummmm." Dee nodded. "We will stay here today and tonight just to see whether we have another nocturnal visit. Maybe if we just sit here they will not feel threatened and will feel that we are safe."

That's what they did. Only this time they let everyone sleep through the night.

And all did just that.

Sleep through the night.

In the morning there were new footprints in and around their camp. The empty coffee pot had been moved and one of the mugs was missing.

Jonathon took the coffee pot and left. He returned with it filled and hot.

As they sat and sipped, Dee suddenly sat up. "Ah ha! That's it!"

Eyes jumped everywhere. No one saw anything.

Dee pointed at Hofga. "Can you tell from which direction they came?"

He nodded and pointed.

She smiled. "I would like a small stone platform of rock made way over there near that large rock."

"Word?" Kitea looked at her, a slight frown creasing her forehead.

"Tonight, just before dark, we will place a large number of mugs and large pot of fresh made coffee over there, a kind of gift just to let them know that we know they are around and that we are nice."

"Hapata!" stated Hofga. He grinned. "I like it."

After eating, they began to construct the stone platform. It was just a single layer of rock to indicate that it was constructed by them. Then they relaxed and talked and waited for the end of the day to arrive.

When the final meal was finished, Jonathon fetched in a very large filled coffee pot. Then he left and returned with two large trays covered with mugs. Everything was placed on the platform. Then Hofga brushed the ground all around their offering clean of any footprints.

And all spend an uneventful night.

In the morning everyone hurried over to see what had happened, if anything. There were lots of footprints.

A small dark green bowl sat in the middle of their platform. All the mugs were gone. The coffee pot was empty.

Dee picked up the bowl and looked inside. She carefully lifted out the necklace, a necklace of deep purple beads. She laughed. "Guess they appreciated the coffee and the mugs."

"Ummmmmm." Jonathon peered over her shoulder at the necklace as she held it high so everyone could see it.

"What?"

"That is the same shade of purple as The Fontala jackets. They know, Dee, who you are, and who the rest of us are."

"Ummmmm."

"Just so."

They walked back to their camping spot, to sit, eat, and talk.

"Tonight," said Dee. "Let's put a bunch of food along with the coffee pot. Jonathon?"

"Ummmmmm."

"I want you to write a very formal note stating that House Darthar and House Darthar Na greets them and gives them welcome and invites them to visit at any time." She smiled at him. "And then sign at the bottom our true names with the rest of the formal titles, all that you can think of."

"Ummmmm." Jonathon nodded.

Then they whiled away the rest of the day, and finally ate the last meal, and prepared the platform.

Jonathon arranged everything just so. Then he set the prepared scroll inside the small dark green bowl, and looked over at Dee. "Most formal."

All settled down for the night and fell asleep wondering

what they would see in the morning and if there was anything else that they could do.

At first light eyes popped open, hands snatched staffs, and The Fontala bounced to their feet.

The strange Feyra sat inside their camp and all around.

Dee sat up and looked at them. Ralph's photographs had suggested that they were large and they were, both the males and the females. All had wound dark cloth around their heads and foreheads to provide shade for their eyes already squinting in the early morning light. Their clothing was loose and of a very dark color brown, an almost black brown. It was a very dull material that seemed to not reflect the light.

She stood and smiled. "Most welcome. I am Daliera Fontala, Head of House Darthar Na." She waited as still as still could be.

One of the men stood and smiled at her. "Daliera Fontala, greetings. I am Moonat, Cluster Head of the Shadow Feyra." His voice was soft, yet carried clearly. "It has been a many long ago time since we last touched Sun Walkers. How come you to be here?"

"Would you share a meal before we talk?" She nodded at Jonathon. "Lord Othara, Head of House Darthar, will bring sufficient here for all."

Jonathon nodded.

Moonat bowed to him and then to her. "Most kind." He walked over and sat near Dee. "Most kind."

She sat and looked at Jonathon.

He nodded and was gone.

And reappeared with Karanly, Janice, Tiela, and Winala.

Some carried large trays covered with bowls and platters

while two trays were stacked with dishes and utensils

The daughters quickly began to hand out dishes and utensils while the others began to set out the food.

The two groups merged and began to share the meal. A number of soft conversations murmured here and there.

Dee nudged Jonathon and said ever so softly in his ear. "Sun Walkers and Shadow Feyra."

"Just so." He refilled her cup.

Then Dee began to tell Moonat and the rest why they had been following them.

Moonat nodded. "We have those few people with us, most safe and mostly calm" He touched the cloth wound around his head. "They do not like not seeing."

Dee nodded.

Then she worked out with Jonathon where he ought to take the people the Shadow Feyra held. Close to some small town in the evening. Moonat agreed. It solved a problem for them.

Finally after everything else had been talked about, Dee asked Moonat to bring all his members to House Darthar Na.

Jonathon said that he would be able to do that in a number of trips.

The Shadow Feyra moved off some distance and sat in a group to softly discuss this idea. Finally they decided to do what she asked. They were anxious to be away from the people.

House Darthar Na.

It was a few days later. Dee and Jonathon were sitting in one of the small rooms with a large outside window.

She took a sip and looked over at him. "They have the floor just below the House Beast Quarters. All the outside rooms on that level have small windows. Ar had those windows fitted with dark drapes to block out daylight."

Jonathon nodded and sipped.

"Ar told the House Beasts that the Shadow Feyra would be coming and going from the house through the beast's outside doors. Everyone else in the house knows that we have nocturnal Feyra living here now."

"Ummmmm."

"What?"

"I left those people in a very small town late at night still blindfolded."

Dee smiled. "I am sure that they soon realized that they were no longer prisoners."

Maryland.

Two large, very capable, very tough, men sat at the table with the three couples.

"We didn't hear or see anything," said one of the men.

The other nodded. "We were mobbed and blindfolded before we could even react."

"It was a no moon night and we were dressed in black and taking it very slowly," added the first. He shook his head. "Pretty amazing when you think about it."

Ralph looked from one to the other. "So, other than the blindfolds, you were treated all right?"

"Yep. Did a lot of walking from some place to some place. Always had someone walking with us on either side holding our arms for support and guidance. Strong grips."

"Until we wound up in that small town," said the other, "we never had a chance to see anything, or hear anything either. Quietist folk we have ever been around."

"Except," laughed the first, "for that local joker with the foul mouth. He said that he worked for some ranchers."

Ralph nodded at them and looked around the table, told them to go home, take a week off, loaf.

"Interesting," said Ralph. "Wonder where they went?"

"Think that we will hear about them again?" asked Charles.

Ralph shrugged. "Any other pressing business?"

"Nope," said Charles. He smiled. "All is quiet on the home front."

"For the moment," added Randy.

Visiting Here and There.

House Patal.

They stood in the narrow canyon and stared up at the vertical orange rock faces and the stairs carved in one face, did Dee and Jonathon.

"Certainly hidden all right," agreed Dee. She had asked Jonathon to take her here. It was the only one of her cousin-houses that she hadn't visited.

Jonathon nodded.

Dee stepped back, great white feather covered wings appeared. "No sense crawling up those stairs when I have a special skill like this."

She watched Jonathon change and shift form, then spread his great grey bat wings. He lifted off and up with Dee following, sun light bouncing off her wing feathers.

They coasted into the narrow opening and settled to the floor. Wings disappeared. Jonathon looked his usual self. They walked into the tunnel.

"Different," observed Dee.

"Ummmmm."

They walked around a tight corner and stopped, facing a door.

He knocked. And waited.

"Who?" asked a voice from the other side.

"Daliera and Jonathon, come to visit," answered Dee,

announcing herself.

The door opened and an eye peered out through the narrow crack. "Daliera?"

"Yes." She nodded. "May we come in?"

"Word said that you were dead. Burned up in a people house."

"Word was wrong," replied Dee. "Because here I am, here I stand."

A different eye peered out at them. Then the door swung wide. "It is you! I know that face! Do come in, Daliera of The Fontala and, oh ah, Jonathon."

They stepped inside as the door closed itself behind them. Soft light glowed from the walls.

One of the two facing them bowed. "Most welcome, Cousin, most welcome."

The pair turned and led them down a narrow and twisting passageway and finally through a door into a broad hall, paneled in wood. And finally into a room.

The one who had spoken to them gestured to the chairs, began to fill mugs, and hand them out.

"I am," he said as he sat, "Candal, Head of House Patal. This is first son, Habal. We are best pleased that you visit us."

Dee nodded and sipped. Her cousin had a dusky skin tone. It seemed to her to be somewhat similar to the rock colors outside in the canyon.

After the appropriate amount of time had passed, Candal looked at her. "Word, strange word, has come of unbelievable happenings. All mentioned House Darthar Na." He looked embarrassed.

She held out her cup and waited until he filled it, took a sip, and nodded.

Then she told him of the several things that had happened to her and Jonathon and House Darthar Na.

The pair smiled as she told them of her daughters. Then they stood and bowed to her and to Jonathon after she had told them of The Fontala and the rebuilding of The Seventh Stand.

She very carefully didn't mention her subsequent interactions with the people. She knew that The Feyra, almost all of them, wished to have nothing to do with them and those that were deeply hidden, such as her cousins, would be greatly bothered.

"All is well with you?" she asked.

Both nodded.

Candal stood. "Now is a small meal, with us?"

Dee stood and bowed to him. "Thank you, we will."

Jonathon and Dee followed the pair down the hall and eventually into a larger room set for the meal. Two other males and two females stood and bowed to her and Jonathon.

Candal introduced everyone and as soon as he finished the youngest female began to serve everyone.

As she ate, Dee smiled. Her cousins liked to use hot chillies in their food. It was delicious. "Very good," she said.

Her cousins grinned and shoved serving dishes here and there.

When they were finished and had sat for some time sipping from their cups, Dee stood. "Many thanks." She bowed deeply to Candal. "Do come visit. If you wish."

Candal stood and returned her bow. "Most kind, Cousin Daliera." He gestured her back into her seat. "Do sit for some moment longer." And hurried from the room.

Habal stood and refilled cups.

They sat in companionable silence. And waited.

Then they heard Candal coming. He entered the room, eyes checking that all the cups were adequately supplied, nodded at Habal, and handed Dee a ring. "This is your's."

Dee took it and held it close to her face. It was a rather plain ring with a band colored a deep green. The gem inset in it was a deep purple. It was a smooth-faced stone set in a plain setting.

Candal wiggled a finger on his left hand. "On this finger. We have kept and guarded that ring from a very much long time ago. It was thought lost forever during the great battle when the Seventh Stand fell to the last member. We, all of House Patal, visited there some small time after and searched, long and long, careful as careful, for some small time using all of our skills. House Patal has a special skill for finding things."

He smiled at her. "Now we return the ring to you, Daliera Fontala, The Word of The Fontala, the voice that directs those who Protect the Innocent. All who truly know, all who understand, will see and sigh happy that the ring is alive and well, that The Word is alive and well. Wear it, never remove it. It is your duty."

Dee slipped the ring on the correct finger and felt the ring adjust to fit.

All of them stood and bowed to her.

"It is our great honor to succeed," said Candal. He smiled broadly. "Our great pleasure to visit with our Cousin Daliera."

Dee stood and bowed to each one of them. "The honor and pleasure is mine. All The Fontala will know of the great thing that you have done."

She bowed again. "But now I must return. Many and much thanks. Be well."

She and Jonathon left the room and were guided to the outer door by Candal.

"Long life, Cousin," said Candal as he opened the door to the outside.

"Long life, Cousin," replied Dee as the door swung closed.

Jonathon took them to her house.

House Darthar Na.

Dee left Jonathon in one of the small rooms after filling a cup and handing it to him and headed up the stairs to the floor occupied by The Fontala after having asked Ar to gather all the staff in a meeting room.

She felt that they all should know of the great thing that House Patal had done.

They could pass on the story to all the members of their Stands.

Farlon, The One Who Remembers of The First Stand, stared at the ring. "It was a great loss. All felt diminished. We searched that fell place but to no avail. All owe great debt to your Cousin-House Patal."

Dee nodded. "It feels, ummm ah, I feel something."

Farlon nodded. "The ring was made when the staff and jackets were made by Zanta the Clever. It was said that the heart and the spirit of The Fontala reside there."

"Ummmmm." Dee watched his face. "Does it do anything?"

Farlon looked into her eyes. "Only The Word can know. Never has anything been said. Ever."

Dee nodded and then congratulated them on their training schedule and efforts, and headed downstairs to ponder this new thing.

Maryland.

They sat in the small kitchen alcove finishing their breakfast, enjoying the start of the day, the quiet, their breakfast, and each other's company.

He popped the last piece of his waffle into his mouth and looked at her, a slight frown creasing his forehead.

"Dear?" She refilled their cups and added just a touch of milk to his.

He smiled at her. "It is just not possible, you know."

"What isn't possible, Dear?"

"You just have to think of it and we are there, wherever there might be."

"True." She nodded.

"So, it is not possible. No one can do that!"

She touched his hand. "But they can do that. Now I can do that."

"And that is the problem."

"Dear?"

"They, and now you, do the impossible."

"Dear, if I do it, then it is not impossible."

He gently stirred his coffee and watched the milk make gentle swirl patterns in the black of the coffee. "You know what it is, don't you?"

"No idea."

"You are now the stuff of fairy tales. Doing things like that is the stuff of fairy tales." He paused, mouth slightly open, and stared off into the distance.

She reached over and gently touched his hand. She knew that look. He had suddenly thought of something that they hadn't thought of before. "Dear?"

He jerked and blinked, and smiled at her. "That is it! We have all been looking in the wrong places."

She leaned back. "Oh?"

His grin widened. "Yep."

"So then where should we have been looking, my ever so clever husband?"

"Fairy tales. That is where. Fairy tales."

"Whose fairy tales. They are everywhere." She added a little more coffee to her cup. And stood. "I thought that a cinnamon roll would be good with our waffles." She opened the oven and slid out a flat sheet, holding it by the edges with her oven gloves. Then she slid the rolls onto a serving platter.

He took a roll, bit into it, and mumbled, "Key words." And swallowed. "We need to decide upon which key words to search with. Just like one of those clever things that you launch into the web every once in awhile."

She carefully cut her roll in half, and then into smaller pieces, before spearing a chunk with her fork. "And you are suggesting?"

He took another large bite from his roll, licked his fingers, and mumbled crumbs, "You and I, my ever so clever wife, are going to decide on the key words. They you are going to send some of your very brightest workers to find the fairy tales that fit."

She nodded. "And?"

"Then you and I are going to read them all and see if there are any threads that are similar, or common, especially if these tales start clustering geographically."

She smiled at him. "You are suggesting that these fairy tales are actually related to some real things that happened, aren't you?"

He laughed and pointed one finger at her. "Sometimes they do, don't they?"

They cleared the table and began their project.

Boston.

They were sitting around a small table in a student hangout not too far from the campus. Charles' daughter and her best friend, Penny, were telling another young woman and a young man all about their recent 'adventure.'

"Her dad and his friend brought a bunch of soldiers with them in the middle of the night and freed us from those creeps," said Penny.

Richlin James nodded vigorously. "Those troops were kinna spooky. They didn't make a sound. We could hardly see them, it was so dark. They cut the door free and we were running through the woods with my father and some others as fast as we could go in the dark, out to some old shack where we had to wait for daylight and a helicopter to take us away from there."

The young man sucked air around the chunk of ice he held in his mouth. "What happened to the guys that grabbed you?" He crunched loudly.

Richlin shrugged. "We couldn't tell. But that place was absolutely quiet when we ran. No lights, no sound."

"Monsters killed our guards," said her friend.

He laughed. "Sasquatch freed you."

She punched his shoulder. "Gigantic paws. They just reached out from the wall and killed them. Both of the guards."

"Uh huh." He looked at Richlin.

She frowned. "Well, it was dark in that room. So I don't

really know." She whispered. "But something killed them before my dad and his friend crashed into that room."

"Maybe you have a guardian angel?" He laughed. "With funny hands." And held up both hands in surrender before they all tossed crushed ice at him from their beverage cups.

House Darthar Na.

Dee ate breakfast and then wandered up to The Training Hall to talk with Ar.

He was standing to one side of the hall watching Armilin take The Third Stand through a complicated series of drills with their staffs.

"Princess," he said as she approached, then bowed.

She held out her hand. "Does this ring do anything?"

He stared at it. "All thought that it was lost forever."

"House Patal had it. They searched that area where The Seventh Stand died and found it. Candal, House Head, gave it to me when I visited them."

Ar nodded. "The ring of The Word of The Fontala. When wearing that ring one can stay awake for very long periods of time without tiring. I believe that the effect covers quite a large area all around you.

"The ring," explained Ar further, "has great meaning to The Fontala as an object that reflects their most long existence and their purpose for being, much more than jackets or staffs do." He smiled at her. "House Patal will now be held in very high regard by all of The Fontala."

Then he looked deep into her eyes. "It is time for you to train in a new skill."

"I do?"

"Just so."

"What?"

"All The Fontala learn this skill early in their training."

"Ah. What?"

"Silent walking."

"Silent walking?"

He nodded. "Just so. Being able to move and make not a sound, soft as a shadow, so silent that it is as if you really aren't there."

"Ummmmmm. Now?"

"In the meadow, Princess."

"Shall we go?"

Ar nodded.

And so it went, day after day after long day.

Dee moved across the meadow and then into the forest and through tall bushes and short bushes and thick bushes and thin bushes.

And finally, one day after too many days to worry about counting, Ar bowed to her. "Very good, Princess, you are now as quiet as a ground fog, as soft as a butterfly's kiss." He bowed again.

Dee bowed in return. Then she realized that this is why she had not heard The Fontala when they rescued those two young women.

They headed up the stairs and into the house. Dee was hungry. "Thanks, Ar.'

"Oh, ummm, you are welcome, Princess." Ar still wasn't used to being thanked for doing things.

As they walked down the hall to the appropriate room Dee suddenly realized that The Fontala always ghosted along. Their conversations had distracted her attention from that aspect of their behavior. But now she realized it. None of them ever made a sound when they moved.

"May I clump if I wish to?"

Ar stopped. "If you wish to ... clump, Princess, just think differently." He opened the door for her.

She clumped into the room and smiled at him.

House Hinterane.

House Head Helsing smiled at them: Dee, Jonathon, and his Third Daughter Janice, a close friend of Dee's.

Janice had told Dee that her father asked to talk to Dee and Dee had asked Jonathon to bring them.

Janice served the coffee and sat.

Helsing waited until all had sipped and settled back into their chairs.

"You know that I deal in very old documents or pieces of old documents of interest to certain types of collectors among the people."

Dee and Jonathon nodded.

"Ummmm," said Jonathon.

Helsing sipped. "Due to my knowledge of that trading group and to my connections world wide, word has come to me of great activity of a strange nature of which I felt you should know."

Dee sipped and looked at him.

"There is," said Helsing, "a sudden and wide spread interest in what the people call fairy tales and early mythological tales."

"Ummmm," said Dee.

"I have spoken to this one and I have spoken to that one of the people dealers such as myself. All have a very high curiosity of such an elaborate nature occurring."

He waited while Janice refilled their cups.

"There have been purchases, many purchases, many purchases of a kind unlike the usual collector dealing. So, I asked here and I asked there and found out a surprising thing."

Dee set her cup down and looked at Jonathon and then back to their host.

Helsing nodded at her. "The trace back was very twisted, much different than the usual collector who wishes to remain private and unknown. It does seem to me that the same few people are involved and that they are part of one of those people groups that try to hide in the shadows."

He shoved a newspaper photo taken at an auction, torn from a page, across the table to Dee. "One of the people dealers recognized this person as a big buyer."

Dee picked it up and nodded. "Sandra. This is Sandra. She is part of a small group of the people that are involved in hidden people government activities in their political entity."

She shoved the picture over to Janice who picked it up and stared at it. "Certainly looks like her. What are they doing?"

"Research," said Jonathon. It was exactly the sort of thing that he would do. He was very good at doing research. He sipped. "They are trying to find us."

Helsing stared at Jonathon.

"In the some long ago past time as the people measure time we know of two recorded instances where we, The Feyra, have had direct contact, direct involvement with one of the people. I think that group is looking for more instances in an effort to locate one, or more, of the houses."

Helsing slumped in his chair and frowned at the table top.

Jonathon looked at Dee. She nodded.

Maryland.

It was mid-day, a bright sunny day.

They pulled into their driveway and walked up to and into the house through the front door.

Four men waited for them in the living room.

"What happened?" asked Ralph.

"Back door is wrecked," said one of the men.

"Your office is a mess," said another.

"Someone apparently searched your house," said the fourth. "The silent alarms went off and we got here as fast as we could without causing a commotion."

"You better look at the kitchen door," said the third.

Ralph walked into the kitchen and stared at his door. One half stood open, still attached to its hinges. The other half lay on the floor, all the bolts and fastenings neatly sliced off.

"Oh my," he said.

"Dear?" His wife slipped up to his side.

He looked around the room and whispered ever so softly into her ear. "What did we do?"

"We better go see what is missing." She headed into the other rooms, thanking the team for their effort as she went.

They sat in the living room and sipped from their wine glasses while a special crew replaced the kitchen door with a heavier, more secure one.

The crew finished, walked by, handed him a new key, and left.

She refilled his glass and sat on the couch. They were the only ones now in the house.

"They took every scrap from everything," she said.

"And we have no duplicates?"

"A closely held project, Dear."

"A mess."

She nudged him in the ribs. "Yes."

Dee and Armilin walked into the room. They wore jackets of a deep purple color and were carrying long staffs that seemed to glow soft purple light.

Dee stomped heavily and stopped in front of him and leaned forward. "NOT NICE!" she snarled.

Armilin stepped around and behind the couch where the pair sat.

Ralph nodded.

"Dee?" said Sandra.

Dee set her end of the staff on the rug, clasped the middle with both hands, and leaned a little toward her.

"We helped you," Dee growled. "I told you that we wanted to be left alone! We are no threat to you! Why do you threaten us?"

"Did we threaten you? How?" Ralph was watching her very carefully.

Dee nodded and rasped at Sandra. "She is trying to find us!" Her frowned darkened. "LEAVE US ALONE!"

They stared at her. Dee seemed to be shimmering.

"DEE! STOP!" Jonathan ran into the room. "DON'T!"

Dee's shoulders sagged. Tears trickled down her face. "Please stop."

Jonathon laid a very cautious hand on her shoulder. "Careful, Dee, careful."

She stared at the floor in front of the pair's feet. "Why won't you . . . people leave us alone?"

"May we talk?" asked Sandra ever so gently.

Dee nodded.

"Please sit," said Ralph.

Dee looked around and sat in a nearby chair and leaned her staff against the handy wall.

"My mistake," said Ralph. "I just thought that we might learn a little more about you." He set his glass on the table next to the couch. He shrugged. "In a way, I think that we just did."

"We weren't really trying to find you," said Sandra. "Just trying to see whether any of your folk had ever, ah, interacted with our people in the past. That's all."

"And," stated Ralph, "we didn't really know how, ah, sensitive you are, eh, about us, uh . . . "

"Prying," said Sandra. "We didn't think that we were, but, apparently we were." She patted her husband's knee. "But no more."

Ralph nodded. "Right!"

Sandra tried a tentative smile. "May we still visit, Dee?"

Dee stood. "One more time. Then we shall decide." She walked from the room followed by Armilin and Jonathon.

Ralph stood. "I'll get the brandy." He did and handed her a glass before he sat down.

She took a slow sip. "Close?"

He took a swallow. "Worse than that. I think that if Jonathon hadn't jumped in when he did, something very bad was about to happen. I could hear it in his voice."

"Well?" She took a large sip.

"A botched burglary as far as The Council will know. Nothing else. I will see that everything, like that door, goes through the appropriate disposal process." He poured more into his glass and nudged her with it. "Good to still be alive."

Another Day, Another Something.

House Darthar Na.

"Dee, you have to be careful. You were shifting into Karthan."

She gulped her coffee and held out her cup. Jonathon filled it. "I was so angry at them. I could feel it. The urge to tear them to pieces."

Jonathon nodded. He knew she had convinced Ar to train her, to teach her how to voluntarily shift into the great, ancient Feyra female predator shape from thousands of years in their past when The Feyra were small roaming families and when the people were few and far between and barely using tools. That form, then and now, would frighten anything alive. Dee was the only one of The Feyra that could now do that on command. And only she, Jonathon, and Ar knew this.

Today that shift, an involuntary shift, only occurred when the females were about to have children, locked and bolted inside the specially built and heavily constructed rooms capable of containing them for the short time required. And any Feyra that ever saw one of them on the loose, a Karthan, would flee for their lives, if they did manage to escape.

If any of the people ever saw one of them they would run screaming and wonder how some great predator lizard from the age of dinosaurs could possibly be here now. The Karthan were great creatures with long thick rear legs, a long neck, a raptor looking face, great claws and fangs. A thing of nightmares.

She looked over at him. "I don't know whether I can trust them. Now."

He nodded. "Ummmmmm. Perhaps they understand now. They looked like they knew that they about to die."

She sighed. "Almost. Almost."

"What did you do to their house?"

"We took everything that we could find. It is all in our library." She sipped. "What do you think?"

"No idea. You grew up thinking that you were one of the people. No other Feyra ever has. Use your people memories and knowledge to decide."

She nodded. "I'll ask Helsing to watch all the major newspapers to see if anything appears. If it doesn't then we will know that the group is serious about staying secret. I will let Ralph and Sandra visit, one more time, and then make a decision."

"What decision?"

"Whether to block them from coming and talking with us ever again."

He nodded. "Perhaps we can get them to do something for us."

"What?"

"To watch for others trying to do the same thing that they were doing. Williams Three was trying. They were trying. If there are other people trying then that group could probably know. If they were watching for that sort of a thing."

"Ummmmm."

He nodded. "Just so. Treat them just like any other house. Houses do favors back and forth."

She smiled. "Do you have a good house name for them?"

He nodded. "I could think of one."

She stood. "Let's go get something to eat."

He stood and followed her from the room.

Maryland.

"You redecorated the place. Pretty nice." Charles smiled at Sandra. "How did you get Ralph to agree?"

She laughed. "Trade secret."

The group was relaxing over dessert and coffee, having finished the usual business some time ago.

Ralph looked around the table. Everyone was looking quite relaxed.

"About our new, eh, friends," he stated.

Sandra looked at him very sharply.

One corner of his mouth twitched, suppressing a smile. Only she realized it.

"What?" asked Randy around a mouthful of cheesecake.

"Welllllll," said Ralph. "They did us a favor, a big favor. So, I think that we should see if there some favor we could do for them."

Charles grinned. "Good idea! I agree. Never hurts. Makes it easier to ask for another."

"What?" asked Randy, after swallowing. "Favor?"

"Oh," replied Ralph. "I thought that I would just ask what sort of a favor they might like. Take it from there. Who knows, maybe they don't what anything from us."

Charles snorted. "Don't see why they wouldn't. Any other group would salivate at the suggestion."

Randy nodded. "Go ahead, Ralph. Ask. We can then decide whether we want to or not."

Ralph smiled at them. "O.K., we will do that. Next couple of days or so. Anything else?"

Randy stood. "Have to go. Small problem trying to become a big problem. I will be rather occupied for a week or so. Thanks for the dinner. Great as usual."

He and his wife hurried away.

Charles shrugged. Randy's organization always got those jobs.

House Darthar Na.

Ralph and Sandra were met as they strolled down the hall looking for Dee.

"In here," called Dee from an open door. As they entered she filled and handed them cups. Then sat. And looked at them from a very blank face. And sipped.

So they sat and sipped as well.

After a little time had passed, Ralph cleared his throat. Sandra nudged him with an elbow.

"Well," he said, "from the dark looks that we received from everyone we saw I would say that we are not exactly welcome here. I am truly sorry that we upset you the way we did and, eh, all the rest. We had no idea how, em, strongly you felt about your, um, privacy. We will not do something like that again. A promise. Never again." He sipped and watched her face. It was still totally blank. He decided that he would never play poker with her.

"We do apologize, Dee, from all of us," added Sandra.

"And, something else," said Ralph.

"Ummmmm." Dee took a sip.

"Well, you did us a great favor getting Charles' daughter and her friend from that place, so we would like to reciprocate."

"How?" She refilled their cups.

"A favor for a favor," explained Ralph. He waggled a

hand. "Not necessarily now. Just whenever we can do something for you, that's all."

Dee nodded. She waved one hand. "This is House Darthar Na. What name shall we call your house?"

She smiled at their startled expressions. "I am Daliera Fontala, Head of House Darthar Na. My formal name is Daliera Fontala a'Anathor a'Mdator a'Zgura a'Winfa a'Relda d'Darthar Na. And you are Head of House . . . ?"

"Oh, well, let's see . . . House Sextet. I think that would be appropriate. Yes." He smiled "House Sextet is just right."

"Why do we require a house name?" asked Sandra.

Dee leaned back in her chair. "All members of a house have obligations to their house. The House Head is responsible for the house and all its members. The House Head is held accountable for the behavior of any in the house."

"I see." Ralph sipped.

"All members and their offspring until they leave the house, if they do, or find another, have that obligation."

"Ahhhhh, O.K." He sipped. "Then as Head of House Sextet I would say that the house owes you a debt for our behavior." He stood and bowed to Dee. "Princess." He had been observing their behavior closely.

Dee smiled at him and Sandra. "House Darthar Na welcomes House Sextet." She stood and bowed to him and Sandra. "Would you like something to eat?"

Maryland.

"Well, I am certainly glad to be home," sighed Ralph.

Sandra looked over at him as she scrambled the eggs.

"I spent two days in what amounted to as a high level graduate seminar taught by Dee's daughter, Winala, on all things House Head. She is, apparently, an authority on this subject and worked my butt off, mentally speaking."

"And?" She scooped a heap of eggs with diced chilli and mushroom onto his plate, then hers, set the skillet on the stove and sat at the table.

He took a mouthful and bit his toast. "Well, from what I learned, their system is sort of like our navy when they are at sea. Each House Head is like the Captain of the ship. They have absolute authority but operate within a larger set of, let's call them, rules. Every house is autonomous. Meddling in others affairs is considered not nice."

He took a swallow of this coffee and laughed. "By the way, that term, not nice, means a heck of a lot worse than it sounds to us. That term encompasses despicable, sleazy, perverted, dirty rotten mean, and all the other awful things that you can think of."

Sandra stopped eating and frowned at him. "That is what Dee called us."

He nodded. "We really made a big mistake. They value their privacy beyond anything we could imagine." He laughed. "Too bad that she doesn't work for us."

"Dear?"

"She co-opted us. When we agreed to become House Sextet we agreed to operate by their cultural values and rules, not ours. Their, ah, political system is very straight forward and quite complicated at the same time."

She refilled his cup and waited.

"Hope you don't mind," he said.

"What?"

"House guest. We are going to have a house guest."

"Oh? We are? Who?"

"Winala. Apparently this is done between houses. She is going to train me in all the things that I need to know and must know to be house head. She is leaving her pet at home."

"Should be interesting."

He laughed. "More than you know. She has never lived outside her, ah, group. You are going to have to put all your anthropological training and knowledge and wisdom to work." He winked at her. "While she is here, she is your responsibility."

"I see." She grinned at him. "Well, House Head, what do you think we should do?"

House Darthar.

Dee was visiting Jonathon and explaining what she had done.

"Winala is visiting them?"

She nodded. "For some small time as the people measure time she will be teaching House Head Ralph as much as she can."

He sipped. "House Sextet?"

"They agreed. When Winala returns we will see if she feels that they really understand, or not, their duties and obligations. If they do, there will be another house, a strange house of people, but a house nevertheless. If Winala feels that they do not properly understand then I shall sever the relationship."

"Ummmm ah."

"What?"

"Strange, most strange. Do you think that people can adjust to something like that?"

She shrugged. "So, what is Hofga doing?"

"Ummmmmm."

Maryland.

She walked into their living room, several large books tucked under one arm.

Ralph and Sandra were sitting on the couch talking quietly, sipping a little red wine.

He jumped up and spun in her direction.

She bowed. "House Head Ralph."

He stared at her. "Winala?"

"Just so." She straightened up. And nodded.

He smiled at her. "Let me show you to your room and then give you a tour of the place."

She nodded and followed him.

Some time later he returned and dropped into the couch. "This will be interesting. I had to show her how to make a sandwich. She acted as if she had never seen anything like most of the stuff in the kitchen."

"I will stay home tomorrow and help her get settled in."

And the next day that is what Sandra did. She carefully demonstrated the various appliances in the kitchen, explained where the various food stuffs were kept, and then took Winala for a walk around the neighborhood.

Then she had her guest help her fix dinner for three.

Sandra decided that it was like having a daughter of a sort.

As they ate dinner, Ralph asked how their day had been and his wife told him, some.

Winala sipped at her coffee, Ralph and Sandra had white wine.

"So many people," said Winala, gesturing toward the outside. "Mother told me. It is real."

Ralph suppressed his smile. "Yes. There are."

"Mother is pleased that I am allowed to visit and to train."

Sandra looked from her husband to Winala. "Aren't house heads usually trained?"

Winala looked at her. "Head to Anointed One."

"Anointed One?" Sandra frowned slightly.

Winala nodded. "The one selected to be the next House Head when the House Head dies. It is usually the First Son or the First Daughter."

"Oh," said Sandra. "I see. Each house head trains the future house head once they are selected."

"Just so." Winala looked from her to Ralph. "I would be most pleased to assist House Head Ralph train the Anointed One of House Sextet."

Ralph's mouth dropped open.

Sandra refilled Winala's cup. "We don't have any children."

"Most sorry." Winala stared at the table top. "Perhaps one of your cousin-houses or sub-houses would agree to a cross-tie so Ralph could mate, keep your house from disappearing."

"Eh, yes." Ralph poured his glass full. "We will have to discuss this."

Winala stood and bowed to them. "Sleep time." And left the room.

"That's interesting," said Sandra.

"Oh." He grinned at her. "Know someone that I can mate with?"

She winked at him. "Their houses seem to be extended families with several generations living together with the office being passed to offspring. It is rather like the Royal Families that used to be all over Europe. At least, the way it was, once upon a time."

He nodded. "She really looked sad."

Sandra poured a little more into her glass. "It appears that the survival of the houses is a strong cultural thing."

"Yes." He stood. "Tomorrow while she is training me in all things house head, I'll try to find out about cross-tie."

Several weeks later he dropped heavily into a chair in the kitchen and watched his wife prepare breakfast.

"My brain is exhausted," he mumbled, fumbling with his coffee cup, taking a swallow.

"She thanked me and left," said Sandra.

"Whew." He sighed. "That bunch has a very byzantine system of relationships."

She began to serve them the pancakes. "So, House Sextet Head Ralph, what do you think?" She sat and began to eat.

"I think that we have to rethink everything. Dee is the Head of House Darthar Na, a great house in their system. We snatched her off the street and her assistant. It would have been as if we had kidnaped The Queen of some small kingdom during the middle ages. Wars and wide spread mayhem happened in those days over lessor errors in judgement."

"I see. You are right. We have been treating her like some leader of a strange commune in the mountains in the west somewhere. There is a lot of culture there that we do not understand. The Council had better go slow and careful."

"Yep." He poured syrup on another stack of pancakes. "Wonder what kind of grade I'll get from my seminar?"

House Darthar Na.

Dee, Jonathon, and Winala sat in one of the small comfortable rooms with the large outside windows.

They watched the lion-sized, cougar-looking feline with the bronze colored fur and white tiger stripes on her shoulders and neck slip across the meadow and into the forest.

"Where is she going?" asked Winala.

"No idea," replied Dee. "The Furleen just like to prowl about at times."

"Ummmm." Jonathon sipped from his cup.

Dee nodded. "What do you think, Winala?"

Winala refilled their cups and took a sip from hers. "I think that House Head Ralph is extremely intelligent and one of the fastest learners that I have yet trained. I believe that he truly understands what House Head means to his house, to the other houses, and to his future." She looked at her mother, her eyes glistening.

"What is it?"

Winala sighed, a soft sob of a sigh. "Ohhhhh, Mother, there are only the two of them, just House Head Ralph and his mate, ah, wife." She wiped her eyes with her sleeve. "That House cannot survive."

Dee reached over and held one of her daughter's hands. "It is the way of the people, most of the time."

Winala stared into her mother's eyes. "That is so very sad."

Dee nodded. "They do not see as we do, Daughter."

Winala sipped. "They are both very nice. I believe that they are determined to behave in well mannered ways."

Dee smiled. "Good. If we are to maintain contact with that small group of the people, a thing never done before, then it is good that they know how to behave."

Jonathon looked at Dee.

"We are The Hidden Ones. The Feyra always have been

from a very long ago time, long before the people were so many, long before the people were barely able to survive in their small numbers." She nodded at him. "I believe that House Sextet will help us remain unknown to the people."

"Ummmmm."

"They, of all of the people," continued Dee, "have a great capability to do that. House Head Ralph said that they owed favor. That is the favor that I shall ask."

"Ah ummmmmm."

"Just so," stated Dee. "Just so."

Ar walked into the room. "House Head Ralph and Sandra are here to visit."

Dee nodded.

Ar opened the door to the room and ushered them inside.

Ralph bowed very formally to Dee and then to Jonathon. "Princess. Lord." And then he bowed to Winala. "Teacher."

Dee filled two cups and set them in front of two empty chairs now set at the table. She stood and bowed to Ralph and to Sandra. And sat. And waited.

Ralph and Sandra sat and sipped.

Then, after the appropriate time had passed, Dee looked from face to face.

"Winala, Second Daughter, Anointed One, is pleased and confident that House Sextet Head Ralph is knowledgeable in much as concerns the obligations and duties of House Head." She stared at Ralph.

He nodded. "Absolutely true, Princess."

Dee looked at Jonathon. He nodded.

"Then House Darthar and House Darthar Na give welcome to House Sextet as one of our sub-houses."

Ralph stood and bowed deeply to her and Jonathon. "A great honor." And sat.

Dee looked at him and then at Sandra. "You do realize that none of the people have ever done this before?"

Ralph nodded. And sipped.

"I wonder why?" He sat back in his chair.

Dee smiled, a very soft smile. "It is because the people believe in too much nonsense and allow that kind of belief to take precedence over knowledge."

"Ummmmm," said Ralph. "Can you be more specific?"

Dee stood. "Come with me. Only you." And walked from the room. She led him up to The Training Hall.

Inside the great open space she ordered everyone out and then told the doors locked.

Ralph looked at the great open space and at the ceiling far over head.

"This is our Training Hall. Every house has one. It is where house members learn skills that are unique to each house. These skills are private and almost never shared. This is where Sandra labored so long and hard. Ar and Dura did something never before tried or accomplished. They gave Sandra the ability to travel. It is a House Darthar house skill but not one of House Darthar Na."

Ralph nodded. And wondered where she was going with this dissertation.

"I thought that you needed to see something that should help you understand what I said some small time before."

He nodded again. It seemed to be something that they did often.

Dee stepped back a few paces.

And hovered ten feet above the floor, great white

feathered wings with long narrow tips beating slowly, just enough to stay overhead.

She looked down at him as she floated back and forth in gentle swoops. "I believe this is what caused the people to believe in angels. Some of you must have seen one of us when we were not being careful in your not so long time ago as you measure time." She thumped to the floor, the wings were gone.

He stared at her, a wobbly smile creasing his face. "Astonishing." He swallowed loudly. "I see." He nodded more to himself than to her. "I see. You, you all, are quite different, aren't you? It is why you see us as the people. It is because you really aren't people at all, are you?"

"No, we are not. A fact that I have been trying to make clear." She smiled at him. "We are a sub-species of you, a long ago developmental split during that period , we believe, as each of the two sub-species were becoming sapient. Jonathon believes it was some peculiar series of mutations, perhaps long before we became sapient. But here we are now. We are what we are. You are what you are. Our members are few. Your members are many."

Ralph sat on the floor. "Oh me, oh my," he mumbled.

Dee watched him carefully.

Ar walked in. Locked doors were not a problem. "Princess?"

"He is all right?"

Ar knelt in front of Ralph. "Badly shocked." He stood. "But recovering."

Ralph lurched to his feet. He stared from her to Ar and back again. "That explains so much, so very much."

He bowed deeply to her and straightened up. "I hardly know what to say." He laughed and smiled at them. "Now I understand why you call yourselves, and are, The Hidden Ones. Perfectly understandable. Absolutely!"

He frowned at her. "May I tell my wife?"

"You are House Head, Ralph."

He nodded. "I see, my decision."

"Just so." She led him to one of the doors. "Let's get something to eat."

Northern Maine.

It was a rather small, rather rustic looking log cabin, next to a small clearing, at the end of a very long and twisting dirt road. A rather dirty pickup truck was parked next to the building.

He sat on the small porch at the front of the building in a badly weathered rocker, slowly rocking back and forth, taking a sip now and then from the water glass he held in one hand. It was half full with red wine.

She walked out and handed him a plate which held a very large cinnamon roll, and a fork. "Careful, Dear, it is hot."

It had been five days of solitude. Every day he sat and rocked and looked out at the meadow or something only he could see.

She was used to this behavior. There were times when her husband required peace and quiet in large quantities. It was why he was the Director of The Council. Certain intractable problems rarely came into their purview but when they did he found a way for them to operate.

She sat on a chair nearby and ate her roll and wondered what it was that he was working on now. It was taking longer than normal.

"Oh me, oh my," he said. These were the first words he

had spoken since they had packed and left Maryland to come up here.

Sandra smiled. "Coffee, Dear?"

"Yes. And another roll, please. Then I will explain. It is for your anthropological ears only, lips forever sealed."

She fetched the coffee pot and two cups and really wondered what it was this time.

A Favor For A Favor.
Or Maybe Two or Three.

Maryland.

The Council had finished their dinner and were working on their dessert prior to talking business.

They were at the house of Randy and Anabelle. As soon as they were done, Anabelle took their twelve year old twins, one boy and one girl, upstairs to tuck them into their beds.

Dinner had been scheduled so bed time would occur at the usual time. They had a baby sitter but she was sick so here they were, The Council, meeting at Randy and Anabelle's house.

She was an excellent cook so they didn't really mind coming here.

Once everyone was settled in their favorite chair with their favorite beverage, the group was ready to discuss business.

Ralph nodded at Randy.

Randy cleared his throat, a nervous gesture that all recognized. "We have, we had, a mole." He shrugged. "Happens in the best of organizations. This one is now residing in rather stark accommodations. By himself."

Charles took a swallow from his glass. "What did he take?"

"He sold to a private research outfit heavily financed by another large company that was into exotic weaponry several of our files describing the destruction at Williams' secret hideout."

"What files, exactly?" asked Ralph.

"All of our analysis of the cuts. The private research outfit is exploring laser technology, exploring new approaches. Our mole thought he was helping spread scientific knowledge that we were trying to hide for some complicated dark reason."

Charles snorted. "So go rescue your stuff. Should be pretty easy for your bunch."

"Gets a little more complicated," grumbled Randy.

"Oh?" Charles sat up.

Randy grimaced. "That research bunch is a linked to the Department of Defense as a sort of satellite research facility. I can't lay hands on any of those folk, national security and all that."

Charles laughed. "We are national security."

His wife patted his hand.

Ralph looked at his friend. "We do not exist." He waggled his hand at the group. "Do we?"

Charles leaned forward and looked at Randy. "Give me the names and tell me where you want them delivered."

"Nope," said Randy. "It is an isolated facility. Everyone lives inside. It is a small town with a very high fence and surrounded by several units of mean nasty soldiers watching the outside. Inside they are all pure research types, paid big bucks by banks. They have guaranteed careers and can do whatever they want to do in terms of research and all that. It is a very secure facility."

"Ummmmm," said Ralph. Then he winked at Sandra as he realized where that vocal mannerism had come from.

"Gets worse," sighed Randy.

Charles refilled his glass and took a big swallow. "Really?"

"Yep." Randy topped up his glass. "We now have good information, very accurate information, that the parent company of these extremely bright researchers is mostly, or totally, funded by people who have tons, literally tons, of money and the morals of a rabid weasel. We are currently trying to get those folks with the strong political fingers to do something smart for a change about that parent company."

He shrugged and took a long swallow, and leaned back. "So, this is a heads up, gang. It is beginning to look like a very complicated piece of garbage to clean up. If that problem happens to float in our direction. It has all the negative features one can imagine. Big money, politicians with their fingers all over the place, and very ugly folk who seem to be pulling the purse strings."

Northern Maine.

He stood outside at the grill, watching things sizzle.

She handed him his wine glass. "What's the problem, Dear?"

"One can't hide things from wives, can they?"

"Not at all."

"We know a lot and not much at all."

"Sounds normal."

"Randy's problem is a hard one."

"It does appear that there are some bad actors involved."

"Ummmm, evil, mean, big resources, no conscience."

She reached in front of him and began to flip things on the grill. "Almost ready."

He turned toward the house. "I'll get the buns."

"Better hurry. I hear company coming."

He ducked into the cabin and stepped back out, a bag of

buns in one hand, a large handgun in the other.

She took the buns and began to assemble lunch.

He watched the road.

"It's Charles," he said. He stepped back inside and back out again, empty handed.

The big rig jolted to a halt next to their truck and Charles leaped out. "Oh good, lunch. Boy, do we have a problem."

"I'll get another chair," said Ralph. "And a glass."

They ate, talked about camping, and other things of no consequence.

Then Ralph said, "Problem."

Charles licked his fingers. "Uh huh. It seems that Randy's mole also sold Randy's home address to the parent company. It appears that person spent a whole lot of time prying into files that he shouldn't have been able to pry into before he was caught."

Charles took a big gulp from his glass and told them that Randy and family had decided, on the spur of the moment, to take in a movie instead of returning home after eating at the kid's favorite restaurant.

He looked at them. "Someone blew up his house. And left a note nailed on the neighbor's tree stating that this is what happens to folk that pry into things better left alone."

"Not funny, Charles," grumbled Ralph.

"So who is joking. We need a place to stash Randy's wife and kids. That only the three of us sitting here eating hamburgers knows about. If we can do that then Randy will calm down."

Ralph nodded. "Might be able to do that."

"Thought so." He handed Ralph a cell phone and a slip of paper. "Throw aways. Just bought them. Tell me when you know. I'll get them there." He hurried to his rig, backed out, and in moments disappeared in the long cloud of dust back the way he had come.

Ralph looked at his wife. "So ask. I will start cleaning up and packing."

He had just finished loading their pickup when she stepped from the house holding a slip of paper. In her hand. "Here. Not far from New York City. Recognize the address?"

He read it. "Oh my." Then he laughed. "Should have considered that." Picking up the cell phone, he called Charles and told him the address. "No one, not even Randy can know about this place. Take every precaution you can take. Yah, see ya."

He smashed the cell phone on the table top with a handy brick and scooped the pieces into a trash bag with their garbage.

"At the rate that we are going I will have to give them my first born child, if I had one."

She winked at him. "Let's go home, Dear. We can talk about that on the way."

The Wild Garden.

Charles pulled up the long driveway in a passenger van whose windows were so dark that the folk in the rear seat could not see out. He told them that it was necessary. Anabelle nodded. She understood and entertained the twins during the drive.

As Charles stepped from the van a man walked from the front door of the house and walked over. He had watched Charles crawl out. "I am Helsing. After your phone call, I spoke with Dee. She agreed that it was necessary. Please come inside."

He ushered Anabelle and the twins toward the house and beckoned to Charles.

"Can't," said Charles. "Have to get back. Thanks."

Helsing nodded. "They will be safe. Do you have a good memory?"

"Sure."

Helsing told him a phone number. "Use only that one." He walked into the house.

As Charles walked back to the van he noticed a number of individuals wandering around the grounds all carrying long purple staffs. Well, well, well, he thought to himself, well, well, well.

Maryland.

They had a meal that Charles had brought from a Thai restaurant.

They were at Ralph's place. With Randy and Charles and Prentice and Charles' daughter, Richlin.

Sandra emptied all the cartons into bowls and platters and served them all their favorite beverage. Richlin had root beer.

"Thanks Ralph," said Randy. "You too, Charles."

Charles laughed and chewed a mouthful. "Yum, yum. Spicy hot."

As they started dessert, Dee and Jonathon walked into the house.

Sandra cut two more pieces of the cheesecake and hurried to the kitchen for the coffee pot and two cups.

"Just in time for dessert," said Ralph, pushing the plates toward two empty chairs, drawing another over for his wife.

"Most kind," said Dee, sitting down.

Jonathon sat and cut a piece from the slice and tentatively ate it. "Ummmmmm."

Dee nodded at him.

Sandra set the filled cups in front of them and sat, setting the pot on a warmer.

"Welcome to our house," said Ralph.

Sandra nodded.

Ralph talked about the food and the dessert and waited.

Dee looked at Ralph. "Word has come that all is very peaceful."

Ralph nodded. He knew that she meant where they had stashed Randy's wife and children.

Sandra refilled cups.

"What will you do now?" asked Dee as she finished her dessert.

Ralph shrugged. "Still working on that. We do not know who is responsible. Yet."

Charles refilled his glass. "But we will find out. Then we will know what to do."

Dee nodded. And stood.

So did Jonathon.

"Always enjoyed cheesecake," said Dee. "Many thanks for the dessert."

Jonathon nodded at Ralph and followed her from the room.

Randy watched them walk down the hall and out the front door. He looked at Ralph.

"Just letting us know that your family is O.K. it seems."

Randy stared at him. "She has a safe house? Somewhere?"

Charles laughed. "I'd say so, yes indeed I would." He

shook his head. "No, I will not tell you. They will come home when we think that it is safe."

Randy held up both hands. "O.K. So, what are we going to do with this problem?"

Northern Maine.

They were sitting on the front porch listing to a CD of classical music. It was a mid-afternoon spent watching the birds jump around and play in the several bird feeders set here and there.

Both looked up at the sound of the approaching vehicle.

"Charles," said Sandra.

"Now what?" grumbled Ralph.

The big rid skidded to a halt throwing up a cloud of dust, the door flew open and Charles jumped out. He hurried up onto the porch and sat next to Ralph. "You probably don't listen to the news up here, do you?"

"Nope."

"What news?" asked Sandra.

Charles grinned widely at them. "According to the news, four very large houses, four lessor sized houses, and a couple or so other structures of some kind all blew up last night. They all apparently belonged to a nasty group of no-goodniks that one hears about now and then. At least that is the story according to the news."

"Interesting," said Ralph.

"Isn't it?" said Charles. "Any cold beer in there." He stood and went inside to see.

"We will wait a week or so, see if anything else pops up on the news," said Ralph. "Randy has a new house. It is being, ah, remodeled. He can move in soon. His wife will like it. It is larger."

Sandra kissed his cheek. "Good to hear."

House Darthar Na.

Janice walked into the room where Dee and Jonathon were sitting, holding a soft conversation.

Dee stood, filled a cup, and handed it to her.

Janice sat and sipped.

Then she looked at Dee. "Father sent word. The woman and her children are settled in. He has been entertaining the children, reading them tales from his collection of fairy tales in his library. The woman spends most of the day working in the flower beds. She said that it was something that she enjoyed doing but rarely had time for before."

Dee nodded. And sipped.

"Some things we can do," said Dee. "Many we will not do."

"Just so." Jonathon sipped.

"We do not want them to expect too much," said Dee to Janice. "There is no place for The Feyra in the affairs of the people. They have a bad habit of thrashing from violent action to violent action."

Janice sipped. And nodded.

"Do you trust that group?" she asked Dee.

"House Sextet?"

Janice nodded.

"Some. Not much. Some."

Maryland.

Charles and Prentice and their daughter Richlin hurried into the room and stopped.

"Charles?" Ralph stared at them.

Charles told them the name of a hotel and the suite number. "Go there now, this instant!" He spun around and hurtled toward the front door, wife and daughter running after him.

Ralph bounced to his feet, grabbed Sandra's hand, and yanked her into motion. "Go! Go! Go!"

He stopped at the door to the dining room. "Move it, Randy! Let's go!"

Suite 421.

Inside the large living room, the three stared, calm or puzzled, at Charles.

He had handed a full wine glass to Ralph and one to Sandra and a wide mouthed goblet of amber liquid to Randy. "O.K. Sit. Better if you heard this sitting down."

They settled into whatever piece of furniture appealed, took a sip or a swallow, and waited.

Prentice sat on the small couch with Richlin, holding one of her daughter's hands.

Charles took a swallow from his beer mug and looked from face to face.

"Here's the problem." He wiped his mouth with the back of his hand. "After Randy's little problem, I had my best and toughest, the ones that I have absolute trust in, run a very deep review of everyone in all our organizations, starting at the top and moving downward. Bad news, folks." he took another swallow.

"It seems that those no-goodniks managed to find someone, some two, and more, that felt that huge amounts of money were irresistible." He dropped into a chair.

"I now have eight people occupying very stark living quarters and another six cooling in drawers with name tags attached to their big toes. But two went missing faster than I could catch them."

Charles smiled at them. "At this very moment, I have absolutely safe crews emptying your houses into moving vans and sticking sold signs on your front lawns. Sorry, Randy, second move for you."

Ralph nodded. "Do you know what information went out the door?"

"Very little apparently. Still checking on that. Randy bagged his mole before the rest heard as far as I can tell, so far. It looks like those not smart folk only had one job to do for all that cash. They were supposed to watch for anything that involved the parent company we are so curious about. Their job was to sidetrack anything that turned up. Randy's exercise was such a select group that nothing leaked out or sideways, pretty much, maybe just a trickle."

"What a mess this is," grumbled Randy.

Ralph laughed. "I'll say."

Charles phone chirped, one of the many in his pockets. He yanked it out. "Yah! O.K." He crushed the phone under a stomped boot heel.

"Warfare in your front yard, Ralph."

"What!"

"Yep. Just as the last van turned a far corner, four car loads of bad nasties turned up and started running up toward your house, loaded to the teeth with all manner of weapons. Poor planning. We had a group inside an ice cream truck parked across the street, another standing around buying from the outside window. The score is we lost one, three wounded to some degree. The bad guys lost their whole crew, sixteen in number, and four cars. We took the car registrations and anything in any pocket and bugged out, ice cream truck and all."

Another phone chirped and was yanked out. "Yah! O.K." And another cell phone was smashed.

"We really have to do something about these guys. Torched my house. My crew threw all of them into the burning house and stole their car. The moving van guys got most of our stuff out before that happened."

A soft voice said something from another pocket and was yanked out. "Yah! O.K."

"We made a clean getaway from Randy's house." He stomped. Then he nodded at Ralph.

Ralph stood. "O.K., we grab the best of the best we have, six to eight from each organization however you have yourselves organized, make them a team, and then we hunt."

He looked around the room. "These quarters will be good enough for us for a few days. Meet back here in, ah, four hours."

Charles beckoned Sandra over. "You, Prentice, and Richlin go with the guy in the blue suit, do some quick shopping for whatever you might need. When you get back, I'll take you to a safe place. O.K.?"

He tossed a cell phone to Ralph. "I bought a whole lot of them." Then he told Ralph what number to call if he had to. "See you in a few." Charles hurtled out the door, followed by his wife, daughter, and Sandra, and their driver.

Ralph sat and stared into nowhere, thinking that they were going to have to make a major overhaul in everything any of the organizations did. This was the worst disaster imaginable. And he was really good at imagining disasters.

Crap, As The Saying Goes.
Or Perhaps, Not Nice.

House Darthar Na.

Dee was sitting with her two daughters talking with them about their studies, activities, and various other items of discussion, just being a mother with two daughters. Tiela was till wearing her purple jacket. Her purple staff leaned against a wall.

Tiela was frowning darkly and Winala was carefully listing the various volumes she had studied and equally carefully explaining some rather arcane little known or quite obscure pointed regarding behaviors that she felt her mother really needed to understand as House Head.

Tiela rolled her eyes and chewed on one corner of her mouth as Winala called in a large volume from the library and cracked it open, shedding dust on Tiela's plate, in order to jab a finger tip at the appropriate sub-section.

Dee suppressed her smile, walked around the table, patted Tiela on the shoulder, and peered past Winala's head to nod at the appropriate thing that she was to read.

"Ummmmmm," she said.

"Just so," agreed Winala.

Tiela stood and refilled their cups.

She suddenly stood there, red-faced, disheveled, and wild-eyed. "Help Dee. We've been kidnaped, me, Prentice, and Richlin."

Dee spun. "Sandra?"

Sandra grabbed her arm. "I don't have much time. I am in a room by myself."

Dee nodded. "Tiela with me. Winala, get Armilin and whoever is handy down here right away."

She handed Sandra a cup and filled it. "We have a minute or two, I am sure." She nodded. The great feline oozed into the room and brushed past Sandra who jerked violently but managed not to slosh coffee everywhere.

"Sandra, this is Purr Cat. Finish your coffee and then take us to wherever you are."

Maryland.

Dee looked around the room. It was just a rather ordinary appearing bedroom. "Where are we?"

"Shhhh," whispered Sandra. "There is a guard just outside the door."

Dee nodded and pointed. The Furleen flowed over to the wall and blended into the wall paper. Sandra stared. Two large green eyes opened and stared back at her. It was all that she could see.

"They have a special skill," explained Dee. "They are very good at that. Tiela prepare. Sandra, go back and bring the next two or three. Now!"

Sandra was gone.

"Mother?" whispered Tiela, clenching her long staff in one hand.

"Something is very not nice." Dee walked over to the door and looked at the wallpaper. "Are any of your clan near the house?"

"Two can be there in small time," softly replied the

wallpaper.

Dee nodded. Tiela stared. She hadn't known that The Furleen could talk.

Sandra appeared with Armilin, Mensta, First Hand, and Udoat, The One Who Remembers, both of The Fifth Stand. They all carried the long staffs.

"One?" asked Armilin.

"Sandra go back and wait. Bring the two Furleen as soon as they get there."

Sandra nodded. And was gone.

Dee explained what little that she knew to the three. "The ones who did this are very not nice people. We have to be careful. The people have terrible weapons, things that you are not familiar with." They nodded.

"Careful careful," ordered Dee.

Armilin bowed. "As The Word says, so will the deed be done."

The three took positions facing the door. It was within reach of their long staffs, all held ready.

"We will wait for Sandra."

Suite 421.

Charles hurtled into the room, a thick sandwich clenched in one hand, chewing loudly. His eyes scanned the room. "Not back yet? What can they be doing?"

Ralph shrugged.

His head jerked as Charles cursed and threw a cell phone across the room. "No answer."

Sandra walked into the room, handed Ralph a piece of paper, and walked out. "Take care, Dear."

Charles stared at him. "What's going on? She was a

mess."

Ralph shrugged, then carefully uncrumpled the paper, read it, and looked up.

"Sandra, Prentice, and Richlin had been kidnaped. Sandra assumes that it is the same people we are concerned with. She is safe and in good company."

Randy banged in, holding a large pizza box. "O.K., things are rolling. We should know in a few hours what we need to know."

Charles frowned at him. "Do you care to explain what I just saw?" Randy stared at Ralph.

Ralph shook his head. "Not now, Charles, not now. It would take much, much too long. But it is interesting, very much so."

"Ralph?"

"We wait," stated Ralph. "Open the box, Randy, I am hungry. And both of you get your number twos in here. While we eat we can plan what to do. Very quickly."

Maryland.

Sandra appeared and dropped heavily on one end of the bed. "I don't think that I am capable of any more trips."

Dee nodded and scratched one fussy ear of the two new Furleen sitting next to her.

Mensta smiled at the tall man. "Over here, Tolar. He is Seventh Stand," she said to Dee.

"Sandra, take a look outside and tell us what you see," said Dee.

Sandra wobbled to her feet and stepped to the door. "It has been a long time since I've felt this wrung out and bone weary." She rattled the knob. "Locked!"

"Stop that!" someone snapped.

She rattled it again.

"You don't stop that, I am going to come in there!" the voice growled.

Dee gently moved Sandra to one side and violently shook the doorknob and kicked the door.

"All right, Lady, now you are in for it."

They could hear fumbling with a key and then the lock snapped.

Dee yanked the door open and jumped back.

"What!" The man with a rifle slung on his back stared at her. "Who are you? How did you get in there?" He stepped into the room, reaching for his sidearm.

Tiela's staff whirled, a flash of dark wood, and bounced off the side of his head.

Tolar dragged the body to one side of the room as Dee gently shut the door after taking a quick peek out the door.

Dee knelt and searched the man's pockets and put everything that she found into her own pockets. Then she stood and beckoned all to stand close to her. "He is still alive." And gave the handgun to Sandra. Sandra disassembled the rifle and kicked that parts under the bed.

She quickly inspected the handgun and nodded. "Much better."

Sandra stepped to the door. "Anabelle and Richlin have the room to the right. I heard them through the wall. There was apparently only the one guard watching us as the rooms are locked. Or were."

"Very quietly," said Dee, easing the door open as she waited for the Furleen to ooze past.

Everyone slipped down the hall to the right and the next

door. Dee wiggled the doorknob. "Locked." And stepped back.

Tolar said something, his staff glowed a faint purple as he swung and carved a large piece of the door containing the doorknob away

Sandra pushed open the door. "Shhhhhhhhh," she hissed at Richlin and Prentice. "No noise."

Prentice nodded. Richlin stared at the Furleen and clenched her mother's arm, and gasped, "Monsters, Mom. It is the monsters!"

Prentice hugged her. "Shhhhhhh. It must be all right. Sandra looks calm."

Richlin's eyes jerked to Sandra's face.

Sandra smiled at her. "Not to worry, dear." She stepped over and kissed her on the forehead. Then she turned away. "Now what do we do, Dee?"

Dee nodded to Mensta. Then she looked at Sandra. "How many of the people are there here?"

Sandra frowned, then said, "I saw four."

Prentice nodded. "I agree."

"Which way?" asked Mensta.

Prentice pointed.

"Can we turn off the hall lights?" asked Dee.

Sandra slipped out the door. "I saw a wall switch."

They heard the snap as the lights went off.

Tiela and Tolar rushed to the opening at the end of the hall and stood to either side of it. She tapped the side of her staff with one finger. He nodded. Both staffs become deep dark wood.

"Hey, dim wit," yelled someone. "Stop playing with the lights in there. Turn them back on!"

They waited.

Heavy foot steps came stomping into the room they could see through the opening. "I am going to kick your butt if you don't turn those lights back on!"" He stepped through the opening "What!"

Tolar's staff across the man's mid-section doubled him over. Tiela's staff drove him to the floor. Mensta quickly dragged him into the first bedroom.

They waited.

Dee spoke softly and the three Furleen oozed into the next room.

They waited.

"YAH!" screamed someone as a gun went off.

They waited.

Then the group slipped into the room, a living room, and spread out.

"In here," called Sandra.

Dee walked into the kitchen. Two bodies lay in awkward positions on the floor.

"Stay here," said Sandra. "I'll check the garage." Gun in hand she slipped through the door.

In a moment, she came back. "We're in luck. They left the keys in the ignition. Let's go. It's time to leave."

In the garage, Sandra laughed. "It is going to be rather cosy in that van. Everyone get in. Now! LET'S GO! It's time to scram."

She climbed into the drivers seat and began to adjust the position of it. Doors slammed. Dee lifted the garage door and then jumped into the van.

Checking her rear view mirror, Sandra backed out of the garage and turned down the street. "Nice neighborhood," she observed. "No one cane out to see what that gun shot was all about."

Ricklin carefully set her hand on the thick fur of the Furleen that was sprawled over her lap and her mother's lap and Teila's lap. The other Furleen were in the rear of the van with its occupants and the small cargo space.

Tiela tickled under a furry chin. "This is Purr Cat. She won't hurt you."

Dee looked back over her shoulder. "Just so."

Suite 421.

Dee handed all the items she had collected from the four men to Ralph. "Two died, two might live."

Sandra sat at the table and wrote on a piece of hotel stationary. "Here's the address, Charles, saw it as we left."

Charles snatched it from her hand. "Come on, Randy, we have some clean up to do." The pair hurried from the room. But first Charles hugged his daughter and kissed his wife.

"We are very fortunate," said Ralph looking at Dee. "Care to tell me how you did that?"

She smiled. "It was Sandra done." She picked up the phone and dialed room service.

As they ate, Ralph poured coffee for Dee and refilled his glass and Sandra's with a not too bad red wine. "It is interesting," he said, "that our involvement with you led to your training Sandra in that strange skill which resulted in her being able to help free herself and the others from those guys." He cut a piece from his steak and chewed very thoughtfully.

Dee sipped, and nodded. "Interesting." Her eyes caught his. "I will ask Jonathon to move everyone back. Sandra has to rest for a number of days. We, ummmm, had no idea of the strain it would put on one of you to do that. I think that there is a a lesson to be learned there."

Ralph nodded and smiled at her. "Just so." And laughed.

After dessert that is what happened. Sandra went to one of the bedrooms to sleep Then Jonathon took Dee, the house beasts, and all the others to House Darthar Na.

House Darthar Na.

Dee had been telling Jonathon all about helping Sandra and the others to escape and the problems that The Council and their organization had been having.

"Ummmmm," said Jonathon.

Tiela poured their cups full.

"Sandra only made a few trips and nearly fell over from fatigue. Just four, I believe." He peered at Jonathon. "Do you get that tired?"

"No."

"How many times can you do that?"

He was gone, taking Tiela and Purr Cat.

"One," he said, was gone again.

"Two."

"Three."

"Four."

. . .

"Fifty-four."

"STOP!" shouted Dee.

Jonathon sat and sipped.

"Must be the difference in our anatomy," suggested Dee.

Jonathon nodded. "Just so."

Tiela and The Furleen left the room.

Ralph and Sandra walked in. She was carrying a large, flat box.

"Cheesecake," said Ralph.

"Minor gift," said Sandra. "Our debt to you grows larger. Charles and Randy are falling over themselves trying figure out something to give you."

Ralph smiled at Dee. "Don't suppose there is really anything that we can give you, is there?"

"No." Dee sipped. "We live differently."

Sandra opened the box and slid out the cheesecake. "It is supposed to be some of the best."

Tiela walked in, carrying plates, forks, and a knife.

Sandra sat and served. As they ate, she said, "I am having a long and rather serious talk with Richlin about what she saw, especially those cougar looking things." She laughed. "Growing up in an urban environment didn't exactly prepare her for such goings on. This is the second time for her."

Ralph smiled. "Good cheesecake." And took another bite. Then he swallowed, took a sip, and looked at Dee.

"I have been urging Charles and Prentice to explain to her what they really do for a living. Richlin is fairly worried for her parents, confused because she grew up in the belief that they merely worked in a big office of some sort of business, and is really having a hard time about those animals, even if one sprawled across her lap and purred at her."

He laughed. "She wanted to know, Dee, whether you were some sort of animal trainer, some sort of Las Vegas type of show. I said that I would ask."

Dee smiled at him. "Could be a new career." Then waggled a hand at Jonathon.

"Ummmmmmm," he said, not sure if she was serious or not.

A True Pain In A Tender Spot.

House Darthar Na.

Some small time had passed and Dee was once again sitting near the bottom of the outside stairs watching her daughters play with their pets, the Ice Cats.

It was the usual game with Tiela and Winala swooping here and there with the Ice Cats leaping and bouncing after them.

Suddenly both Ice Cats stopped and hurtled in opposite directions and leaped high in the air at Tiela.

"OOOOOF!" She hadn't seen the one behind her.

Both Ice Cats licked her face as Winala thumped to the ground next to her sprawled sister and smiled down. "Very clever," she said.

Dee laughed and applauded the Ice Cats.

"Mother!" Tiela shoved at one Ice Cat while Winala called the other off her sister.

The small group walked up the stairs, into the house, and down the hallway to have a snack. Then Dee stopped and turned into a different room. She had felt Sandra arrive.

"What is he doing here?" growled Dee, frowning darkly at Sandra. "And how did you do that."

He was looking out the window at the large meadow and turned around.

"I am not sure," replied Sandra.

"Morning, Dee," said Charles. "I talked her into it." He

grabbed a pot and filled three cups and handed them around. "Whatever it is that she did."

Dee sat in a chair, and sipped, never taking her eyes off him.

He sat and sipped. And sighed, a very loud sigh.

"Speak!" snapped Dee.

He took another sip. "My daughter, Richlin, sleeps with the lights on in her room." He looked at Dee. "She is much too old to be doing something like that."

"And?" snarled Dee.

His sigh was even louder. "We, my wife and I, explained, a little, about our jobs, and nothing else. So, she kinna understands that and why we live the way we do. And after being kidnaped twice, she really does understand why certain things must be done in ways that are different than things her friends might do."

Dee nodded and sipped.

"Well," he said, "that is not the problem."

Dee nodded and sipped.

He frowned. "Her best friend, Penny, the one that was with her on that camping trip has been telling Richlin that those, ehh, cat things are demons, and that the ones that rescued her and Richlin are working for the dark one in order to corrupt her, Richlin."

He refilled his cup. "Penny claims that she is protected because she belongs to this, ahhh, church and that they are praying for Richlin in order to protect her as well. She says that all Richlin needs to do is, ahh, to accept their beliefs and then she can sleep with her lights off again."

He stared at Dee. "I do not want my daughter getting messed up by those folks. They are narrow-minded bigots full of righteous zeal to make everyone be like them"

"And," growled Dee.

Charles set his cup down and leaned in her direction, hands on his knees. "Can you, will you, talk to her, just talk to her?"

Dee banged her cup on the table top and leaped to her feet. "That is why we have avoided contact and involvement with the people for thousands of years, as you measure time!"

Charles slammed back in this chair, staring at the finger jabbed at him. He thought that he had heard it just crackle.

"You people believe in nonsense. You place mythology over knowledge. You have no honor, you have no morals, you always try to make, MAKE, others do what ever you might believe is the only way to think, without any foundation to those beliefs at all! You are just ignorant, ignorant, ignorant, ignorant, ahhhhhh . . . people! And you give credence to those people that insist in believing all that blather about whatever mythological story telling they wish was real as if it is meaningful!"

She stomped from the room.

"Well, Charles," said Sandra. "Any idea, after that, why she might want to help you?"

She stood. They were gone.

Maryland.

"Forget it!"

They were eating dinner. It was the third dinner in a row that Charles had said that. To his daughter.

It was the third evening that she said that she wanted to go with Penny to her church.

"I do not care what your buddy or any of that crowd thinks! They are full of crap! It wasn't Satan's minions that saved your butt and her's. It was just Ralph and me and some well trained others!"

Prentice filled his glass and looked at her daughter. "Her church is really quite uninformed. They are deliberately ignorant of almost everything, it appears."

"A very bad habit of the people in general," stated Dee as she walked into the room.

"Have some dessert," said Charles.

Dee sat and Prentice slid a plate across the table to her.

"Thank you," said Dee, taking a bite. "It is very good."

Richlin stared at her.

Dee stared back. "What?"

"I don't know," mumbled Richlin. "About anything." She shook her head.

"Ummmmm." Dee sipped from her cup, just filled by Prentice.

She nodded to Richlin. "I was raised among the people and, thus, have a better understanding of your strange beliefs and behaviors than most."

"Strange beliefs and behaviors?" Richlin frowned at her. "Among the people?"

"Just so." Dee nodded.

"Why are you here?" demanded Richlin.

Dee glowered at her. "Both of your parents are very intelligent. Therefore, you are probably very intelligent as well. True?"

Richlin glared at her parents and then slowly nodded.

"Good! With that agreement I believe that you may learn, a little, about me. Your parents already do."

Richlin stared at them. "Dad? Mom?"

Charles shrugged.

"We do," replied Prentice.

"And you will tell me?" asked Richlin.

Dee nodded. And held up one finger. "Listen carefully now and believe what I tell you."

Richlin slowly nodded. Her eyes darted to her father, then to her mother. Prentice smiled at her.

"O.K.," said Richlin.

"Then understand that what I tell you is a secret that your parents hold close. Among, ah, my, ummmm, folk, we have what we call a true promise. In certain cases, we ask this one or that one to make a true promise about this or that. If the one asked gives a true promise then the problem is resolved." She paused. "However," she looked from face to face, "if the one who gave the true promise breaks that promise, they die. It has nothing to do with their belief in anything at all, it merely happens." She looked at Richlin. "A broken true promise and, poof, they die!"

Dee eyes searched each face. Then she took another bite from her dessert and a sip from her cup.

Richlin sat straighter in her chair. "What kind of, ahh, true promise do you want?"

"Small thing," replied Dee.

"What?" asked Richlin.

Dee smiled at her. "Anything that I tell you may not be told to anyone else, not anyone else, no matter who, no matter what kind of friend they might be. You may not hedge, or hint, or indirectly indicate, or in any other manner tell." She nodded. "You may, however, talk with your parents. But only to them, Richlin."

Dee looked at Charles and Prentice. "You will promise the same thing. Except that you may talk with one another and your daughter. Thus, it becomes a family secret."

Charles looked at Prentice. She looked at her daughter. "Your call, Richlin."

Richlin frowned at the table top and pushed a piece of her dessert around on her plate with her fork.

Finally, she looked up at Dee. "Is it going to hurt?"

Dee laughed. "Of course not."

"O.K., what do I do?"

"Do you, Richlin, agree to everything that I just told you?"

"Yes, I do."

"True promise?"

"Yes."

"Say it."

"OH!" She nodded. "True promise." Richlin jerked. "Was that it? My skin just tingled for an instant."

"You felt the true promise binding." Dee looked over. "Charles. Prentice. Do you agree to everything I just told you? True promise?"

Charles smiled at her. "True promise, Dee." He twitched.

Prentice said, "True promise. Oh my, it does, it did."

Dee scanned their faces. "Please remember, to break a true promise is to die. Instantly. There is no time to change your mind."

Dee stood. And nodded.

She slipped into the room and sat next to Richlin, who jerked.

"This is Purr Cat. You have met her before. She is a Furleen. They avoid being seen by the people, who have a bad tendency to want to hunt things or shoot things that they haven't seen before. Lions, tigers, cougars, and all the other cat-like species are not some sort of mythological boogie man or monster, are they? She is just a different species. Hardly a reason to sleep with your room lights on at night."

Richlin tentatively reached out and scratched one furry ear. The great cat purred at her. Richlin smiled. "And I can't tell anyone about her either, right?"

"Just so," said Dee.

The purr rumbled louder.

Richlin laughed and looked at Dee. "Was she one of them that seemed to reach out from the wall in that ugly camp?"

"Just so." Dee sat in her chair and picked up her cup.

"How can they do something like that?"

Dee nodded. Purr Cat stood, walked over to the wall, and faded into it. "They have chameleon-like skills."

"Whoa," gasped Charles.

"You might call them Chameleon Cats, I suppose," said Dee.

"I'll say." Charles drained his glass. He stood, walked over to a cabinet, and took a bottle of wine that had been sitting on the top, and began to remove the cork.

Two large green eyes looked out at him. He almost dropped the bottle. "Holy cow!" Sitting back in his chair he poured for Prentice, then himself. "Now that is pretty spooky."

Richlin laughed at her father's expression. The Furleen seemed to flow from the wall and walked past him to sit next to Dee.

Dee smiled at her. "No more religious nonsense?"

Richlin nodded and mumbled, "Penny sounded so sure and everything."

"But now you know better?"

"Yes. I do."

Dee stood. "Good. Otherwise this might have frightened you." She looked at the doorway. "Let's go home, Sandra."

She walked into the room. "Hi Charles, Prentice, Richlin."

"You have been listening all this time?" asked Charles, frowning at her.

"Yep." She stood next to Dee and scratched Purr Cat on top of the head. They were gone.

Richlin stared at her father. "Daddy?"

He poured some red wine into his glass. "Want some?"

She shook her head. "Is Mrs. Fredrickson, ummmm, one of them? Like Dee?"

"Nope!" Charles laughed. "No. Somehow they taught her how to do that." He looked at her. "All this is part of your promise as well. Please remember that." His expression softened. "I really don't want to loose my only daughter."

Richlin jumped up, ran around the table, and hugged him and stared to cry. "You won't Dad, I promise."

He looked at his wife who winked at him and poured a little wine into a clean glass. "Here, Richlin. Bout time that we treated you like an adult."

Boston.

They were in between classes, sitting around a table, eating and drinking various beverages that were available in the snack shop, all non-alcoholic.

"We made copious notes for you," said Penny.

"Yah," said the young man. "Everyone wondered where you were."

"It was rather sudden," said Richlin. "Thanks for the notes. Really appreciate it."

Penny looked at her. "Looks like you caught up on your

sleep."

Richlin smiled at her. "Certainly did." Purr Cat sprawling on her rug for a few nights had really helped.

"An affiliate church is meeting tonight. You really ought to come. Help you out."

"Thanks, Penny. But, no, I don't need any help."

"You should come," she insisted. She leaned close and whispered. "Those demons must be held off."

Richlin shook her head. "No, I really don't believe that." She smiled broadly. "I am perfectly safe."

"How can you say that!" gasped her friend.

Richlin shook her head. "Can't tell you that. I promised. But it is true. Anyone watch the game last night?"

Book Tour and Adventure.
Sort Of.

Just Another Small Town.

She had been wandering the United States for a number of months, popping into a number of the larger urban areas, visiting the bookstores. It was a book tour that had been arranged by her publisher. It was a new book, just as she had promised. The pair of them, the author and her tour organizer, were beginning to get just some small amount of tired from answering the same old questions, asked over and over and over again. It was interesting in a strange sort of a way. But tiring.

She had suggested to Janice, one again, that maybe they could just create a handout with those same questions and the usual answers printed on it. That way, she hoped, someone would ask something new. Her companion had argued that it wasn't a good idea and she had agreed. Once again.

Finally, the author had suggested, quite forcefully, that she was going to visit some small towns and their bookstores, often the only bookstore, and give the stores and whoever might be there more of an unprepared show and tell than the usual thing that they did. It was fun to be spontaneous and relaxed rather than programmed.

So, there they were, two females, Dee and Janice, in that same small town in one of the western states, well off the main road, having a meal in the only restaurant.

"Much better than the usual hotel restaurant stuff." She licked the frosting off her lips and smiled at her traveling companion. "Much better."

Janice nodded. "I agree. But why are we doing this? Way out here in the middle of nowhere again? In this town again? You are not going to shove some large guy through a window again, are you?"

"There is more variety out here, in the middle of nowhere. Or haven't you noticed? All those big urban book stores all look alike. Out here I can see open spaces, talk with a few people at a time, listen to the quiet, and begin to think, ummm ah, about a new novel." She laughed. "So when you call home again, you can tell them that. It will make them happy."

She waved at the only waitress, who strolled over, and looked down at her. "Somethin?"

"Yes. I would like another piece of that pie. And more coffee, please." She looked across the table.

"Just coffee, please."

The waitress shuffled over to the pie case, a circular pie container with a number of shelves inside a clear plastic shell, cut a chunk from the appropriate pie, slid it onto a plate, and returned, and set it on the table.

"Here ya go, Dearie. Coffee is just finishing. I'll bring you a pot." She winked. "I do enjoy seeing someone who enjoys what we fix. I remember you. Welcome back." She wandered away, came back, refilled their coffee cups, and headed into the back to speak with the cook.

Dee smiled and cut a big chunk off the slice with her fork. And finished her coffee. "Nice country. Lots of open space and mountains. So, Janice, how much more of this are we going to do?"

"Two more big places to go, Dee. Then we can go home. Let's just stroll around for awhile. We can cruise the main drag, such as it is. See if anything has changed."

"Sure."

As soon as they were finished, they paid the bill, left a generous tip, and walked outside.

Janice pointed. "As I remember, the edge of town is over there."

They strolled that way in the gathering dusk. And as they wandered down the sidewalk the sky darkened and the few street lights came on. They heard no traffic or any other sounds. It was a very quite town.

"Still a small place," said Dee. They had hit the edge of town. So they turned and wandered back toward the other edge of town.

"Certainly is," agreed Janice. "With one not too bad motel, one pretty good restaurant, the same and only bar in town with a rather unkempt exterior and a brand new large window, and a new, but little bookstore."

They walked over to the bookstore and introduced themselves to the owner and the few customers.

Then they talked, the author and the few customers, about the usual things. Dee smiled to see that her books were on display. "Thanks," she said to the owner.

And they walked in. Two very large men, who stopped, and stared at them. One mouth dropped open. Both men were wearing heavy, badly worn work boots, dirty denim jeans and denim jackets over faded shirts of some barely visible pattern. Both stomachs were threatening of overflow wide leather belts.

One stepped up to Dee and looked down at her.

"I, we, would really like to apologize about our behavior,

ehh, before. Right, Little Fred?"

Little held out a well thumbed book. "Ahhhh, Ms. Grant, would you sign my book?"

Rance did the same thing with the book that he held as he stepped back. The pair had heard that Dee and her friend were in the bookstore.

Dee laughed. "I would be most happy to do so, gentlemen."

The book store owner stared at her. No one ever called Rance and Little Fred gentlemen, not to their faces.

Dee signed their books. "And I am sorry about what happened last time as well. May I buy both of you a beer or two or three?"

Rance held out his arm. She took it.

"Come into my parlor," laughed Rance, "and we will just do that. Come on, Little. Let's go drink some beer. And show off our favorite author"

General Bits and Pieces

House Darthar

Jonathon - Othara a'Anathor a'Mdator a'Zgura a'Winfa a'Relda d'Darthar - Head of House Darthar, and Lord of the Darthar family, both branches (Darthar and Darthar Na).

Karanly - Karanalador, first sister. She is the Damadon (sort of an Aunt) to Dee's daughters.

Jant - second brother - cross-tie to Nerela, Head, House Tartarnon.

Silneana - second sister.

Hakar - third brother.

Rinil - fourth brother.

Aberly - third sister.

Antel - fourth sister.

House Darthar Na

Dee - Daliera Fontala a'Anathor a'Mdator a'Zgura a'Winfa a'Relda d'Darthar Na. Head of House Darthar Na.

Ar - Ar'ga'da'fazza'din'ban'ahm'na. Dee's Advisor and Teacher.

Tiela - first daughter

Winala - second daughter, Anointed One.

The House Beasts of Darthar Na.

Kartar - a great grizzly bear looking animal with thick, light green scales. One of them was named Gooda by Dee when she was a very young child.

The Inferno Hounds - horse sized animals that vaguely look like dogs. The four that are permanent residents of House Darthar Na, Dee named Manny, Moe, Jack, and Peter.

Furleen - lion-sized, cougar-looking, feline creatures with bronze colored fur and white tiger stripes on their shoulders and neck. Dee named the one of the house, Purr Cat.

Tarken - giant eagle-like birds who stand taller than most men, the pair of the House are called Hack and Jack by Dee.

Sub-Houses of the Darthar

suta Namel

suta Ean

suta Zbtan

suta Dundar

suta Milaton

- who gifted the *Hamel*, the Ice Cats.

suta Ocedaron

suta Farbin

suta Sextet - The Council members of the people.

House Hinterane

Hesling - House Head

Janice - Third Daughter

Dee's Cousin-Houses and their Heads.

    Dalir - Parlente

    Namata - Fam

    Induna - Armilin.

    Patal - a deeply hidden house - Candal.

    Angorson - Pardosh

    Anathor - Fraz

The Council

    Ralph and Sandra Fredrickson.

    Charles and Sandra James

        Richlin - their daughter

    Randy and Anabelle Anders

        Samuel and Samantha - their twins

The Fontala - Organization.

> Daliera Fontala - The Word of The Fontala
> Armilin ♀ - The One of the All - House Induna.

First Stand.

> Amadur ♂ - First Hand - House Argonar.
> Farlon ♂ - The One Who Remembers - House Faradon.

Second Stand

> Meludo ♀ - First Hand - House Telat.
> Delat ♀ - The One Who Remembers - House Trillmar.

Third Stand

> Cantala ♀ - First Hand - House Zbtan.
> Trakatar ♂ - The One Who Remembers - House Nerian.

Fourth Stand

> Stregt ♂ - First Hand - House Overer.
> Wisuot ♀ - The One Who Remembers - House Zilan.

Fifth Stand

> Mensta ♀ - First Hand - House Darunat.
> Udoat ♀ - The One Who Remembers - House Hantaz.

Sixth Stand

> Oatut ♀ - First Hand - House Quartep-Vierda.
> Uztal ♂ - The One Who Remembers - House Abalam.

Seventh Stand

> Kitea ♀ - First Hand - House Induna
> Anagon ♀ - The One Who Remembers - House Naztan.
> Yallan ♂ - The Seeker - House Farback.

> ♂ = male.
> ♀ = female.

About the Author

George R. Mead began to study anthropology in 1962 after being discharged (honorably) from the U. S. Army, Combat Engineers. He eventually received his degrees, a B.A., a M. A., and a Ph. D. in his chosen field. And many years later an M. S. W. in Clinical Social Work. He has worked in aerospace, taught at the college and university levels, worked in a community action agency, ran a restaurant, been unemployed, and worked for the U. S. Forest Service. He is now retired from the work-a-day world but does a certain amount of consulting, writing, and research. He lives seven miles outside of the small town of La Grande, Oregon, with his wife, one cat, and a German Shepard dog named Katy who firmly believes that staring into his face at nine-o-clock in the evening is a statement that popcorn should be made. A new dog joined the house as an eight-week old puppy found by Katy under some brush in the middle of the American Southwest desert. Rez now weighs 107 pounds (some puppy).

www.ingramcontent.com/pod-product-compliance
Lightning Source LLC
Chambersburg PA
CBHW060941030726
47503CB00003B/686